RAGTIME

RAGTIME

BY

E. L. Doctorow

RANDOM HOUSE • *New York*

All rights reserved under International and Pan-American Copyright Conventions. Published in
the United States by Random House, Inc., New York, and simultaneously in Canada by Random
House of Canada Limited, Toronto.

Library of Congress Cataloging in Publication Data
Doctorow, E   L   1931–
Ragtime.
I. Title.
PZ4.D6413Rag [PS3554.03] 813'.5'4 75–9613
ISBN 0–394–46901–1 Trade
ISBN 0–394–49937–7 Limited
Manufactured in the United States of America
6 8 9 7

Portions of this book appeared, in somewhat different form, in American Review 20 and
American Review 21.

The author thanks the John Simon Guggenheim Memorial Foundation and the Creative Artists Program Service for fellowships awarded during the period in which this novel was written.

RESPECTFULLY DEDICATED TO
ROSE DOCTOROW BUCK

Do not play this piece fast.
It is never right to play Ragtime fast . . .

—SCOTT JOPLIN

1

In 1902 Father built a house at the crest of the Broadview Avenue hill in New Rochelle, New York. It was a three-story brown shingle with dormers, bay windows and a screened porch. Striped awnings shaded the windows. The family took possession of this stout manse on a sunny day in June and it seemed for some years thereafter that all their days would be warm and fair. The best part of Father's income was derived from the manufacture of flags and buntings and other accoutrements of patriotism, including fireworks. Patriotism was a reliable sentiment in the early 1900's. Teddy Roosevelt was President. The population customarily gathered in great numbers either out of doors for parades, public concerts, fish fries, political picnics, social outings, or indoors in meeting halls, vaudeville theatres, operas, ballrooms. There seemed to be no entertainment that did not involve great swarms of people. Trains and steamers and trolleys moved them from one place to another. That was the style, that was the way people lived. Women were stouter then. They visited the fleet carrying white parasols. Everyone wore white in summer. Tennis racquets were hefty and the racquet faces elliptical. There was a lot of sexual fainting. There were no Negroes. There were no immigrants. On Sunday afternoon, after dinner, Father and Mother went upstairs and closed the bedroom door. Grandfather fell asleep on the divan in the parlor. The Little Boy in the sailor blouse sat on the screened porch and waved away the flies. Down at the bottom of the hill Mother's Younger Brother boarded the streetcar and rode to the end of the line. He was a lonely, withdrawn young man with blond moustaches, and was thought to be having difficulty finding himself. The end of the line was an empty field of tall marsh grasses. The air was salt. Mother's Younger Brother in his white linen suit and boater rolled his trousers and walked barefoot in the salt marshes. Sea birds started and flew up. This was the time in our history when Winslow Homer was doing his painting. A certain light was still available along the Eastern seaboard. Homer painted the light. It gave the sea a heavy dull menace and shone coldly on the rocks and shoals of the New England coast. There were unexplained shipwrecks and brave towline rescues. Odd things went on in lighthouses and in shacks nestled in the wild beach plum. Across America sex and death were barely distinguishable. Runaway women died in the rigors of ecstasy. Stories were hushed up and reporters paid off by rich families. One read between the lines of the journals and gazettes. In New York City the papers were full of the shooting of the famous architect Stanford White by Harry K. Thaw, eccentric scion of a coke and railroad fortune. Harry K. Thaw was the husband of Evelyn Nesbit, the celebrated beauty who had once been Stanford White's mistress. The shooting took place in the roof garden of the Madison Square Garden on 26th Street, a spectacular block-long building of yellow brick and terra cotta that White himself had designed in the Sevillian style. It was the opening night of a revue entitled *Mamzelle Champagne*, and as the chorus sang and danced the eccentric scion wearing on this summer night a straw boater and heavy black coat pulled out a pistol and shot the famous

architect three times in the head. On the roof. There were
screams. Evelyn fainted. She had been a well-known artist's
model at the age of fifteen. Her underclothes were white. Her
husband habitually whipped her. She happened once to meet
Emma Goldman, the revolutionary. Goldman lashed her with
her tongue. Apparently there *were* Negroes. There *were* immigrants. And though the newspapers called the shooting the
Crime of the Century, Goldman knew it was only 1906 and
there were ninety-four years to go.

Mother's Younger Brother was in love with Evelyn Nesbit.
He had closely followed the scandal surrounding her name and
had begun to reason that the death of her lover Stanford
White and the imprisonment of her husband Harry K. Thaw
left her in need of the attentions of a genteel middle-class
young man with no money. He thought about her all the time.
He was desperate to have her. In his room pinned on the wall
was a newspaper drawing by Charles Dana Gibson entitled
"The Eternal Question." It showed Evelyn in profile, with a
profusion of hair, one thick strand undone and fallen in the
configuration of a question mark. Her downcast eye was em-
bellished with a fallen ringlet that threw her brow in shadow.
Her nose was delicately upturned. Her mouth was slightly
pouted. Her long neck curved like a bird taking wing. Evelyn
Nesbit had caused the death of one man and wrecked the life
of another and from that he deduced that there was nothing
in life worth having, worth wanting, but the embrace of her
thin arms.

The afternoon was a blue haze. Tidewater seeped into his
footprints. He bent down and found a perfect shell specimen,
a variety not common to western Long Island Sound. It was
a voluted pink and amber shell the shape of a thimble, and
what he did in the hazy sun with the salt drying on his ankles
was to throw his head back and drink the minute amount of
sea water in the shell. Gulls wheeled overhead, crying like

oboes, and behind him at the land end of the marsh, out of
sight behind the tall grasses, the distant bell of the North
Avenue streetcar tolled its warning.

Across town the little boy in the sailor suit was suddenly
restless and began to measure the length of the porch. He trod
with his toe upon the runner of the cane-backed rocking chair.
He had reached that age of knowledge and wisdom in a child
when it is not expected by the adults around him and conse-
quently goes unrecognized. He read the newspaper daily and
was currently following the dispute between the professional
baseballers and a scientist who claimed that the curve ball was
an optical illusion. He felt that the circumstances of his family's life operated against his need to see things and to go places.
For instance he had conceived an enormous interest in the
works and career of Harry Houdini, the escape artist. But he
had not been taken to a performance. Houdini was a headliner
in the top vaudeville circuits. His audiences were poor people
—carriers, peddlers, policemen, children. His life was absurd.
He went all over the world accepting all kinds of bondage and
escaping. He was roped to a chair. He escaped. He was chained
to a ladder. He escaped. He was handcuffed, his legs were put
in irons, he was tied up in a strait jacket and put in a locked
cabinet. He escaped. He escaped from bank vaults, nailed-up
barrels, sewn mailbags; he escaped from a zinc-lined Knabe
piano case, a giant football, a galvanized iron boiler, a rolltop
desk, a sausage skin. His escapes were mystifying because he
never damaged or appeared to unlock what he escaped from.
The screen was pulled away and there he stood disheveled but
triumphant beside the inviolate container that was supposed
to have contained him. He waved to the crowd. He escaped
from a sealed milk can filled with water. He escaped from a
Siberian exile van. From a Chinese torture crucifix. From a
Hamburg penitentiary. From an English prison ship. From a
Boston jail. He was chained to automobile tires, water wheels,

[6]

cannon, and he escaped. He dove manacled from a bridge into the Mississippi, the Seine, the Mersey, and came up waving. He hung upside down and strait-jacketed from cranes, biplanes and the tops of buildings. He was dropped into the ocean padlocked in a diving suit fully weighted and not connected to an air supply, and he escaped. He was buried alive in a grave and could not escape, and had to be rescued. Hurriedly, they dug him out. The earth is too heavy, he said gasping. His nails bled. Soil fell from his eyes. He was drained of color and couldn't stand. His assistant threw up. Houdini wheezed and sputtered. He coughed blood. They cleaned him off and took him back to the hotel. Today, nearly fifty years since his death, the audience for escapes is even larger.

The little boy stood at the end of the porch and fixed his gaze on a bluebottle fly traversing the screen in a way that made it appear to be coming up the hill from North Avenue. The fly flew off. An automobile was coming up the hill from North Avenue. As it drew closer he saw it was a black 45-horsepower Pope-Toledo Runabout. He ran along the porch and stood at the top of the steps. The car came past his house, made a loud noise and swerved into the telephone pole. The little boy ran inside and called upstairs to his mother and father. Grandfather woke with a start. The boy ran back to the porch. The driver and the passenger were standing in the street looking at the car: it had big wheels with pneumatic tires and wooden spokes painted in black enamel. It had brass head-lamps in front of the radiator and brass sidelamps over the fenders. It had tufted upholstery and double side entrances. It did not appear to be damaged. The driver was in livery. He folded back the hood and a geyser of white steam shot up with a hiss.

A number of people looked on from their front yards. But Father, adjusting the chain on his vest, went down to the sidewalk to see if there was something he could do. The car's

owner was Harry Houdini, the famous escape artist. He was
spending the day driving through Westchester. He was thinking of buying some property. He was invited into the house
while the radiator cooled. He surprised them with his modest,
almost colorless demeanor. He seemed depressed. His success
had brought into vaudeville a host of competitors. Conse-
quently he had to think of more and more dangerous escapes.
He was a short, powerfully built man, an athlete obviously,
with strong hands and with back and arm muscles that suggested themselves through the cut of his rumpled tweed suit
which, though well tailored, was worn this day inappropriately.
The thermometer read in the high eighties. Houdini had un-
ruly stiff hair parted in the middle and clear blue eyes, which
did not stop moving. He was very respectful to Mother and
Father and spoke of his profession with diffidence. This struck
them as appropriate. The little boy stared at him. Mother had
ordered lemonade. It was brought into the parlor and Houdini
drank it gratefully. The room was kept cool by the awnings on
the windows. The windows themselves were shut to keep out
the heat. Houdini wanted to undo his collar. He felt trapped
by the heavy square furnishings, the drapes and dark rugs, the
Oriental silk cushions, the green glass lampshades. There was
a chaise with a zebra rug. Noticing Houdini's gaze Father
mentioned that he had shot that zebra on a hunting trip in
Africa. Father was an amateur explorer of considerable reputation. He was past president of the New York Explorers Club
to which he made an annual disbursement. In fact in just a few
days he would be leaving to carry the Club's standard on the
third Peary expedition to the Arctic. You mean, Houdini said,
you're going with Peary to the Pole? God willing, Father replied. He sat back in his chair and lit a cigar. Houdini became
voluble. He paced back and forth. He spoke of his own travels,
his tours of Europe. But the Pole! he said. Now that's something. You must be pretty good to get picked for that. He

turned his blue eyes on Mother. And keeping the home fires burning ain't so easy either, he said. He was not without charm. He smiled and Mother, a large blond woman, lowered her eyes. Houdini then spent a few minutes doing small deft tricks with objects at hand for the little boy. When he took his leave the entire family saw him to the door. Father and Grandfather shook his hand. Houdini walked down the path that ran under the big maple tree and then descended the stone steps that led to the street. The chauffeur was waiting, the car was parked correctly. Houdini climbed in the seat next to the driver and waved. People stood looking on from their yards. The little boy had followed the magician to the street and now stood at the front of the Pope-Toledo gazing at the distorted macrocephalic image of himself in the shiny brass fitting of the headlight. Houdini thought the boy comely, fair like his mother, and tow-headed, but a little soft-looking. He leaned over the side door. Goodbye, Sonny, he said holding out his hand. Warn the Duke, the little boy said. Then he ran off.

2

As it happened Houdini's unexpected visit had interrupted
Mother and Father's coitus. There was no sign from Mother
that it was now to be resumed. She fled to her garden. As the
days passed and the time for Father's departure approached,
he waited for the mute sign that he might visit her bed. He
knew that to make an overture of his own was to threaten the
occasion. He was a burly man with strong appetites, but he
appreciated his wife's reluctance to assume the indelicate attitudes that answered to his needs. In the meantime the entire
household girded for his departure. His gear had to be packed,
arrangements had to be made for his absence from his business, and a thousand other details had to be seen to. Mother
lifted the back of her wrist to her forehead and pushed aside
a strand of hair. No one in the family was unmindful of the
particular dangers to which Father would be exposed. Yet no
one would have him stay because of them. The marriage
seemed to flourish on Father's extended absences. At dinner
the night before he was to leave, the cuff of Mother's sleeve
brushed a spoon off the table, and she grew flushed. When the
entire house was asleep he came to her room in the darkness.
He was solemn and attentive as befitted the occasion. Mother

shut her eyes and held her hands over her ears. Sweat from Father's chin fell on her breasts. She started. She thought: Yet I know these are the happy years. And ahead of us are only great disasters.

The next morning everyone rode down to the New Rochelle railroad station to see Father off. Some of the office staff was there, and Father's chief assistant made a short speech. There was a spattering of applause. The New York train arrived, five varnished dark green cars pulled by a Baldwin 4–4–0 with spoked engine truck wheels. The little boy stared as the wiper with his oilcan checked the brass drive pistons. He felt a hand on his shoulder, turned, and his smiling Father took his hand and shook it. Grandfather had to be restrained from lifting the bags. With the porter's help Father and Mother's Younger Brother laid the trunks aboard. Father shook the young man's hand. He had given him a raise and a more responsible position with the firm. Keep your eye on things, Father said. The young man nodded. Mother beamed. She gently embraced her husband, who kissed her on the cheek. Standing on the rear platform of the last car, Father doffed his skimmer and waved goodbye as the train went around the bend.

The next morning, after a champagne breakfast with the press, the men of Peary's polar expedition cast off the lines and their sturdy little ship, the *Roosevelt,* backed out of her berth into the East River. Fireboats sent up sprays of water which misted in rainbows as the early morning sun rose over the city. Passenger liners tooted their basso horns. It was not until some time later, when the *Roosevelt* had reached the open sea, that Father was persuaded of the actuality of the trip. As he stood at the railing there was transmitted to his bones the awesome unalterable rhythm of the ocean. A while later the *Roosevelt* passed an incoming transatlantic vessel packed to the railings with immigrants. Father watched the prow of the scaly broad-beamed vessel splash in the sea. Her decks were packed with people. Thousands of male heads in derbies. Thousands of female heads covered with shawls. It was a rag ship with a million dark eyes staring at him. Father, a normally resolute person, suddenly foundered in his soul. A weird despair seized him. The wind came up, the sky had turned overcast, and the great ocean began to tumble and break upon itself as if made of slabs of granite and sliding terraces of slate. He watched the ship till he could see it no longer. Yet aboard her were only more customers, for the immigrant population set great store by the American flag.

3

Most of the immigrants came from Italy and Eastern Europe. They were taken in launches to Ellis Island. There, in a curiously ornate human warehouse of red brick and gray stone, they were tagged, given showers and arranged on benches in waiting pens. They were immediately sensitive to the enormous power of the immigration officials. These officials changed names they couldn't pronounce and tore people from their families, consigning to a return voyage old folks, people with bad eyes, riffraff and also those who looked insolent. Such power was dazzling. The immigrants were reminded of home. They went into the streets and were somehow absorbed in the tenements. They were despised by New Yorkers. They were filthy and illiterate. They stank of fish and garlic. They had running sores. They had no honor and worked for next to nothing. They stole. They drank. They raped their own daughters. They killed each other casually. Among those who despised them the most were the second-generation Irish, whose fathers had been guilty of the same crimes. Irish kids pulled the beards of old Jews and knocked them down. They upended the pushcarts of Italian peddlers.

Every season of the year wagons came through the streets

and picked up bodies of derelicts. Late at night old ladies in babushkas came to the morgue looking for their husbands and sons. The corpses lay on tables of galvanized iron. From the bottom of each table a drainpipe extended to the floor. Around the rim of the table was a culvert. And into the culvert ran the water sprayed constantly over each body from an overhead faucet. The faces of the dead were upturned into the streams of water that poured over them like the irrepressible mechanism in death of their own tears.

But somehow piano lessons began to be heard. People stitched themselves to the flag. They carved paving stones for the streets. They sang. They told jokes. The family lived in one room and everyone worked: Mameh, Tateh and The Little Girl in the pinafore. Mameh and the little girl sewed knee pants and got seventy cents a dozen. They sewed from the time they got up to the time they went to bed. Tateh made his living in the street. As time went on they got to know the city. One Sunday, in a wild impractical mood, they spent twelve cents for three fares on the streetcar and rode uptown. They walked on Madison Avenue and Fifth Avenue and looked at the mansions. Their owners called them palaces. And that's what they were, they were palaces. They had all been designed by Stanford White. Tateh was a socialist. He looked at the palaces and his heart was outraged. The family walked quickly. The police in their tall helmets looked at them. On these wide empty sidewalks in this part of the city the police did not like to see immigrants. Tateh explained that this was because an immigrant some years before had shot the steel millionaire Henry Frick in Pittsburgh.

A crisis came to the family when somebody delivered a letter telling them the little girl would have to go to school. This meant they could not make ends meet. Helplessly, Mameh and Tateh took their child to the school. She was enrolled and went off each day. Tateh roamed the streets. He didn't know what to do. He had a peddler's business. Never could he find a place at the curb that was profitable. While he was gone Mameh sat by the window with her stack of cut cloth and pedaled the sewing machine. She was a petite dark-eyed woman with wavy brown hair which she parted in the middle and tied behind her neck in a bun. When she was alone like this she sang softly to herself in a high sweet thin voice. Her songs had no words. One afternoon she took her finished work to the loft on Stanton Street. The owner invited her into his office. He looked at the piece goods carefully and said she had done well. He counted out the money, adding a dollar more than she deserved. This he explained was because she was such a good-looking woman. He smiled. He touched Mameh's breast. Mameh fled, taking the dollar. The next time the same thing happened. She told Tateh she was doing more work. She became accustomed to the hands of her employer. One day with two weeks' rent due she let the man have his way on a cutting table. He kissed her face and tasted the salt of her tears.

At this time in history Jacob Riis, a tireless newspaper reporter and reformer, wrote about the need of housing for the poor. They lived too many to a room. There was no sanitation. The streets reeked of shit. Children died of mild colds or slight rashes. Children died on beds made from two kitchen chairs pushed together. They died on floors. Many people believed that filth and starvation and disease were what the immigrant got for his moral degeneracy. But Riis believed in air shafts. Air shafts, light and air, would bring health. He went around climbing dark stairs and knocking on doors and taking flash photos of indigent families in their dwellings. He held up the flash pan and put his head under the hood and a picture exploded. After he left, the family, not daring to move, remained in the position in which they had been photographed. They waited for life to change. They waited for their transformation. Riis made color maps of Manhattan's ethnic populations. Dull gray was for Jews—their favorite color, he said. Red was for the swarthy Italian. Blue for the thrifty German. Black for the African. Green for the Irishman. And yellow for the cat-clean Chinaman, a cat also in his traits of cruel cunning and savage fury when aroused. Add dashes of color for Finns, Arabs, Greeks, and so on, and you have a crazy quilt, Riis cried, a crazy quilt of humanity!

One day Riis decided to interview Stanford White the eminent architect. He wanted to ask White if he'd ever designed housing for the poor. He wanted his ideas on public housing, on air shafts, on light. He found White down at the docks looking at arriving shipments of architectural furnishings. Riis marveled at what was coming out of the holds of the ships: whole façades of Florentine palaces and Athenian atria, stone by marked stone; paintings, statuary, tapestries, carved and painted ceilings in crates, tiled patios, marble fountains, marble stairs and balustrades, parqueted floors and silk wall panels; cannon, pennants, suits of armor, crossbows and other ancient weaponry; beds, armoires, chaises, refectory tables, sideboards, harpsichords; barrels of glassware, silver, goldplate, porcelain and china; boxes of church ornaments, boxes of rare books, snuffboxes. White, a robust burly man with reddish brush-cut hair turning gray, went about smacking the backs of the handlers with his rolled-up umbrella. Careful, you fools! he shouted. Riis wanted to ask him his questions. Housing for the poor was Riis's story. But he had a vision of the dismantling of Europe, the uncluttering of ancient lands, the birth of a new aesthetic in European art and architecture. He himself was a Dane.

That evening White went to the opening night of *Mamzelle Champagne* at the roof garden at Madison Square. This was early in the month of June and by the end of the month a serious heat wave had begun to kill infants all over the slums. The tenements glowed like furnaces and the tenants had no water to drink. The sink at the bottom of the stairs was dry. Fathers raced through the streets looking for ice. Tammany Hall had been destroyed by reformers but the hustlers on the ward still cornered the ice supply and sold little chips of it at exorbitant prices. Pillows were placed on the sidewalks. Families slept on stoops and in doorways. Horses collapsed and died in the streets. The Department of Sanitation sent drays around the city to drag away horses that had died. But it was not an efficient service. Horses exploded in the heat. Their exposed intestines heaved with rats. And up through the slum alleys, through the gray clothes hanging listlessly on lines strung across air shafts, rose the smell of fried fish.

4

In the killing summer heat politicians up for reelection invited their followers to outings in the country. Toward the end of July one candidate led a parade through the streets of the Fourth Ward. He wore a gardenia in his lapel. A band played a Sousa march. The members of the candidate's Benevolent Association followed the band and the entire procession made its way to the river where everyone boarded the steamer *Grand Republic*, which then set a course up the Long Island Sound to Rye, New York, just beyond New Rochelle. The steamer, overloaded with perhaps five thousand men, listed badly to starboard. The sun was hot. The passengers jammed the decks and crowded the railing for a breath of air. The water was like glass. At Rye everyone disembarked for another parade to the Pavilion, where at picnic tables the traditional fish chowder was served by a small army of waiters in white full-length aprons. After the luncheon speeches were made from a band shell. The band shell was decorated with patriotic bunting. This had been provided by Father's firm. There were also banners with the candidate's name spelled in gold and small American flags on gold sticks that were given as favors at each table. The men of the Benevolent Association spent the afternoon consuming beer from kegs on tap, playing baseball and throwing horseshoes. The meadows of Rye were dotted with men dozing on the grass under their derbies. In the evening another meal was served and a military band played a concert, and then came the culmination of the entertainment: a display of fireworks. Mother's Younger Brother had come here to supervise personally this aspect of the event. He liked to design fireworks. They were the only part of the business that really interested him. Rockets went up booming in the close electric evening air. Heat lightning flashed over the Sound. A great wheel of spinning fire seemed to roll over the water. A woman's profile, like a new constellation, embossed the night sky. Showers of light, red and white and blue, fell like stars and burst again, like bombs, over the old steamer down at the water. Everyone cheered. When the fireworks were concluded torches were lit to mark the way to the dock. On the trip home the old steamer listed to port. Among her passengers was Mother's Younger Brother, who had leapt lightly aboard at the last possible moment. He stepped over men lying asleep on the deck. He stood at the rail up at the prow and lifted his head to the breeze coming up over the black water. He turned his intense eyes on the black night and thought of Evelyn.

Now at this time Evelyn Nesbit was daily rehearsing the testimony she would give in her husband's forthcoming trial for the murder of Stanford White. She had not only to deal with Thaw in her almost daily visits to the Tombs, the city jail where he was kept, but with his lawyers, of whom there were several; with his mother, a regal Pittsburgh dowager who despised her; and with her own mother, whose greediest dreams of connived wealth she had surpassed. The press followed her every move. She tried to live quietly in a small residential hotel. She tried not to think how Stanford White looked with his face shot away. She took her meals in her rooms. She rehearsed her lines. She retired early believing that sleep would improve her skin tone. She was bored. She ordered clothes from her dressmaker. The key to the defense of Harry K. Thaw would be that he had become temporarily deranged by the story she had told him about her ruination at the age of fifteen. She was an artist's model and aspiring actress. Stanford White had invited her to his apartments in the tower of Madison Square Garden and offered her champagne. The champagne was drugged. When she woke up the following morning the effulgence of White's manhood lay over her thighs like a baker's glaze.

But it was going to be difficult to persuade a jury that Harry K. Thaw became deranged only upon the telling of that tale. He was a violent man who all his life had created incidents in restaurants. He drove cars up sidewalks. He was suicidal and had once consumed an entire bottle of laudanum. He kept syringes in a silver case. He injected things into himself. He had a habit of clenching his fists and beating them against his temples. He was imperious, possessive and insanely jealous. Before they were married he had concocted a scheme whereby Evelyn was to sign an affidavit accusing Stanford White of beating her. She refused and told White about it. Harry's next move was to take her to Europe where he could have her without worrying if White was to have his turn when he was through. Her mother went along as chaperone. They sailed on the *Kronprinzessin Cecile.* In Southampton Harry paid off Evelyn's mother and took Evelyn alone to the Continent. Eventually they arrived at an ancient mountain castle in Austria that Harry had rented—the Schloss Katzenstein. Their first night in the Schloss he pulled off her robe, threw her across the bed and applied a dog whip to her buttocks and the backs of her thighs. Her shrieks echoed down the corridors and stone stairwells. The German servants in their quarters listened, grew flushed, opened bottles of Goldwasser and copulated. Shocking red welts disfigured Evelyn's flesh. She cried and whimpered all night. In the morning Harry returned to her room, this time with a razor strop. She was bedridden for weeks. During her convalescence he brought her stereopticon slides of the Black Forest and the Austrian Alps. He was gentle when he made love to her and mindful of the tender places. Nevertheless she decided their relationship had gone beyond its tacit understanding. She demanded to be sent home. She sailed back to America alone on the *Carmania*, her mother having long since returned. When she reached New York she immediately went to see Stanford White and told him what had happened. She showed him the traces of a laceration across the flesh of the inside of her right thigh. Oh my, oh my, Stanford White said. He kissed the spot. She showed him a tiny yellow and purple discoloration on the face of her left buttock where it curved toward the cleft. How awful, Stanford White said. He kissed the spot. The following morning he sent her to a lawyer who prepared an affidavit as to what happened in the Schloss Katzenstein. Evelyn signed the affidavit. Now, darling, when Harry comes home you show him that, Stanny White said smiling broadly. She followed his instructions. Harry K. Thaw read the affidavit, turned pale and immediately proposed marriage. She had only been in the chorus but she had done as well as any of the Floradora girls.

And now Harry, in jail, was on public display. His cell was on Murderer's Row, the top tier of the cavernous Tombs. Each evening the guards brought him the papers so that he could follow his favorite team, the Pittsburgh Nationals, and their star Honus Wagner. Only when he had read about the ball games would he read about himself. He went through every paper—the *World*, the *Tribune*, the *Times*, the *Evening Post*, the *Journal*, the *Herald*. When he finished reading a paper he would fold it up, stand at the bars and flip it over the rail of the cellblock promenade so that it came apart, fluttering in pieces six stories down through the central vault, or well, around which the cellblock tiers were arranged. His behavior fascinated the guards. It was seldom they had people of this class. Thaw was not really fond of the jail fare so they brought in his meals from Delmonico's. He liked to feel clean so they passed along a change of clothes delivered each morning to the jail doors by his valet. He disliked Negroes so they made sure no Negro prisoner was lodged near his cell. Thaw was not unmindful of the guards' kindnesses. He showed his gratitude not discreetly but with impeccable style, crumpling and tossing twenty-dollar bills at his feet and telling them what swine they were as they stooped to retrieve the money. They were very happy. Reporters asked their views when they left the Tombs at the end of a shift. And each afternoon when Evelyn arrived looking crisp in her high-collared shirtwaist and pleated linen skirt the husband and wife would be permitted to stroll back and forth across the Bridge of Sighs, the iron catwalk that connected the Tombs with the Criminal Courts Building. Thaw walked with a dipping, pigeon-toed gait, like someone with brain damage. He had the wide mouth and doll eyes of a Victorian closet queen. Sometimes they saw him gesticulate wildly while Evelyn stood with her head bowed, her face in shadow under her hat. Sometimes he would ask for use of the consultation room. The guard whose station was just outside the consultation room door with its small porthole window claimed that Thaw sometimes cried and sometimes he held Evelyn's hand. Sometimes he paced back and forth and beat his fists against his temples while she gazed through the barred window. Once he demanded proof of her devotion and it turned out nothing else would do but a fellatio. Abutted by Thaw's belly Evelyn's broad-brimmed hat with its topping of dried flowers in tulle slowly tore away from her coiffure. After-wards he brushed the sawdust from the front of her skirt and gave her some bills from his money clip.

Evelyn told reporters who met her outside the Tombs that

her husband Harry K. Thaw was innocent. His trial will prove my husband Harry K. Thaw is innocent, she said one day stepping into the electric hansom provided her by her august mother-in-law. The chauffeur closed the door. In the privacy of the car she wept. She knew better than anyone how innocent Harry was. She had agreed to testify in his behalf for the sum of two hundred thousand dollars. And her price for a divorce was going to be even higher. She ran her fingertips over the car upholstery. Her tears dried. A strange bitter exaltation suffused her, a cold victory grin of the heart. She had grown up playing in the streets of a Pennsylvania coal town. She was the Gaudens statue Stanny White had put at the top of the tower of Madison Square Garden, a glorious bronze nude Diana, her bow drawn, her face in the skies.

Coincidentally this was the time in our history when the morose novelist Theodore Dreiser was suffering terribly from the bad reviews and negligible sales of his first book, *Sister Carrie*. Dreiser was out of work, broke and too ashamed to see anyone. He rented a furnished room in Brooklyn and went to live there. He took to sitting on a wooden chair in the middle of the room. One day he decided his chair was facing in the wrong direction. Raising his weight from the chair, he lifted it with his two hands and turned it to the right, to align it properly. For a moment he thought the chair was aligned, but then he decided it was not. He moved it another turn to the right. He tried sitting in the chair now but it still felt peculiar. He turned it again. Eventually he made a complete circle and still he could not find the proper alignment for the chair. The light faded on the dirty window of the furnished room. Through the night Dreiser turned his chair in circles seeking the proper alignment.

5

The impending Thaw trial was not the only excitement down at the Tombs. Two of the guards in their spare time had fashioned new leg irons that they claimed were better than the standard equipment. To prove it they challenged Harry Houdini himself to put them to the test. The magician arrived one morning at the office of the Warden of the Tombs and was photographed shaking the hand of the Warden and standing between the two smiling guards with his arms around their shoulders. He traded quips with reporters. He gave out lots of free tickets. He held the leg irons under the light and examined them carefully. He accepted the challenge. He would escape from the irons at the following night's performance at the Keith Hippodrome. With the press crowded around, Houdini now proposed his own challenge: that then and there he be stripped and locked in a cell and his clothing placed outside the cell; if everyone would then leave he would contrive to escape from the cell and appear fully dressed in the Warden's office within five minutes. The Warden demurred. Houdini professed astonishment. After all he, Houdini, had accepted the guards' challenge without hesitation: was the Warden not confident of his own jail? The reporters took Houdini's side.

Knowing what the newspapers could do with his refusal to go along with the stunt the Warden gave in. He believed in fact his cells were secure. The walls of his office were pale green. Photographs of his wife and his mother stood on the desk. A humidor with cigars and a decanter of Irish whiskey stood on a table behind his desk. He picked up his new phone and holding the shaft in one hand and the earpiece with the other he looked significantly at the reporters.

A while later Houdini was led, stark naked, up the six flights of stairs to Murderer's Row on the top tier of the jail. There were fewer inhabitants on this tier and the cells were believed to be escape-proof. The guards locked Houdini in an empty cell. They placed his clothing in a neat pile on the promenade, beyond his reach. Then the guards and the accompanying reporters withdrew and, as they had agreed, went back to the Warden's office. Houdini carried in various places on his person small steel wires and bits of spring steel. This time he ran his palm along the sole of his foot and extracted from a slot in the callus of his left heel a strip of metal about a quarter-inch wide and one and a half inches long. From his thick hair he withdrew a piece of stiff wire which he fitted around the strip metal as a handle. He stuck his hand through the bars, inserted the makeshift key in the lock and twisted it slowly clockwise. The cell door swung open. At that moment Houdini realized that across the vault of gloom the cell directly opposite was lighted and occupied. A prisoner sat there staring at him. The prisoner had a broad flat face with a porcine nose, a wide mouth, and eyes that seemed unnaturally bright and large. He had coarse hair combed back from an oddly crescent hairline. Houdini, a vaudevillian, thought of the face of a ventriloquist's dummy. The prisoner was sitting at a table laid with linen and service. On the table were the remains of a large meal. An empty bottle of champagne was stuck upside down in a cooler. The iron cot was covered with a quilted spread and throw pillows. A Regency armoire stood against the stone wall. The ceiling fixture had been ornamented with a Tiffany lampshade. Houdini could not help staring. The prisoner's cell glowed like a stage in the perpetual dusk of the cavernous prison. The prisoner stood up and waved, a stately gesture, and his wide mouth offered the trace of a smile. Quickly Houdini began to dress. He put on his briefs, his trousers, his socks and garters and shoes. Across the well the prisoner began to undress. Houdini put on his undershirt, his shirt, his collar. He tied his tie and set the stock pin. He snapped his suspenders in place and pulled on his jacket. The prisoner was now as naked as Houdini had been. The prisoner came up to the front of his cell and raising his arms in a shockingly obscene manner he thrust his hips forward and flapped his penis between the bars. Houdini rushed down the promenade, fumblingly unlocked the cellblock door and closed it behind him.

Houdini was to tell no one of this strange confrontation. He went through the celebrations of his jailhouse feat in an uncharacteristically quiet, even subdued manner. Not even the lines at the box office following the stories in the evening papers could cheer him up. Escaping from the leg irons in two minutes gave him no pleasure at all. Days passed before he realized that the grotesque mimic on Murderer's Row had to have been the killer Harry K. Thaw. People who did not respond to his art profoundly distressed Houdini. He had come to realize they were invariably of the upper classes. Always they broke through the pretense of his life and made him feel foolish. Houdini had high inchoate ambition and every development in technology made him restless. On the shabby confines of a stage he could create wonder and awe. Meanwhile men were beginning to take planes into the air, or race automobiles that went sixty miles an hour. A man like Roosevelt had run at the Spanish on San Juan Hill and now sent a fleet of white battleships steaming around the world, battleships as white as his teeth. The wealthy knew what was important. They looked on him as a child or a fool. Yet his self-imposed training, his dedication to the perfection of what he did, reflected an American ideal. He kept himself as trim as an athlete. He did not smoke or drink. Pound for pound he was as strong as any man he had ever run up against. He could tighten his stomach muscles and with a smile invite anyone at all to punch him there as hard as they liked. He was immensely muscular and agile and professionally courageous. Yet to the wealthy all this was nothing.

New in Houdini's act was an escape in which he released himself from an office safe and then opened the safe to reveal, handcuffed, the assistant who had been onstage a moment before. It was a great success. One evening after the performance Houdini's manager told him of being called by Mrs. Stuyvesant Fish of 78th Street, who wanted to book Houdini for a private party. Mrs. Fish was one of the Four Hundred. She was famous for her wit. Once she had given a ball at which everyone had to talk baby talk. Mrs. Fish was throwing a commemorative ball in honor of her friend the late Stanford White, the architect of her home. He had designed her home in the style of a doge palace. A doge was the chief magistrate in the republic of Genoa or Venice. I won't have nothing to do with those people, Houdini told his manager. Dutifully the manager reported to Mrs. Fish that Houdini was not available. She doubled the fee. The ball was held on a Monday evening. It was the first big event of the new season. At about nine o'clock Houdini drove up in a hired Pierce Arrow. He was accompanied by his manager and his assistant. Behind the car was a truck carrying his equipment. The entourage was shown to the trade entrance.

Unknown to Houdini, Mrs. Stuyvesant Fish had also engaged for the evening the entire sideshow of the Barnum and Bailey circus. She liked to shock fuddy-duddies. Houdini was led into some sort of waiting room where he found himself encircled by a mob of freaks all of whom had heard of him and wanted to touch him. Creatures with scaled iridescent skins and hands attached to their shoulders, midgets with the voices of telephones, Siamese twin sisters who leaned in opposite directions, a man who lifted weights from iron rings permanently attached to his breasts. Houdini removed his cape and his top hat and his white gloves and handed them to his assistant. He slumped in a chair. His grips were waiting for instructions. The freaks yattered at him.

But the room itself was very beautiful, with carved wood ceilings and Flemish tapestries of Actaeon being torn apart by dogs.

Early in his career Houdini had worked in a small circus in western Pennsylvania. He recalled his loyalties now in order to regain his composure. One of the midgets, a woman, separated herself from the rest and got everyone to step back a few paces. She turned out to be the eminent Lavinia Warren, the widow of General Tom Thumb, the most famous midget of all. Lavinia Warren Thumb was dressed in a magnificent gown supplied by Mrs. Fish: it was supposed to be a joke on Mrs. Fish's nemesis, Mrs. William Astor, who had worn the identical design the previous spring. Lavinia Thumb was coiffed in the Astor manner and wore glittering copies of the Astor jewels. She was nearly seventy years old and carried herself with dignity. Upon her wedding fifty years before she and Colonel Thumb had been received in the White House by the Lincolns. Houdini wanted to cry. Lavinia was no longer working in the circus but she had come down to New York from her home in Bridgeport, a clapboard house with escalloped bargeboards and a widow's walk, which cost something to maintain. That was why she had taken this evening's job. She lived in Bridgeport to be near the grave of her husband, who had died many years before and was commemorated in stone atop a monumental column in Mountain Grove Cemetery. Lavinia was two feet tall. She came to Houdini's knees. Her voice had deepened with age and she now spoke in the tones of a normal twenty-year-old girl. She had sparkling blue eyes, silver-white hair and the finest of wrinkles on her clear white skin. Houdini was reminded of his mother. Come on, kid, do a coupla numbers for us, Lavinia said.

Houdini entertained the circus folk with sleight of hand and some simple tricks. He put a billiard ball in his mouth, closed his mouth, opened it, and the billiard ball was gone. He closed his mouth and opened it again and removed the billiard ball. He stuck an ordinary sewing needle into his cheek and pulled it through the inner side. He opened his hand and produced a live chick. He withdrew from his ear a stream of colored silk. The freaks were delighted. They applauded and laughed. When he felt he had discharged his responsibilities, Houdini rose and told his manager he would not perform for Mrs. Stuyvesant Fish. There were remonstrations. Houdini stormed out the door. Crystal light dazzled his eyes. He was in the grand ballroom of the doge palace. A string orchestra played from a balcony. Great pale red drapes framed the clerestory windows and four hundred people were waltzing on a marble floor. Shading his eyes he saw bearing down on him Mrs. Fish herself, a clutch of jeweled feathers rising from her piled hair, ropes of pearls swinging pendulously from her neck, a witticism forming on her lips like the bubbles of an epileptic.

Despite such experiences Houdini never developed what we think of as a political consciousness. He could not reason from his own hurt feelings. To the end he would be almost totally unaware of the design of his career, the great map of revolution laid out by his life. He was a Jew. His real name was Erich Weiss. He was passionately in love with his ancient mother whom he had installed in his brownstone home on West 113th Street. In fact Sigmund Freud had just arrived in America to

[29]

give a series of lectures at Clark University in Worcester, Massachusetts, and so Houdini was destined to be, with Al Jolson, the last of the great shameless mother lovers, a nineteenth-century movement that included such men as Poe, John Brown, Lincoln and James McNeill Whistler. Of course Freud's immediate reception in America was not auspicious. A few professional alienists understood his importance, but to most of the public he appeared as some kind of German sexologist, an exponent of free love who used big words to talk about dirty things. At least a decade would have to pass before Freud would have his revenge and see his ideas begin to destroy sex in America forever.

6

Freud arrived in New York on the Lloyd liner *George Washington*. He was accompanied by his disciples Jung and Ferenczi, both some years his junior. They were met at the dock by two more younger Freudians, Drs. Ernest Jones and A. A. Brill. The entire party dined at Hammerstein's Roof Garden. There were potted palms. A piano violin duo played Liszt's *Hungarian Rhapsody*. Everyone talked around Freud, glancing at him continuously to gauge his mood. He ate cup custard. Brill and Jones undertook to play host for the visit. In the days following they showed Freud Central Park, the Metropolitan Museum and Chinatown. Catlike Chinamen gazed at them out of dark shops. There were glass cabinets filled with litchi nuts. The party went to one of the silent films so popular in stores and nickelodeons around the city. White smoke rose from the barrels of rifles and men wearing lipstick and rouge fell backwards clutching their chests. At least, Freud thought, it is silent. What oppressed him about the New World was its noise. The terrible clatter of horses and wagons, the clanking and screeching of streetcars, the horns of automobiles. At the wheel of an open Marmon, Brill drove the Freudians around Manhattan. At one point, on Fifth Avenue, Freud felt as if he was being observed; raising his eyes he found some children staring down at him from the top of a double-decker bus.

Brill drove the party down to the Lower East Side with its Yiddish theatres and pushcarts and elevated trains. The fearsome elevated rumbled past the windows of tenements in which people were expected to live. The windows shook, the very buildings shook. Freud had to relieve himself and nobody seemed to be able to tell him where a public facility could be found. They all had to enter a dairy restaurant and order sour cream with vegetables so that Freud could go to the bathroom. Later, back in the car, they pulled up to a corner to watch a street artist at work, an old man who with nothing but a scissors and paper made miniature silhouette portraits for a few cents. Standing for her portrait was a beautiful well-dressed woman. The excitable Ferenczi, masking his admiration for the woman's good looks, declared to his colleagues in the car his happiness at finding the ancient art of silhouette flourishing on the streets of the New World. Freud, clamping his teeth on his cigar, said nothing. The motor idled. Only Jung noticed the little girl in the pinafore standing slightly behind the young woman and holding her hand. The little girl peeked at Jung and the shaven-headed Jung, who was already disagreeing on certain crucial matters with his beloved mentor, looked through his thick steel-rimmed spectacles at the lovely child and experienced what he realized was a shock of recognition, although at the moment he could not have explained why. Brill pressed the gear pedal and the party continued on its tour. Their ultimate destination was Coney Island, a long way out of the city. They arrived in the late afternoon and immediately embarked on a tour of the three great amusement parks, beginning with Steeplechase and going on to Dreamland and finally late at night to the towers and domes, outlined in electric bulbs, of Luna Park. The dignified visitors rode the shoot-the-chutes and Freud and Jung took a boat together through the Tunnel of Love. The day came to a close only when Freud tired and had one of the fainting fits that had lately plagued him when in Jung's presence. A few days later the entire party journeyed to Worcester for Freud's lectures. When the lectures were completed Freud was persuaded to make an expedition to the great natural wonder of Niagara Falls. They arrived at the falls on an overcast day. Thousands of newly married couples stood, in pairs, watching the great cascades. Mist like an inverted rain rose from the falls. There was a high wire strung from one shore to the other and some maniac in ballet slippers and tights was walking the wire, keeping his balance with a parasol. Freud shook his head. Later the party went to the Cave of Winds. There, at an underground footbridge, a guide motioned the others back and took Freud's elbow. Let the old fellow go first, the guide said. The great doctor, age fifty-three, decided at this moment that he had had enough of America. With his disciples he sailed back to Germany on the *Kaiser Wilhelm der Grosse*. He had not really gotten used to the food or the scarcity of American public facilities. He believed the trip had ruined both his stomach and his bladder. The entire population seemed to him over-powered, brash and rude. The vulgar wholesale appropriation of European art and architecture regardless of period or country he found appalling. He had seen in our careless commingling of great wealth and great poverty the chaos of an entropic European civilization. He sat in his quiet cozy study in Vienna, glad to be back. He said to Ernest Jones, America is a mistake, a gigantic mistake.

At the time of course not a few people on these shores were ready to agree with him. Millions of men were out of work. Those fortunate enough to have jobs were dared to form unions. Courts enjoined them, police busted their heads, their leaders were jailed and new men took their jobs. A union was an affront to God. The laboring man would be protected and cared for not by the labor agitators, said one wealthy man, but by the Christian men to whom God in His infinite wisdom had given the control of the property interests of this country. If all else failed the troops were called out. Armories rose in every city of the country. In the coal fields a miner made a dollar sixty a day if he could dig three tons. He lived in the company's shacks and bought his food from the company stores. On the tobacco farms Negroes stripped tobacco leaves thirteen hours a day and earned six cents an hour, man, woman or child. Children suffered no discriminatory treatment. They were valued everywhere they were employed. They did not complain as adults tended to do. Employers liked to think of them as happy elves. If there was a problem about employing children it had to do only with their endurance. They were more agile than adults but they tended in the latter hours of the day to lose a degree of efficiency. In the canneries and mills these were the hours they were most likely to lose their fingers or have their hands mangled or their legs crushed; they had to be counseled to stay alert. In the mines they worked as sorters of coal and sometimes were smothered in the coal chutes; they were warned to keep their wits about them. One hundred Negroes a year were lynched. One hundred miners were burned alive. One hundred children were mutilated. There seemed to be quotas for these things. There seemed to be quotas for death by starvation. There were oil trusts and banking trusts and railroad trusts and beef trusts and steel trusts. It became fashionable to honor the poor. At palaces in New York and Chicago people gave poverty balls. Guests came dressed in rags and ate from tin plates and drank from chipped mugs. Ballrooms were decorated to look like mines with beams, iron tracks and miner's lamps. Theatrical scenery firms were hired to make outdoor gardens look like dirt farms and dining rooms like cotton mills. Guests smoked cigar butts offered to them on silver trays. Minstrels performed in blackface. One hostess invited everyone to a stockyard ball. Guests were wrapped in long aprons and their heads covered with white caps. They dined and danced while hanging carcasses of bloody beef trailed around the walls on moving pulleys. Entrails spilled on the floor. The proceeds were for charity.

7

One day after a visit to the Tombs Evelyn Nesbit happened to notice through the rear window of the electric hansom that for the first time in days none of the reporters were following. Usually Hearst and Pulitzer reporters dogged her in packs.

On an impulse she told the driver to turn and go east. A servant of Harry Thaw's mother, the driver permitted himself a frown. Evelyn took no notice. The car moved through the city, its motor humming in the warm afternoon. It was a black Detroit Electric with hard rubber tires. After a while through the window Evelyn saw the peddlers and pushcarts of the Lower East Side.

Dark-eyed faces peered into the hansom. Men with big moustaches smiled through their gold teeth. Street workers sat on the curbs in the heat and fanned themselves with their derbies. Boys in knickers ran alongside the car with bulky loads of piecework on their shoulders. Evelyn saw stores with Hebrew signs in the windows, the Hebrew letters looking to her eyes like arrangements of bones. She saw the iron fire escapes on the tenements as tiers of cellblocks. Nags in their yokes lifted their bowed necks to gaze at her. Ragmen struggling with their great junk-loaded two-wheeled carts, women selling breads from baskets carried in their arms: they all looked. The driver was nervous. He wore gray livery with black leather jodhpurs. He nosed the shiny car through the narrow filthy streets. A girl in a pinafore and high-laced shoes sat playing in the muck along the curbstone. A little dirty-faced girl. Stop the car, Evelyn said. The driver ran around and opened her door. Evelyn stepped into the street. She knelt down. The girl had straight black hair that fitted her head like a helmet. She had olive skin and eyes so brown they were black. She gazed at Evelyn without curiosity. She was the most beautiful child Evelyn had ever seen. A piece of clothesline was tied around her wrist. Evelyn stood up, followed the clothesline, and found herself looking into the face of a mad old man with a closely cropped gray beard. The end of the line was tied around the old man's waist. He wore a threadbare coat. One sleeve was torn. He wore a soft cap and a collar with a tie. He stood on the sidewalk in front of a display cart of framed silhouette portraits pinned to a black velvet curtain. He was a silhouette artist. With nothing but a small scissors and some glue he would make your image by cutting a piece of white paper and mounting it on a black background. The whole thing with the frame cost fifteen cents. Fifteen cents, lady, the old man said. Why do you have this child tied with a rope, Evelyn said. The old man gazed at her finery. He laughed and shook his head and talked to himself in Yiddish. He turned his back to her. A crowd had gathered when the car stopped. A tall working-man stepped forward and removed his hat with respect before translating for Evelyn what the old man had said. Please, missus, he said, so the little girl is not stolen from him. Evelyn had the feeling the translator was also something of a diplomat. The old artist was laughing bitterly and thrusting his chin in her direction, obviously commenting on her. He says the rich lady may not be aware that young girls in the slums are stolen every day from their parents and sold into slavery. Evelyn was shocked. This child can't be more than ten, she said. The old man began to shout and pointed across the street at a tenement house, and turned and pointed toward the corner and turned and pointed to the other corner. Please, missus, the tall workingman said, married women, children, anyone they can get their hands on. They defile them and then in shame the female gives her life to vagrancy. Houses on this very street are used for this purpose. Where are the child's parents, Evelyn demanded. The old man was now talking to the crowd, beating his breast and pointing his finger in the air. A woman in a black shawl shook her head and moaned in sympathy. The old man took off his hat and tugged at his hair. Even the tall workingman forgot to translate, so moved was he by the account. Please, missus, he finally said, this man himself is the child's father. He pointed to the artist's torn sleeve. His own wife, to feed them, offered herself and he has now driven her from his home and mourns her as we mourn the dead. His hair has turned white in the last month. He is thirty-two years old.

The old man, weeping and biting his lip, turned to Evelyn and saw now that she too was moved. For a moment everyone standing there on the corner shared his misfortune—Evelyn, the chauffeur, the workingman, the woman in the black shawl, the onlookers. Then one person walked away. Then another. The crowd dispersed. Evelyn made her way to the little girl still sitting at the curb. She knelt down, her eyes dewy, and looked into the face of the dry-eyed girl. Hey pumpkin, she said.

Thus began Evelyn Nesbit's concern for the thirty-two-year-old geriatric artist and his daughter. The man had a long Jewish name that she couldn't pronounce so she took to calling him Tateh, the name by which the little girl called him. Tateh was president of the Socialist Artists' Alliance of the Lower East Side. He was a proud man. Evelyn discovered that there was no way to approach him except by coming to have her silhouette done. Over a period of two weeks the old man executed a hundred and forty silhouette portraits of Evelyn. After each one she would hand him fifteen cents. Sometimes she demanded a portrait of the little girl. Tateh executed over ninety of these, and he took more time with them. Then Evelyn asked for double portraits of herself and the little girl. At this the old man looked directly at her and a terrible Hebraic judgment seemed to flash from his eyes. Nevertheless he did as he was asked. As time went on it became apparent to Evelyn that while people sometimes stopped to watch the old man work, very few people asked to have their portraits done. He began to create more and more intricate silhouettes, full-figured, with backgrounds, of Evelyn, of the little girl, of a drayman's horse plodding by, of five men in stiff collars sitting in an open car. With his scissors he suggested not merely outlines but textures, moods, character, despair. Most of these are today in private collections. Evelyn came nearly every afternoon and stayed for as long as she could. She dressed down to be as inconspicuous as possible. Following a Thaw practice she paid great sums of money to the chauffeur to keep him quiet. Gossip columnists began to infer from Evelyn's disappearances that she was engaging in reckless liaisons, and her name was linked with dozens of men around town. The less she was seen the more slanderous the reports became. She didn't care. She sneaked off to her new love interest on the Lower East Side. She wore a shawl over her head and a tattered black moth-eaten sweater over her shirtwaist; the chauffeur kept these for her under the car rug. She went to Tateh's corner, stood for her portrait and feasted her eyes on the little girl at the end of the clothesline. She was infatuated. And all this time there was no man in her life other than her mad husband, Harry K. Thaw. Unless she wanted to consider her secret admirer, the young man with the high cheekbones and blond moustaches who followed her everywhere she went. She had seen him first at Tateh's corner, standing across the street and turning his eyes away when she challenged him with her gaze. She knew her mother-in-law employed private detectives but she decided he was too shy to be a detective. He had learned where she lived and what her daily routine was, but he never approached her. She felt not intimidated by his attention but protected. Intuitively she felt his admiration like a keenness in her own breath. At night she dreamed of the little girl, woke up, thought of her. Plans for the future flashed in her mind like fireworks and quickly disappeared. She was anxious, over-wrought, aroused, unaccountably happy. She would testify on her husband's behalf and do it well. She was hopeful that he would be found guilty and locked up for life.

The little girl in the pinafore held her hand but would not say anything to her. Even to Tateh she spoke few words. Tateh said no one mourns like a child, not even a lover. Evelyn realized that the old man's pride would have driven her off long ago if he had not perceived that her attentions to the little girl were helpful. One day Evelyn came for her portrait and neither father nor daughter was to be seen. Fortunately she had learned where they lived, on Hester Street, over a public bath. She went there now, walking quickly, not daring to think what was the matter. Hester Street was a teeming marketplace of peddlers who sold vegetables and fruits and chickens and breads from pushcarts lined up along the curb. The sidewalks were glutted with shoppers, overflowing garbage cans stood in ranks beside the entrance stairs of every house. Bedding hung from fire escapes. Evelyn rushed up a flight of iron stairs and into a dark incredibly foul-smelling hallway. Tateh and the little girl lived on the top floor, in two small rooms in the back. She knocked on the door. She knocked again. A moment later it opened a crack; there was a chain latch in place. What is the matter, Evelyn said. Let me in.

Tateh was scandalized by her visit. He stood in only his shirt and pants held up by suspenders and he wore house slippers.

He insisted that the front door be left open despite the rank winds that blew up the stairwell, and quickly put on his jacket and shoes. He hurriedly made up his cot, throwing over it a brightly colored spread. The little girl lay on a brass bed in the other room. She was ill with a fever. The two rooms were lit by candle. The bedroom, although it had a window, was almost as dark as the front room. It looked out on an air shaft. The whole place was no bigger than a closet. Yet as Evelyn's eyes accustomed themselves to the darkness she perceived that the home was scrupulously clean. Her arrival had caused a storm of consternation in the old artist, who paced up and down in the candlelight and did not know what to do about her. In great agitation he smoked a cigarette which he held between his thumb and forefinger, palm up, in the European style. I will stay with the child, Evelyn insisted, while you go to work. Finally the old man gave in, if only to avoid the terrible strain on himself of her presence in his home. He rushed out carrying his display stand with its black velvet curtains folded over his arms and his wooden box, like a suitcase, that held his materials. Evelyn closed the door after him. She looked at the glass cabinet, at the few cups and plates of chipped crockery. She examined the bedding in the drawers, the scrubbed oak table and chairs where the family ate. There was a pile of unfinished knee pants on a sewing machine by the bedroom window. The machine had a filigreed iron treadle. The window in the bedroom sparkled with the reflection of the candle. The brass of the thin little bed was shining. Evelyn felt a strong kinship with the departed mother. The girl looked at her from the pillows and neither smiled nor said anything. Evelyn removed the shawl, the old sweater, and put them down on a chair. In a packing crate laid on its end beside the bed, like an end table, books in Yiddish were stacked tightly. There were books in English too, on socialism, and pamphlets on the covers of which workingmen with powerful linked arms were marching forward. None of them looked like the frail white-haired Tateh. There were no mirrors on the walls and no photographs anywhere of the family, of the missing wife and mother. She found a tub of galvanized tin in the front room. She found a pail and went down the stairs and drew from the sink on the ground floor a pail of water. She warmed the water on the coal stove in the front room and went into the bedroom with the tub, the pail of water and a thin starched towel. The little girl clutched the covers about her. Evelyn gently removed the covers and sat her up on the edge of the bed and raised her nightgown and stood her up and lifted the nightgown over her head, feeling like the sun the warm exhalations of her young body. Come stand a moment in the tub, she said and knelt in front of the girl and bathed her with the warm water scooping it in her hands and caressing the child with her hands of water and doing it again, on her tawny shoulders, her nut-brown budded nipples, her face, her downy back, her thin thighs, the smooth slope of her stomach, her girlhood, the sluiced water from her young fevered body falling like rain in the tub as Evelyn bathed her with her hands. Then with the towel folded in quarters she gently patted the little girl dry and dressed her afresh in another gown she had found in the drawer—a larger gown this time of thin cotton, much too big, funny, so that the girl laughed. Evelyn smoothed the sheets and plumped up the pillows and settled the girl in the bed again and felt her forehead and it was cool. The little girl's dark eyes shone in the dusk. Evelyn combed her black hair and touched her face and leaned over her, and the little girl's arms went around Evelyn's neck and she kissed her on the lips.

This was the day Evelyn Nesbit considered kidnapping the little girl and leaving Tateh to his fate. The old artist had never inquired of her name and knew nothing about her. It could be done. Instead she threw herself into the family's life with redoubled effort, coming with food, linens and whatever else she could move past the old man's tormented pride. She was insane with the desire to become one of them and drew Tateh out in conversation and learned from the girl how to sew knee pants. For hours each day, each evening, she lived as a woman in the Jewish slums, and was driven home by the Thaw chauffeur from a prearranged place many blocks away, always in despair. She was so desperately in love that she could no longer see properly, something had happened to her eyes, and she blinked constantly as if to clear them of the blur. She saw everything through a film of salt tears, and her voice became husky because her throat was bathed in the irrepressible and continuous crying which her happiness caused her.

8

One day Tateh invited her to a meeting of which the Socialist Artists' Alliance of the Lower East Side was a part sponsor, along with seven other organizations. It was an important event. The featured speaker was to be none other than Emma Goldman. Carefully Tateh explained that although he was unalterably opposed to Goldman, she being an anarchist and he a socialist, he had great respect for her personal courage and integrity; and that he had therefore agreed that some sort of temporary accord between the socialists and the anarchists was advisable, if only for the evening, because the funds raised for the occasion would go to support the shirtwaist makers, who were then on strike, and the steelworkers at McKeesport, Pennsylvania, who were on strike, and the anarchist Francisco Ferrer, who was going to be condemned and executed by the Spanish government for fomenting a general strike in Spain. In five minutes Evelyn was immersed in the bracing linguistics of radical idealism. She didn't dare confess to Tateh that she had had no idea socialism and anarchism were not the same thing, or that the thought of seeing the notorious Emma Goldman frightened her. She pulled her shawl over her head, and holding the little girl's hand tightly, walked behind Tateh as he strode north to the Workingmen's Hall on East 14th Street. But she did at one point turn around to see if her strange shy admirer was following, and he was, half a block behind, his lean face hidden in the shadow of his straw boater.

Emma Goldman's subject was the great dramatist Ibsen in whose work, she said, lay all the instruments for the radical dissection of society. She was not a physically impressive woman, being small, thick-waisted, with a heavy-jawed masculine face. She wore horn-rimmed glasses that enlarged her eyes and suggested the constant outrage to her soul of the sights she saw. She had immense vitality and her voice rang, and Evelyn, after getting over her relief to discover that Goldman was simply a woman, and a rather small woman at that, was swept up by the oratory of powerful ideas that lifted her mind like a river. In the heat and constant excitement rising from the audience she allowed her shawl to drop to her shoulders. There were perhaps a hundred people present, all sitting on benches or standing along the walls while Goldman spoke from behind a table at the end of the room. The police department had stationed men prominently at the doors and at one point a police sergeant tried to stop Emma's address, claiming she had been advertised to speak on the subject of the drama but instead was talking about Ibsen. Jeers and catcalls drove him from the hall. Goldman, however, did not join the laughter, knowing from experience what an embarrassed police force inevitably did. She spoke now with great rapidity and as she spoke her eyes ranged restlessly over the audience and came to stop, again and again, on the alabaster face of Evelyn Nesbit, who sat between Tateh and the little girl in the first row on the right, a position of honor as befitted Tateh's office as president of the Socialist Artists' Alliance. Love in freedom! Goldman cried. Those who like Mrs. Alving have paid with blood and tears for their spiritual awakening, repudiate marriage as an imposition, a shallow empty mockery. Some of the audience, including Tateh, shouted No! No! Comrades and brothers, Goldman said, can you socialists ignore the double bondage of one-half of the human race? Do you think the society that plunders your labor has no interest in the way you are asked to live with women? Not through freedom but through bondage? All the reformers talk today of the white slavery problem. But if white slavery is a problem, why is marriage not a problem? Is there no connection between the institution of marriage and the institution of the brothel? At mention of this word cries of Shame! Shame! filled the hall. Tateh had put his hands over his daughter's ear and pressed her head to his side. A man stood and shouted. Goldman held up her hands for quiet. Comrades, let us disagree, of course, but not by losing our decorum to the extent that the police may have an excuse to interrupt us. People turning in their seats indeed saw now a dozen policemen in the crowd at the doors. The truth is, Goldman went on quickly, women may not vote, they may not love whom they want, they may not develop their minds and their spirits, they may not commit their lives to the spiritual adventure of life, comrades they may not! And why? Is our genius only in our wombs? Can we not write books and create learned scholarship and perform music and provide philosophical models for the betterment of mankind? Must our fate always be physical? There sits among us this evening one of the most brilliant women in America, a woman forced by this capitalist society to find her genius in the exercise of her sexual attraction—and she has done that, comrades, to an extent that a Pierpont Morgan and a John D. Rockefeller could envy. Yet her name is scandal and their names are intoned with reverence and respect by the toadying legislators of this society. Evelyn went cold. She wanted to pull the shawl over her head but was afraid she would draw attention to herself. She sat perfectly still, staring at her hands in her lap. At least the woman had had the grace not to look in her direction as she spoke. People in the audience who were craning their necks trying to locate the object of Goldman's remarks were diverted now by a shout from the back of the hall. A phalanx of blue coats jammed through the doors. There was a scream. And suddenly the hall was pandemonium. It was a typical conclusion to an Emma Goldman speech. Police poured down the center aisle. The anarchist stood calmly behind her table and put her papers in her brief case. Evelyn Nesbit felt Tateh's eyes upon her and turned into the glare of his judgment. He was looking at her as she had seen him look upon a roach before he stepped on it. Then his old face seemed to collapse into another, more complex set of wrinkles and lines, his entire being settled into the last age before death, and his eyes, from the depths of his ancient skull, translated for her the whispered Yiddish that came from his broken lips: My life is desecrated by whores, is what he said. And grasping the hand of the little girl in the pinafore, he disappeared into the crowd.

Evelyn stood staring after them. It seemed to her that the light was racing away from her eyes. Her hand went out for something to hold. A now familiar voice said in her ear This way, come with me, and her arm was in the grip of Goldman herself. It was a grip of iron. Goldman led her through a small door behind the speaker's table and just before the door closed Evelyn, letting a high thin wail from her throat, looked back and saw her shy blond young shadow fighting his way furiously in her direction. I am an old hand at this, Emma Goldman said leading her down a dark stairs. This is just an ordinary evening. The stairs gave onto the street around the corner from the entrance to the meeting hall. A police van passed them, its bell clanging; it turned the corner. Come, Emma Goldman said, linking her arm, and she walked Evelyn quickly away in the opposite direction.

When Mother's Younger Brother reached the street he just managed to see the two female figures passing under a streetlight two blocks away. He hurried after them. The evening was cool. The perspiration on his neck chilled him. A breeze whipped his duck trousers. He came to within a half-block of the two women and for some minutes followed them at this distance. They turned, suddenly, and went up the stone stairs of a brownstone. He ran now and when he reached the brownstone saw that it was a rooming house. He went inside and quietly went up the stairs, not knowing what room he was looking for but sure somehow he'd find it. On the second landing he backed into the shadowed recess of a door. Goldman, carrying a basin, passed on her way to the bathroom. He heard the sound of water running and found the open door to Goldman's room. It was a small room and peeking around the door he saw Evelyn Nesbit sitting on the bed, her face in her hands. Sobs shook her body. The walls were a faded lilac print. An electric lamp at the bedside provided the only light. Hearing Goldman coming back Younger Brother soundlessly darted into the room and slipped into the closet. He left the closet door slightly ajar.

Goldman placed the basin of water on the bedtable and shook out a thin starched face towel. Poor girl, she said, poor girl. Why don't you let me refresh you a bit. I'm a nurse, you know, that's how I support myself. I've followed your case in the newspapers. From the beginning I found myself admiring you. I couldn't understand why. She unlaced Evelyn's high-top shoes and slipped them off. Don't you want to put your feet up? she said. That's the way. Evelyn lay back on the pillows rubbing her eyes with the heels of her hand. She took the towel offered by Goldman. Oh, I hate to cry, she said. Crying makes me ugly. She wept into the towel. After all, Goldman went on, you're nothing more than a clever prostitute. You accepted the conditions in which you found yourself and you triumphed. But what kind of a victory has it been? The victory of the prostitute. And what have your consolations been? The consolations of cynicism, of scorn, of contempt for the human male. Why, I thought, should I feel such strong sisterhood with this woman? After all I have never accepted servitude. I have been free. I have fought all my life to be free. And I have never taken a man to bed without loving him, without taking him in love as a free human being, his equal, giving and taking in equal portions in love and freedom. I've probably slept with more men than you have. I've loved more men than you have. I bet it would shock you to know how free I've been, in what freedom I've lived my life. Because like all whores you value propriety. You are a creature of capitalism, the ethics of which are so totally corrupt and hypocritical that your beauty is no more than the beauty of gold, which is to say false and cold and useless.

No other words could have so quickly stemmed Evelyn's tears. She lowered the towel from her face and stared at the stout little anarchist who now paced back and forth in front of the bed as she spoke. So why should I have felt such strong bonds between us? You are the embodiment in woman of everything I pity and abhor. When I saw you at my meeting I was ready to accept the mystical rule of all experience. You came because in such ways as the universe works, your life was destined to interact with my own. Through the vile depths of your own existence your heart has directed you to the anarchist movement.

Nesbit shook her head. You don't understand, she said. Tears filled her eyes once again. She told Goldman about the little girl in the pinafore. She told her of Tateh and her secret life in the slums. And now I have lost them, she said. I have lost my urchin. She wept bitterly. Goldman sat down in the rocking chair beside the bed and placed her hands on her knees. She leaned toward Evelyn Nesbit. All right, if I had not pointed you out your Tateh wouldn't have run off. But what of it? Don't worry. Truth is better than lies. When you find them again you'll be able to deal with them honestly, as the person you really are. And if you don't find them, perhaps *that* will be for the best. Who can say who are the instrumentalities and who are the people. Which of us causes, and lives in others to cause, and which of us is meant thereby to live. That is exactly my point. Do you know at one time in my life I walked the streets to sell my body? You are the first person I have ever told. Fortunately I was spotted for the novice that I was and sent home. It was on 14th Street. I tried to look like a street-walker and I fooled no one. I don't suppose the name Alexander Berkman means anything to you. Evelyn shook her head. When Berkman and I were in our early twenties we were lovers and revolutionaries together. There was a strike in Pittsburgh. At the Homestead steel plant of Mr. Carnegie. And Mr. Carnegie decided to break the union. So he ran off for a European vacation and had his chief toady, that infamous piece of scum Henry Clay Frick, do the job. Frick imported an army of Pinkertons. The workers were on strike to protest the cutting of wages. The plant is on the Monongahela River and Frick towed his Pinkertons up the river and landed them at the plant from the river. There was a pitched battle. It was a war. When it was over ten were dead and dozens and dozens were wounded. The Pinkertons were driven off. So then Frick was able to get the government working for him and the state militia came in to surround the workers. At this point Berkman and I decided on our *attentat.* We would give the beleaguered workers heart. We would revolutionize their struggle. We would kill Frick. But we were in New York and we had no money. We needed money for a railroad ticket and for a gun. And that's when I put on embroidered underwear and walked 14th Street. An old man gave me ten dollars and told me to go home. I borrowed the rest. But I would have done it if I had to. It was for the *attentat.* It was for Berkman and the revolution. I embraced him at the station. He planned to shoot

Frick and take his own life at his trial. I ran after the departing train. We only had money for one ticket. He said only one person was needed for the job. He barged into Frick's office in Pittsburgh and shot the bastard three times. In the neck, in the shoulder. There was blood. Frick collapsed. Men ran in. They took the gun. He had a knife. He stabbed Frick in the leg. They took the knife. He put something in his mouth. They pinned him to the ground. They pried open his jaws. It was a capsule of fulminate of mercury. All he had to do was chew on the capsule and the room would have blown up and every-one in it. They held his head back. They removed the capsule. They beat him unconscious.

Evelyn had sat up in bed, drawing her knees up to her chest. Goldman stared at the floor. He was in prison eighteen years, she said, many of them in solitary, in a dungeon. I visited him once. I could never bear to visit him again. And that bastard Frick survived and became a hero in the press and the public turned against the workers and the strike was broken. It was said we set back the American labor movement forty years. There was another anarchist, Most, an older man whom I revered. He denounced Berkman and me in his newspaper. The next time I saw Most at a meeting I was prepared. I had bought a horsewhip. I horsewhipped him in front of everyone. Then I broke the whip and threw it in his face. Berkman got out only last year. His hair is gone. He is the color of parch-ment. My darling young man walks with a stoop. His eyes are like coal pits. We are friends in principle only. Our hearts no longer beat together. What he endured in that prison I can only imagine. Living in darkness, in wet, tied up and left to lie in his own filth. Evelyn's arm had gone out to the older woman and Goldman now took her hand and held it tightly. We know, don't we, both of us, what it means to have a man in jail. The two women looked at each other. There was silence for some moments. Of course, your man is a pervert, a parasite, a leech, a foul loathsome sybarite, Goldman said. Evelyn laughed. An insane pig, Goldman said, with a twisted shrunken little pig's mentality. Now they were both laughing. Yes, I hate him, Evelyn cried. Goldman grew reflective. But there are correspondences, you see, our lives correspond, our spirits touch each other like notes in harmony, and in the total human fate we are sisters. Do you understand that, Evelyn Nesbit? She stood and touched Nesbit's face. Do you see that, my beautiful girl?

As she had been talking Goldman's eyes reacted to something in Evelyn's posture. Are you wearing a corset? she now asked. Evelyn nodded. You ought to be ashamed of yourself. Look at me, even with my figure I have not one foundation garment, I wear everything loose and free-flowing, I give my body the freedom to breathe and to be. That's what I mean, you're a creature of their making. You have no more need of stays than a wood nymph. She took Nesbit's hands and sat her up on the edge of the bed. She felt her waist. My God, stays like steel. Your waist is pinched tighter than a purse string. Stand up. Evelyn stood up obediently and Goldman with a nurse's expertise swiftly unbuttoned her shirtwaist and removed it. She unclasped Evelyn's skirt and had her step out of it. She untied the strings of her petticoat and removed it. Evelyn wore a light corset around her waist. The top of the corset pushed up her bosom. The bottom was attached to straps which went between her thighs. The corset was laced in the back. It is ironic that you are thought of in homes all over America as a licentious shameless wanton, Goldman said pulling the laces out of the grommets, loosening the garment and pulling it down Evelyn's legs. Step out, she said. Evelyn obeyed. Her undershift remained stuck to her body in the pattern of the stays. Breathe, Goldman commanded, raise your arms, stretch your legs and breathe. Evelyn obeyed. Goldman plucked at the shift, then lifted it over her head. Then she knelt and slid Evelyn's lace-trimmed underdrawers to her feet. Step out, she commanded. Evelyn did so. She now stood nude in the lamplight except for her black embroidered cotton stockings which were held up by elastic bands around the thighs. Goldman rolled the stockings down and Evelyn stepped out of her stockings. She held her arms across her breasts. Goldman stood and turned her around slowly for inspection, a frown on her face. Look at that, it's amazing you have any circulation at all. Marks of the stays ran vertically like welts around Nesbit's waist. The evidence of garters could be seen in the red lines running around the tops of her thighs. Women kill themselves, Goldman said. She turned back the bedcovers. She took from the top of the bureau a small black bag of the kind that doctors carried. A superb body like this and look what you do to it. Lie down. Evelyn sat down on the bed and looked at what was coming out of the black bag. On your stomach, Goldman said. She was holding a bottle and tilting the contents of the bottle into her cupped hand. Evelyn lay down on her stomach and Goldman applied the liquid where the marks of the stays reddened the flesh. Ow, Evelyn cried. It stings! This is an astringent—the first thing is to restore circulation, Goldman explained as she rubbed Evelyn's back and buttocks and thighs. Evelyn was squirming and her flesh cringing with each application. She buried her face in the pillow to smother her cries. I know, I know, Goldman said. But you will thank me. Under Goldman's vigorous rubbing Evelyn's flesh seemed to spring into its fullest conformations. She was shivering now and her buttocks were clenched against the invigorating chill of the astringent. Her legs squeezed together. Goldman now took from her bag a bottle of massage oil and began to knead Evelyn's neck and shoulders and back, her thighs and calves and the soles of her feet. Gradually Evelyn relaxed and her flesh shook and quivered under the emphatic skill of Goldman's hands. Goldman rubbed the oil into her skin

[53]

until her body found its own natural rosy white being and began to stir with self-perception. Turn over, Goldman commanded. Evelyn's hair was now undone and lay on the pillow about her face. Her eyes were closed and her lips stretched in an involuntary smile as Goldman massaged her breasts, her stomach, her legs. Yes, even this, Emma Goldman said, briskly passing her hand over the mons. You must have the courage to live. The bedside lamp seemed to dim for a moment. Evelyn put her own hands on her breasts and her palms rotated the nipples. Her hands swam down along her flanks. She rubbed her hips. Her feet pointed like a dancer's and her toes curled. Her pelvis rose from the bed as if seeking something in the air. Goldman was now at the bureau, capping her bottled emollient, her back to Evelyn as the younger woman began to ripple on the bed like a wave on the sea. At this moment a hoarse unearthly cry issued from the walls, the closet door flew open and Mother's Younger Brother fell into the room, his face twisted in a paroxysm of saintly mortification. He was clutching in his hands, as if trying to choke it, a rampant penis which, scornful of his intentions, whipped him about the floor, launching to his cries of ecstasy or despair, great filamented spurts of jism that traced the air like bullets and then settled slowly over Evelyn in her bed like falling ticker tape.

9

In New Rochelle, Mother had for days brooded about her brother. He had called on the telephone from New York once or twice but would not say why he had gone away or where he was staying or when he would return. He mumbled. He was close-mouthed. She was furious with him. He did not respond to anger. Since his calls she had taken the extreme step of going into his room and looking around. As always it was neat. There was his table with the machine for stringing tennis racquets. There were his scull oars in brackets on the wall. He kept his own room and there was not a speck of dust even now in his absence. His hairbrushes on the bureau top. His ivory shoehorn. A small shell shaped like a thimble, with some grains of sand stuck to it. She had never seen that before. A picture from a magazine pinned to the wall, the drawing by Charles Dana Gibson of that Evelyn Nesbit creature. He had packed nothing, his shirts and collars filled the drawer. She closed the door guiltily. He was a strange young man. He never made friends. He was solitary and impassive except for a streak of indolence which he either could not hide or did not care to. She knew Father found that indolence disturbing. Nevertheless he had promoted him to greater responsibility.

She could not share her worries with Grandfather, who had sired the young man at a late age and was now totally separated from any practical perception of life. Grandfather was in his nineties. He was a retired professor of Greek and Latin who had taught generations of Episcopal seminarians at Shady Grove College in central Ohio. He was a country classicist. He had known John Brown when he was a boy in Hudson County in the Western Reserve and would tell you that twenty times a day if you let him. More and more since Father's departure Mother thought of the old Ohio homestead. The summers there were gravid with promise and red-winged blackbirds flew up from the hay meadows. The furnishings of the house were spare, and country-made. Ladderback chairs of pine. Polished wood floors of wide boards fastened with dowels. She had loved that house. She and Younger Brother played on the floor by the light of the fire. In their games she always instructed him. In winter their horse Bessie was hitched to the sleigh and bells were tied to her collar and they skimmed over the thick wet Ohio snowfalls. She remembered Brother when he was younger than her own son. She took care of him. On rainy days they played secret pretending games in the hayloft, in the sweet warmth, with the horses snorting and nickering below them. On Sunday morning she wore her pink dress and the purest white pantaloons and went to church with a heart beating with excitement. She was a large-boned child with high cheekbones and gray eyes that slanted. She had lived in Shady Grove all her life except for four years at boarding school in Cleveland. She had always presumed she would marry one of the seminarians. But in her last year at school she had met Father. He was traveling through the Midwest to make local sales connections for his flag and bunting business. He called on her at Shady Grove on two successive business trips. When they married and she came East she brought her father with her. And then because Brother had not been able to settle himself he too had joined the household in New Rochelle. And now in this season of life, alone in her modern awninged home at the top of the hill on fashionable Broadview Avenue with only her small son and her ancient father, she felt deserted by the race of males and furious with herself for the nostalgia that swept through her without warning at any hour of the day or night. A letter had arrived from the Republican Inaugural Committee inquiring if the firm would care to bid on the decoration and fireworks contract for the inauguration parade and ball the following January, when Mr. Taft was expected to succeed Mr. Roosevelt. It was an historic moment for the business and neither Father nor Younger Brother was on hand. She fled to the garden for solace. This was the late September of the year and all the heavy swaying flowers were in bloom, salvia, chrysanthemum and marigold. She walked along the borders of the yard, her hands clasped. From an upstairs window the little boy watched her. He noted that the forward motion of her body was transmitted to her clothes laterally. The hem of her skirt swayed from side to side, brushing the leaves of grass. He held in his hand a letter from his father that had been posted from Cape York in northwest Greenland. It had been brought back to the United States by the supply ship *Erik*, which had transported to Greenland thirty-five tons of whale meat for Commander Peary's dogs. Mother had copied the letter and thrown the original in the garbage because it strongly suggested the smell of dead whale. The boy had retrieved the letter and as time passed, the grease spots on the envelope were worked into every fiber of the paper by his small hands. The letter was now translucent.

As the boy watched his mother she came out of the dappled shade of the maple trees, and her golden hair, which she wore piled on her head in the style of the day, flared like the sun. She stood for a moment as if listening to something. She brought her hands up to her ears and slowly, by the flower bed, dropped to her knees. Then she began to paw the ground. The little boy left the window and raced downstairs. He went through the kitchen and out the back door. He found himself following the Irish housemaid, who was running through the yard wiping her hands on her apron.

Mother had dug something up. She was brushing the dirt from a bundle which she held on her lap. The maid let out a scream and crossed herself. The little boy tried to get a look at it, whatever it was, but Mother and the maid were on the ground, brushing the dirt off, and for a moment he couldn't get past them. Mother's face had turned so pale and suffered such an intense expression that all the bones of her face appeared to have grown and the opulently beautiful woman he revered was shockingly haggard, like someone ancient. He saw, as they brushed the dirt away, that it was an infant. Dirt was in its eyes, in its mouth. It was small and wrinkled and its eyes were closed. It was a brown baby and had been bound tight in a cotton blanket. Mother freed its arms. It made a small weak cry, and the two women grew hysterical. The maid ran into the house. The boy followed his mother to the house, running alongside her as the small arms of the brown baby waved in the air.

The women washed the baby in a basin on the kitchen table. It was bloody, an unwashed newborn boy. The maid examined the cord and said it had been bitten. They swaddled it in towels, and Mother ran to the front hall to phone the doctor. The boy watched the infant closely to see if it was breathing. It barely moved. Then its tiny fingers grasped the towels. Its head slowly turned as if through its closed eyes it had found something to look at.

When the doctor came in his Ford Doctor's Car he was shown into the kitchen. He held his stethoscope to the small bony rib cage. He opened the mouth and poked his finger down the throat. These people, he said. He shook his head.

The muscles of his cheeks pulled in his mouth at the corners. Mother described for him the circumstances of the discovery: how she had heard a cry coming from her feet, from the earth, and thought at the moment she had heard it that she had not heard it at all. And what if I had walked on, she said to herself. The doctor asked for some hot water. He removed an instrument from his bag. The maid tightly clutched the small cross that hung from her neck on a chain. The doorbell rang and the boy followed her into the front hall. The police had arrived. Mother came out and explained the circumstances once again. The policeman asked if he could use the telephone. The telephone was on a table near the front door. He removed his helmet, picked up the phone and put the receiver to his ear and waited for the operator. He winked at the boy.

Within an hour a black woman was found in the cellar of a home on the next block. She was a washwoman who worked in the neighborhood. She sat outside the house in the police ambulance and Mother brought the baby out to her. When the woman took the baby in her arms she began to cry. Mother was shocked by her youth. She had a child's face, a guileless brown beautiful face. She was the color of dark chocolate and her hair looked chopped and uncared for. She was being attended by a nurse. Mother stepped back on the sidewalk. Where will you take her, she said to the doctor. To the charity ward, he said. And eventually she will have to stand charges. What charges, Mother said. Well, attempted murder, I should think. Does she have family, Mother said. No, ma'am, the policeman said. Not so's we know. The doctor pulled down on the rim of his derby and walked to his car and put his bag on the seat. Mother took a deep breath. I will take the responsibility, she said. Please bring her inside. And despite the best advice of the doctor and the remonstrations of the police, she would not change her mind.

So the young black woman and her child were installed in

a room on the top floor. Mother made numbers of phone calls. She canceled her service league meeting. She walked back and forth in her parlor. She was very agitated. She felt keenly her husband's absence and condemned herself for so readily endorsing his travels. There was no way to communicate with him any of the problems and concerns of her life. She would not hear from him till the following summer. She stared at the ceiling as if to see through it. The Negro girl and her baby had carried into the house a sense of misfortune, of chaos, and now this feeling resided here like some sort of contamination. She was frightened. She went to the window. Every morning these washwomen came up the hill from the trolley line on North Avenue and fanned into the houses. Traveling Italian gardeners kept the lawns trim. Icemen walked alongside their wagons, their horses straining in their traces to pull the creaking ice wagons up the hill.

When the sun set that evening it lay at the bottom of the hill as if it had rolled there. It was blood red. Late at night the boy woke and found his mother sitting beside the bed looking at him, her golden hair plaited and her large breasts soft against his arm when she leaned over to kiss him.

10

Actually Father wrote every day during the long winter months, letters for delayed transmission which took the form of entries in his journal. In this way he measured the uninterrupted flow of twilight darkness. The members of the expedition lived in surprising comfort aboard the *Roosevelt*, which had been lifted in its berth by the winter floes until it sat like a walnut in icing. Peary lived the most comfortably of all. He had a player piano in his stateroom. He was a large man with a heavy torso and thick red hair turning gray. He wore a long moustache. In a previous expedition he had lost his toes. He walked with an odd gait, a kind of shuffle, pushing his feet along the floor without lifting them. He pedaled his player piano with toeless feet. He was supplied with rolls of the best Victor Herbert and Rudolf Friml numbers as well as a medley of Bowdoin College songs and a version of *The Minute Waltz* of Chopin which he could pump out in forty-eight seconds. But the winter months were not given to idleness. There were hunting sorties for musk ox; there were sledges to be built, and the base camp had to be set up ninety miles away, at Cape Columbia, the point from which the actual polar dash across the sea ice would be made. Everyone had to get used to handling dog teams and building igloo shelters. Peary's Negro assistant, Mathew Henson, supervised the training. After numbers of expeditions, Peary had developed a system. Every last detail of their lives in the Arctic represented his considered judgment and was part of the system. The material and designs of the sledges, the food that was to be eaten, the tins in which the food was to be carried, the manner in which the tins were to be lashed to the sledges, the kind of under- and over-clothing that was to be worn, the means of harnessing the dogs, the kinds of knives and guns to carry, the kinds of matches and the means of keeping them dry, the design of the eye guards to be used against snow blindness, and so on. Peary loved to discuss his system. In its essentials—that is, in the use of dogs and sledges and the wearing of fur clothing and the living off local fauna—Peary's system merely adopted the Esquimo way of life. Father realized this with a start one day. As it happened he had been standing on the quarter-deck observing Peary soundly scold one of the Esquimo men who had not done his assigned chore properly. Then Peary shuffled back along the deck, passing Father and saying to him They're children and they have to be treated like children. Father tended to agree with this view, for it suggested a consensus. He recalled an observation made in the Philippines ten years before where he had fought under General Leonard F. Wood against the Moro guerrillas. Our little brown brothers have to be taught a lesson, a staff officer had said, sticking a campaign pin in a map. There was no question that the Esquimos were primitives. They were affectionate, gentle, emotional, trustworthy and full of pranks. They loved to laugh and sing. In the deepest part of the winter of continuous night, when terrible storms tore rocks from the cliffs, and winds shrieked, and it was so desolately cold that Father hallucinated that his skin was burning, Peary and most of the men withdrew to the theoretical considerations of his system and so protected themselves against their fear. The

Esquimos, who had no system but merely lived here, suffered the terrors of their universe. Sometimes the Esquimo women would unaccountably tear off their clothes and run into the black storms howling and rolling on the ice. Their husbands had forcibly to restrain them from killing themselves. Father kept himself under control by writing in his journal. This was a system too, the system of language and conceptualization. It proposed that human beings, by the act of making witness, warranted times and places for their existence other than the time and place they were living through.

But there seemed in this icebound winter night a force that gripped you by the neck and faced you into it. The Esquimo families lived all over the ship, camping on the decks and in the holds. They were not discreet in their intercourse. They cohabited without even undressing, through vents in their furs, and they went at it with grunts and shouts of fierce joy. One day Father came upon a couple and was shocked to see the wife thrusting her hips upwards to the thrusts of her husband. An uncanny animal song came from her throat. This was something he could not write in his journal except in a kind of code. The woman was actually pushing back. It stunned him that she could react this way. This filthy toothless Esquimo woman with the flat brow and the eyes pressed upwards by her cheekbones, singing her song and pushing back. He thought of Mother's fastidiousness, her grooming and her intelligence, and found himself resenting this primitive woman's claim to the gender.

The spring came, finally, and it was Peary's assistant, Mathew Henson, who called to Father one morning and pointed aft. A thin ray of light was in the southern sky. In the days that followed, distinctions in the kinds of darkness could be made, and these became more and more pronounced. Finally one morning there rose above the horizon a blurred and blood-red sun, not round but elliptically misshapen, like something born. Everyone became happy. Glorious colors, pink and green and yellow, lay upon the snow peaks, and the entire bleak magnificent world offered itself to who would take it. The sky gradually turned blue and Peary said the time had come to conquer the Pole.

The day before the expedition was to leave, Father went along with Mathew Henson and three of the Esquimos to the bird cliffs half a day's journey from the coast. They climbed the cliffs with sealskin bags hung over their shoulders and collected dozens of eggs, a great delicacy in the Arctic. When the birds flew up, chattering and circling, it was as if a portion of the rock cliff had come away. Father had never seen so many birds. They were fulmar and auk. The Esquimos held out nets between them and the birds flew into the nets and became entangled. The nets were taken up at the corners and became sacks of immobile weighted feathers chirping piteously. When the men had caught all they could carry, they made the descent and straightaway slaughtered the birds. The fulmar, about the size of gulls, were wrung at the neck. But what amazed Father was the means by which the small and inoffensive auk was done in. One simply nudged the tiny heart in its breast. Father watched it done and then tried it himself. He held an auk in one hand and with his thumb gently squeezed the beating breast. Its head slumped and it was dead. The Esquimos loved the auklet and customarily pickled it in sealskins.

On the way back to camp Father and Mathew Henson discussed what the men under Peary always discussed—who would have the honor of actually going to the Pole with him. Before the embarkation from New York the Commander had made it quite clear to everyone that he and he alone was to discover the Pole: their glory would be in support. I've spent my life planning for that moment, Peary said, and I'm going to have it for myself. This seemed to Father a reasonable point of view. He had the diffidence of the amateur before the professional. But it was Mathew Henson's view that someone besides Esquimos would have to go to the top with the Commander, and he thought, with all due respect, it would be himself. Actually Father believed Henson had a good case. Henson had been with Peary on his previous expeditions and he was an astute and formidable Arctic explorer in his own right. He knew how to drive the dogs almost as well as an Esquimo, he knew how to repair sledges, build camps, he had great physical strength and boasted many skills. But Father found himself unaccountably resenting Henson's presumption and he asked the Negro how he knew he would be chosen. They had breasted a ridge along the trail and stood resting the dogs for a moment as they looked over a great white plain of snow. At that moment the sun broke through the overcast and the entire earth flashed like a mirror. Well, sir, Mathew Henson said with a smile, I just know.

The next day the expedition set out due north across the polar ice. They were arranged in separate parties consisting of a white man or two, a group of Esquimo boys, a pack of dogs and four or five sledges. Each party except Peary's was to serve for a week as pioneer or trailbreaker to the rest of the expedition. Eventually, each of them was to peel off and head back to land, leaving Peary and his boys to make the last hundred miles or so in fresh, relatively rested condition. That was the system. The big work was in breaking trail. This was hazardous and backbreaking labor. Ridges of ice had to be hacked away with a pickax, heavy sledges had to be hauled and pushed up ice inclines and then held against precipitous descents. Each sled carried over six hundred pounds of tools and provisions. When it broke, it had to be unloaded and repaired by lashing the broken parts together—work that required an ungloved hand. There were leads of water that had to be crossed or waited out. The ice floes came together with great cracks, like the sound of cannon, and rumbled underfoot like the voice of the ocean itself. Inexplicable fogs blocked out the sun. Sometimes there was nothing to do but crawl across thin sheets of forming ice; no one wanted to be caught on a drifting ice floe. The weather was a constant torment, the wind blowing so sharply at fifty or sixty degrees below zero that the air itself seemed to have changed its physical nature, being now unassimilable crystals in one's lungs. Each breath left its solid residue in the beard or on the frozen edges of the fur hoods. Everyone wore the prescribed soft sealskin shoes, the bear fur trousers and the hooded caribou jackets, but even these indigenous materials turned brittle in the frost. The sun now stood above the horizon twenty-four hours a day. At the end of a day's travel, perhaps fifteen miles of arduous effort, the pioneer group would make camp, build igloos for the pursuing expedition, feed the dogs, untangle their iced-up traces, light the alcohol cooker to brew tea, and fall to a meal of frozen pemmican and crackers. Slowly through the month of March the Peary expedition made its way due north. One by one a party would turn back, its obligations now to beat the return trail as thoroughly as possible to make it easier for the parties who would follow. Peary would bring up the lag each day on the outgoing run and immediately occupy one of the igloos built for him by Henson. In the meantime Henson took care of Peary's dogs, repaired broken sledges, made supper, dealt with the Esquimos, many of whom were now becoming difficult. Peary defined the virtues of Esquimos as loyalty and obedience, roughly the same virtues one sought in the dogs. When the time came for the final run for the Pole, now only a hundred miles away, Peary did indeed choose Henson to go with him; and Henson chose the Esquimos who in his judgment were the best boys, the most loyal and devoted to the Commander. The balance of the party was turned around and sent home.

Father had long since gone back. He had pioneered the very first week. He had proven not the sturdiest member of the expedition. This was from no lack of heart, as Peary told him before sending him home, but from the tendency of his extremities to freeze easily. Father's left heel, for instance, froze every day, no matter what he did to protect it. Each evening in camp he would thaw it out painfully and treat it as best he could, and each morning it would freeze up again. So too with one of his knees and a small area on the top of his hand. Pieces of Father froze very casually and Peary said this was the fate of some men in the North and nothing could be done about it. Peary was not an unkind commander, and he liked Father. During the long winter months aboard the *Roosevelt,* they had discovered themselves members of the same national collegiate fraternity, and this was no light bond between them. But after a lifetime of effort Peary was impatient to get his task done. Father's society had paid a good sum into the Peary chest, and for it they got their man to seventy-two degrees, forty-six minutes, a very respectable way. Before he left, Father presented the Commander with an American flag he had manufactured for the occasion. It was pure silk and a good size; but when folded had no more bulk than a large handkerchief. Peary thanked him, put the flag inside his furs and, after warning Father to look out for the leads, sent him on his return journey to the *Roosevelt* in the company of three bad-tempered Esquimos.

But now Peary was within a day's travel of his lifelong goal. Driving Henson and the Esquimos mercilessly, he had refused to let them sleep more than an hour or two at the end of each arduous day. Now the sun shone brightly, the sky was clear; there was a full moon in the blue sky and the great ice thighs of the earth heaved and shuddered and rose toward the moon. At midmorning of April 9, Peary called a halt. He ordered Henson to build a snow shield to protect him while he took his observations. Peary lay on his stomach and with a pan of mercury and a sextant, some paper and a pencil, he calculated his position. It did not satisfy him. He walked further along the floe and took another sighting. This did not satisfy him. All day long Peary shuffled back and forth over the ice, a mile one way, two miles another, and made his observations. No one observation satisfied him. He would walk a few steps due north and find himself going due south. On this watery planet the sliding sea refused to be fixed. He couldn't find the exact place to say this spot, here, is the North Pole. Nevertheless there was no question that they were there. All the observations together indicated that. Give three cheers, my boy, he told Henson. And let's fly the flag. Henson and the Esquimos cheered loudly but could not be heard in the howling wind. The flag snapped and rippled. Peary posed Henson and the Esquimos in front of the flag and took their picture. It shows five stubby figures wrapped in furs, the flag set in a paleocrystic peak behind them that might suggest a real physical Pole. Because of the light the faces are indistinguishable, seen only as black blanks framed by caribou fur.

11

Back home a momentous change was coming over the United States. There was a new President, William Howard Taft, and he took office weighing three hundred and thirty-two pounds. All over the country men began to look at themselves. They were used to drinking great quantities of beer. They customarily devoured loaves of bread and ate prodigiously of the sausage meats of poured offal that lay on the lunch counters of the saloons. The august Pierpont Morgan would routinely consume seven- and eight-course dinners. He ate breakfasts of steaks and chops, eggs, pancakes, broiled fish, rolls and butter, fresh fruit and cream. The consumption of food was a sacrament of success. A man who carried a great stomach before him was thought to be in his prime. Women went into hospitals to die of burst bladders, collapsed lungs, overtaxed hearts and meningitis of the spine. There was a heavy traffic to the spas and sulphur springs, where the purgative was valued as an inducement to the appetite. America was a great farting country. All this began to change when Taft moved into the White House. His accession to the one mythic office in the American imagination weighed everyone down. His great figure immediately expressed the apotheosis of that style of man. Thereafter fashion would go the other way and only poor people would be stout.

In this regard, as in most others, Evelyn Nesbit was ahead of her time. Her former chief lover Stanford White had been a fashionably burly man, and her husband Harry K. Thaw though not as large was nevertheless soft and wide, but her new lover, Mother's Younger Brother, was as lean and hard as a young tree. They made love slowly and sinuously, humping each other into such supple states of orgasm that they found very little reason to talk the rest of the time they were together. It was characteristic of Evelyn that she could not resist some-one who was so strongly attracted to her. She led Younger Brother around the Lower East Side in a futile search for Tateh and the little girl. The flat on Hester Street had been abandoned. Evelyn took up the lease and paid the landlord for the pitiful furnishings. She spent hours sitting by the window on the air shaft. She would touch things, a blanket, a plate, like a blind person trying to read with her fingers. Then she would break down and be soothed by Mother's Younger Brother in the narrow brass bed.

When the trial of Harry K. Thaw began, Evelyn was photo-graphed arriving at the courthouse. In the courtroom, where no photographers were allowed, she was drawn by artists for the illustrateds. She could hear the scratching of the steel pens. She took the witness stand and described herself at fifteen pumping her legs in a red velvet swing while a wealthy ar-chitect caught his breath at the sight of her exposed calves. She was resolute and held her head high. She was dressed in impec-cable taste. Her testimony created the first sex goddess in American history. Two elements of the society realized this. The first was the business community, specifically a group of accountants and cloak and suit manufacturers who also dab-bled in the exhibition of moving pictures, or picture shows as they were called. Some of these men saw the way Evelyn's face on the front page of a newspaper sold out the edition. They realized that there was a process of magnification by which news events established certain individuals in the public consciousness as larger than life. These were the individuals who represented one desirable human characteristic to the exclusion of all others. The businessmen wondered if they could create such individuals not from the accidents of news events but from the deliberate manufactures of their own medium. If they could, more people would pay money for the picture shows. Thus did Evelyn provide the inspiration for the concept of the movie star system and the model for every sex goddess from Theda Bara to Marilyn Monroe. The second group of people to perceive Evelyn's importance was made up of various trade union leaders, anarchists and socialists, who correctly prophesied that she would in the long run be a greater threat to the workingman's interests than mine owners or steel manufacturers. In Seattle, for instance, Emma Goldman spoke to an I.W.W. local and cited Evelyn Nesbit as a daughter of the working class whose life was a lesson in the way all daughters and sisters of poor men were used for the pleasure of the wealthy. The men in her audience guffawed and shouted out lewd remarks and broke into laughter. These were militant workers, too, unionists with a radical awareness of their situation. Goldman sent off a letter to Evelyn: I am often asked the question How can the masses permit themselves to be exploited by the few. The answer is By being persuaded to identify with them. Carrying his newspaper with your picture the laborer goes home to his wife, an exhausted workhorse with the veins standing out in her legs, and he dreams not of justice but of being rich.

Evelyn didn't know what to do with such remarks. She continued to testify as she had contracted to do. She made appearances with the Thaw family and produced by means of glances and small gestures of devotion images of a wife. She portrayed Harry as the victim of an irrepressible urge to find honor for himself and his young bride. She performed flawlessly. She heard the scratch scratch of the steel drawing pens. Legal bystanders in spectacles and celluloid collars stroked their moustaches. Everyone in the courtroom wore black. She wondered at this huge establishment of legal people who lay waiting in their lives for conventions such as this. Judges and lawyers and bailiffs and policemen and wardens and jurymen: they had all known there would be a trial for them. She heard the scratches. Waiting in the corridors were alienists prepared to testify that Harry was insane. This was the one line of defense he would not permit. He could not bring himself to do it. His august mother wanted him to make that plea. She was afraid that if he did not he would go to the electric chair. Evelyn watched him at the defense table. She wondered what in the world could ever put to ease that enraged heart. Harry kept his facial expressions keyed to the testimony. When something was funny he smiled. When it was sad he dropped his eyes. When Stanford White's name was mentioned he furrowed his brow. He arranged himself in attitudes of contrition alternated with heads-up confidence and even burning righteousness. This activity required all his concentration. Going in and out of the courtroom he was calm and courteous, the picture of rationality.

It occurred to Evelyn one day that Harry might indeed love her. She was stunned. She tried to make a determination of the real truth of their relationship. Of the relationship of the three of them. For the first time she experienced acutely the sense of Stanford White's death, the loss of Stanny. He would have been able to tell her what the truth was. He would have made a joke out of it. That was his way. He was a lusty old fuck and he loved a good laugh. She could drive him out of his mind, just as she could drive Harry out of his. But she felt more comfortable with Stanny White. He would leave her alone to go out and build something, whereas Harry would never leave her because he had nothing else to do. Harry was merely wealthy. She needed desperately to talk to someone and the only person she had ever been able to talk to was the man for whose death she was directly responsible. On her blue vellum Mrs. Harry K. Thaw stationery with raised letters she wrote Emma Goldman. What have I done? she said in the letter. The reply came back from California where Goldman was raising funds in defense of the militant McNamara brothers who were accused of blowing up the Los Angeles *Times* building: Don't overestimate your role in the relationship those two men had with each other.

In the meantime Harry's trial went to the jury. They could not come to a verdict. A new trial was ordered. Evelyn testified again, with the same words and the same gestures. When it was all over Harry K. Thaw was remanded for an indefinite period to the Matteawan Hospital for the Criminally Insane. Almost immediately his lawyers negotiated for his divorce. Evelyn was ready. Her price was a million dollars. Then the private detectives came forward with their record of her infidelities with Mother's Younger Brother and some others they had made up and the divorce was quietly concluded by the payment to Evelyn of twenty-five thousand. Evelyn sat on the bed in her hotel suite which she now had to give up and gazed at her evening slippers which she held in her hand. On this particular occasion Younger Brother's endearments left her cold. She remembered what Goldman had told her on her last visit to New York. However much money you have gotten from Thaw it is only as much as he wanted to give you. It is the law of wealth that such people only profit from the money that is taken from them. It is the way things work. Somehow every dollar paid over to you has resulted in his profit. And you will be left with a finite amount of money that you will spend and waste until you are as poor as when you started. She knew this was true. Even such money as she had, still the bulk of her fortune, left her with strange and inconclusive feelings. Some man would feign love, steal the money and break her heart. For this bitter insight she had only Goldman to thank, who had painted for her two pictures, one of greed and barbarity, starvation, injustice and death, as in the present national organizations of private capital, and the other of utopian serenity, as in the loose ungoverned combinations of equals sharing their work and their wealth sensibly with one another. Evelyn made donations to Goldman's anarchist magazine *Mother Earth*, to keep it going. She supported radical appeals that came to her from all over the country once it became underground gossip that she had been politicized. She gave money to the legal defense of labor leaders who had been thrown in jail. She gave money to the parents of children mutilated in mills and factories. Listlessly she doled out her hard-earned fortune. The public never knew this because she insisted on anonymity. She had no joy. She looked into the mirror and saw the unmistakable lineaments of womanhood coming into her girlish face. Her long beautiful neck seemed to her like an ungainly stalk upon which was perched a sad-eyed ridiculous head of a whore past her prime. She cried for the snuggling opportunities of a body like Stanford White's. And all the while Mother's Younger Brother solemnly and in his doggish silent way stood to wait upon her. He didn't know the meaning of comfort. He couldn't tease her or talk baby talk to her. He couldn't tell her how to look at a diamond, or take her to a restaurant where the maître d' fawned over him. All he could do was commit his life to hers and work to satisfy her smallest whim. She loved him but she wanted someone who would treat her badly and whom she could treat badly. She longed for a challenge to her wit, she longed to have her ambitions aroused once again.

12

And what of Tateh and his little girl? After that meeting the old artist sat one night and one day in his flat and he did not eat or say anything, brooding, as he smoked endlessly his Sobrany cigarettes, on the brutal luck of his life. Every once in a while he would look at his child, and seeing the sure destruction of her incredible beauty in his continuing victimization he would clutch her to him and tears would fill his eyes. The little girl quietly prepared their simple meals in ways so reminiscent of the movements of his wife that finally he could bear the situation no longer. Throwing their few clothes in a musty suitcase whose strap had long since rotted away, he tied a piece of clothesline around the suitcase, took the girl by the hand and left the two-room flat on Hester Street forever. They walked to the corner and boarded the No. 12 streetcar for Union Square. At Union Square they transferred to the No. 8 and rode north up Broadway. The early evening was warm and all the windows of the trolley were lowered. The streets were crowded with cabs and cars and their horns blew at one another. Trolleys went along in clusters, their bells ringing, the flashes of electricity from their pantographs crackling along the overhead wires in minute intensifications of the heat lightning that flattened the sky over the darkening, sultry city. Tateh had no idea where he was going. The little girl held his hand tightly. Her dark eyes stared solemnly at the parades of people strolling along Broadway, the men in boaters and blue blazers and white ducks, the women in white summer frocks. The electric light bulbs of each vaudeville house rippled in a particular pattern. A ring of light spun around the rims of her pupils. Three hours later they were on a streetcar moving north along Webster Avenue in the Bronx. The moon was out, the temperature had dropped, and the trolley clipped along the broad reaches of this wide boulevard with only occasional stops. They passed grassy lots interspersed with blocks of row houses still under construction. Finally the lights disappeared entirely and the little girl realized they were traveling along the edges of a great hillside cemetery. The stones and vaults standing against the cold night sky suggested to her the fate of her mother. For the first time she asked her Tateh where they were going. He pulled the window shut against the cold wind whistling now through the ratcheting, rocking trolley. They were the only passengers. Sha, he said to her. Close your eyes. Distributed in his pockets and in his shoes were his life savings, some thirty dollars. He had decided to leave New York, the city that had ruined his life. There was in these days of our history a highly developed system of interurban street railway lines. One could travel great distances on hard rush seats or wooden benches by taking each line to its terminus and transferring to the next. Tateh did not know anything about the routes. He only planned to keep on going as far as each streetcar would take him.

In the early hours of the first morning of their trip they crossed the city line into Mount Vernon, New York, and there learned that the next service would not begin till daylight. They found a small park and slept in the band shell. In the morning they washed and refreshed themselves in a public facility. As the sun came up they boarded a bright red and yellow streetcar, and the conductor greeted them cheerfully. Tateh paid a nickel for himself, two cents for the child. On the wooden floor of the car, at the rear, were stacked crates filled with wet and glistening quart bottles of milk. Tateh offered to buy one. The conductor looked at him and then at the little girl and told him to take one out but did not wait to be paid for it. He pulled a cord, the trolley bell rang, and the car lurched into motion. The conductor sang. He was a robust big-bellied man with a tenor voice. He had a change-making machine strapped to his belt. A while later the streetcar en-tered the city of New Rochelle, New York, and slowly made its way up Main Street. Traffic was heavier now, the sun was up, and the small city was abustle. It was explained to Tateh that if he wanted to ride through he had to transfer to the Post Road Shore Line at the corner of North Avenue. This was done by paying another penny for each transfer. Tateh and the little girl got off at the corner of Main Street and North Avenue and waited for the connecting trolley. A boy and his mother passed by. The little girl looked at the boy. He was tow-headed. He wore a sailor blouse, dark blue knickers, white socks and polished white shoes. His hand was in his mother's hand and as he passed the little girl standing with her ancient father, the boy's eyes looked into hers. At this moment the Post Road streetcar appeared and Tateh holding the little girl firmly by the wrist walked into the street and stepped aboard. As the car moved off, the little girl watched the boy pass backward in her sight. She stood on the rear platform of the trolley car and watched him until she could no longer see him. His eyes had been blue and yellow and dark green, like a school globe. The streetcar went up the Post Road, along the Long Island Sound shoreline to the Connecticut border. In Green-wich, Connecticut, they transferred to another car. This took them up through the cities of Stamford, Norwalk and then to

[77]

Bridgeport, the burial place of Tom Thumb. By now they knew how to tell when the end of the line was approaching. The conductor would walk back through the car and reverse the empty seats, going along the aisle and yanking the handles attached to the seat backs without breaking stride. At Bridgeport they transferred again. The tracks turned inland. They stopped for the night in New Haven, Connecticut. They slept in a rooming house and had breakfast in the landlady's dining room. Tateh furiously brushed his trousers and jacket and soft cap before going downstairs. He tied a bow tie around his frayed collar. He made sure the little girl wore her clean pinafore. It was a rooming house for university students and some of them were at the table. They wore gold spectacles and turtleneck sweaters. After breakfast the old artist and his daughter walked to the streetcar tracks and resumed their journey. A car of the Springfield Traction Company took them to New Britain and then to the city of Hartford. The car slowly swung through the narrow streets of Hartford, the clapboard houses of the city seemingly close enough to reach out and touch. Then they were on the outskirts and racing along north to Springfield, Massachusetts. The great wooden car swayed from side to side. The wind flew in their faces. They sped along the edges of open fields from which birds started and settled as they passed. The little girl saw herds of grazing cows. She saw brown horses loping in the sun. A thin layer of chalk dust settled on her face, like a mask, whitening her complexion, bringing out her large moist eyes, the redness of her mouth, and Tateh was momentarily shocked by a vision of her maturity. The car barreled along its tracks down the side of the road, and whenever it approached an intersection its air horn blew. Once it stopped and took on a load of produce. Riders crowded the aisle. The little girl could not wait for the speed to be up. Tateh realized she was happy. She loved the trip. Holding the suitcase on his lap with just one arm Tateh put the other around his child. He found himself smiling. The wind blew in his face and filled his mouth. The car threatened to jump off the tracks. It banged from side to side and everyone laughed. Tateh laughed. He saw the village of his youth going by now, some versts beyond the meadow. There was a church steeple seen above a hill. As a child he loved wagons, he loved the rides on the big tumbrils in summer moonlight, the bodies of children falling over one another in the hard bumping wagons. He looked around at the riders on the trolley and for the first time since coming to America he thought it might be possible to live here. In Springfield they bought bread and cheese and boarded a modern dark green car of the Worcester Electric Street Railway. Tateh realized now that he was going at least as far as Boston. He computed the cost of all the fares. It would come to two dollars and forty cents for him, just over a dollar for the child. The trolley hummed along the dirt roads, the sun behind it now going down in the Berkshires. Stands of fir trees threw long shadows. They passed a single oarsman in a scull on a very quiet broad stream. They saw a great dripping millwheel turning slowly over a creek. The shadows deepened. The little girl fell asleep. Tateh clutched the suitcase on his lap and kept his eyes on the tracks ahead, shining now in the single beam of the powerful electric headlamp on the front of the car.

13

Tracks! Tracks! It seemed to the visionaries who wrote for the popular magazines that the future lay at the end of parallel rails. There were long-distance locomotive railroads and interurban electric railroads and street railways and elevated railroads, all laying their steel stripes on the land, crisscrossing like the texture of an indefatigable civilization. And in Boston and New York there were even railroads under the streets, new rapid-transit subway systems transporting thousands of people every day. In New York, in fact, the success of the Manhattan subway had created a demand for a line to Brooklyn. Accordingly an engineering miracle was taking place, the construction of a tunnel under the East River from Brooklyn to the Battery. Sandhogs working behind a hydraulic shield excavated river-bed silt inch by inch and installed linking sections of cast-iron tubes as they went. The digging chamber was filled with compressed air pumped in from the surface. The work was dangerous. The men who did the work, the sandhogs, were considered heroes. Working under the river they were subject to horrible destinies. One typical hazard was the blowout, a situation in which the compressed air found a weakness in the roof of the tunnel and escaped with a violent rush. One day there was a blowout so explosive that it sucked four workmen out of the tunnel and blew them through twenty feet of river silt and shot them up through the river itself forty feet into the air on the crest of a geyser. Only one of the men survived. The freak accident made headlines in all the papers, and when Harry Houdini read the accounts over his morning coffee he hurriedly dressed and rushed downtown to Bellevue Hospital where it was said the surviving worker had been taken. I'm Harry Houdini, he told the admissions desk, and I've got to see that sandhog. Two nurses conferred behind the desk and while they did he stole a glance at the charts and ran up the stairs. You can't come up here, a flinty nurse told him as he strode down a ward filled with sick and dying men. Chutes of cheerful morning sun leaned like buttresses from the high dirty windows of the ward. Clustered about the bed of the heroic sandhog was his family—a wife, an old mother in a babushka, two strapping sons. A doctor was in attendance. The man in the bed was swathed in bandages from his head to his feet. His arms, in casts, were supported in traction as was one encased leg. Every few moments there would issue from his head bandages a weak or perhaps only decorous groan. Houdini cleared his throat. I'm Harry Houdini, he said to the family, I escape for a living, that's my profession, I'm an escapologist. But let me tell you I've never done an escape that can touch this one. He pointed to the bed. The family looked at him without expression on their stolid Slavic faces. The grandmother without taking her eyes off Houdini said something in a foreign language—a question it was, because one of the sons answered in kind and said Houdini's name. They continued to look at him. I came to offer my respects, Houdini said. They all had flat faces, broad brows, eyes set widely apart. They did not return his smile. How did you get in here, the doctor said. I'll only be a minute, Houdini said, I just want to ask him something. I think you better leave, the doctor said. Houdini turned to the family. I want to know how it felt. I want to know what he did to get to the surface. He was the only one to make it. He must have done something. I would like to know, it means a lot to me to know. He took out his wallet, removed some bills. I think you could probably use this. Go ahead, take it, I would like to help. The family continued to gaze at him. A sound came from the figure on the bed. One of the sons leaned over and put his ear down. He listened a moment and nodded. He went to the other son and said something to him. They were big fellows, over six feet, with chests like barrels. No rough stuff, the doctor said. Houdini found himself lifted by the arms and walked down the aisle of the ward with his feet just failing to touch the floor. He made a decision not to resist. He knew the tricks of self-defense, there were ways he could best these oafs; but this was a hospital after all.

Houdini walked through the streets. His ears burned with humiliation. He wore a hat with the brim turned down. He wore a tight-fitting double-breasted linen jacket and he kept his hands in the pockets of the jacket. He wore tan trousers and brown and white shoes with pointed toes. It was a chilly autumn afternoon and most people wore coats. He moved swiftly through the crowded New York streets. He was incredibly lithe. There was a kind of act that used the real world for its stage. He couldn't touch it. For all his achievements he was a trickster, an illusionist, a mere magician. What was the sense of his life if people walked out of the theatre and forgot him? The headlines on the newsstand said Peary had reached the Pole. The real-world act was what got into the history books.

Houdini decided to concentrate on his outdoor exploits. Going on tour he escaped from a packing case nailed shut and tied with ropes that had been lowered into the freezing Detroit River. He had himself lowered into rivers in Boston and Philadelphia. Ice floated in the rivers. He practiced for the freezing river escapes by sitting in his bathtub at home with blocks of ice dropped in there by the iceman. But nothing was changed. He decided to do a European tour. He had gotten his start in Europe when he had been unable to crack the big-time vaudeville circuits in the States. In some peculiar way, he still felt, the people in Europe understood him better than his own countrymen. A few days before his departure he agreed to do a benefit for old magicians and retired theatre folk. He wanted to surprise them with a new escape. He hired a team of orderlies from Bellevue to come up on the stage and wrap him from head to foot in bandages. This was done. Then they wound him in numbers of sheets and then they strapped him to a hospital bed. Then they poured water over him to weigh down the wrappings. Houdini escaped. The old theatre people went wild. He was unsatisfied.

Houdini was to sail for Europe on the *Imperator*, an immense German vessel with a figurehead—an odd thing for a modern three-stack passenger liner. The figurehead was a crowned eagle with its claws embedded in the world. Houdini's ancient mother, Mrs. Weiss, came down to the pier to see him off. She was a neat little woman in black. He kissed her and hugged her and kissed her hands and went up the gangplank. He ran back down the gangplank and kissed her again, holding her face in his hands and kissing her eyes. She nodded and patted him. He ran up the gangplank and waved. He wasn't sure she could see him. As the great liner backed into the river he stood at the rail and waved. He waved his cap to attract her attention. It was obvious she could not see him. He shouted, ridiculously, because the ship's engines were churning up the river water. He continued to watch her small black figure and ran around to the port deck when tugs faced the ship downriver. She stood on the pier, a frail sweet old lady, and watched the ship drift out of her vision. She enjoyed her son's devotions. Once he had come to her and had her hold out her apron. Into the apron he poured fifty shiny gold dollars. He was a good boy.

She returned by cab to their home on 113th Street to wait for him.

Houdini opened his European tour at the Hansa Theatre in Hamburg. The audiences were enthusiastic. The papers gave him lots of space. He had never known such feelings of dissatisfaction. He wondered why he had devoted his life to mindless entertainment. The audiences cheered. After every show there was always a small crowd at the stage entrance. He was short with them. Then one day he attended the public demonstration of a French-made flying machine, a Voisin, a beautiful biplane with boxed wings, a box rudder and three delicately strutted bicycle wheels. The aviator flew it over a race track and landed on the infield, and the next day his feat was described in the newspapers. Houdini moved decisively. Within a week he was the owner of a new Voisin biplane. It had cost him five thousand dollars. It came complete with a French mechanic who gave instruction in the art of flying. He secured the use of an army parade grounds outside of Hamburg. In all the countries in which he played he always got on well with the military. Soldiers everywhere were fans of his. Each morning at dawn he would drive to the parade grounds and sit at the controls of the Voisin while the French mechanic lectured him on the function and purpose of the levers and pedals within reach of the pilot. The plane was directed by means of a large steering wheel mounted in the vertical position and attached by a shaft to the front rudder. The pilot sat behind the front rudder on a little seat between the two wings. Behind him was the engine, and behind the engine was the propeller. The Voisin was made of wood. The wings were covered in fabric stretched taut and sized with varnish. The struts connecting the double wings were paneled with the same material. The Voisin looked like a box kite. Houdini had his name painted in block letters on the outside panels of the wings and on the rear elevators. He could hardly wait for his first flight.

The patient mechanic drilled him in the various operations
required to get the machine aloft, maintain it in flight and land
it. Every night Houdini did his act and every morning at dawn
he went out for his lessons. Finally one morning when the red
sky was clear and the mechanic judged the wind conditions to
be right, they pushed the machine out of its shed and faced
it into the breeze. Houdini climbed into the pilot's seat, turned
his cap backwards and pulled it down tight. He clutched the
wheel. His eyes narrowed in concentration, he set his jaw
firmly and he turned his head and nodded to the mechanic,
who spun the wood propeller. The engine fired. It was an
Enfield 80-horsepower job, supposedly better than the one the
Wrights themselves were using. Hardly daring to breathe,
Houdini throttled the engine, idled it, throttled it again. Finally he held up his thumb. The mechanic ducked under the
wings and pulled the wheel chocks. The craft slowly moved
forward. Houdini breathed faster and faster as the Voisin
picked up speed. Soon it was bumping along the ground and
he could feel the sensitive wings take on an intelligence of their
own, as if a disembodied presence had joined the enterprise.
The machine lifted off the ground. He thought he was dream-
ing. He had to willfully restrain his emotions, commanding
himself sternly to keep the wings level, to keep the throttle
continuously in touch with the speed of the flight. He was
flying! His feet worked the pedals, he clasped the control wheel
and gently the rudder in front of him tilted down and the
machine climbed the sky. He dared to look down: the earth
was fifty feet below him. He no longer heard the ratcheting
engine behind his ear. He felt the wind in his face and discovered he was shouting. The guy wires seemed to sing, the great
wings above and below him nodded and dipped and played in
the air with their incredibly gentle intelligence. The bicycle
wheels spun slowly, idly in the breeze. He was flying over a
stand of trees. Gaining confidence he put the craft into a

difficult maneuver, a bank. The Voisin described a wide circle around the parade grounds. Then he could see the mechanic standing in the distance, by the shed, raising both arms in salute. Coolly, Houdini leveled the wings, slipped under his breeze and began his descent. The moment the wheels touched down, the crudeness of the impact offended him. And when the machine rolled to a stop he wanted only to be airborne again.

On subsequent flights Houdini stayed in the air as much as ten or twelve minutes. That was virtually to challenge the fuel capacity of the plane. He seemed at times to drift as if suspended from the clouds over his head. He was able to see whole villages nestled below in the German countryside, and to follow his own shadow down incredibly straight roads lined with hedgerows. Once he flew high enough to be able to see in the distance the medieval skyline of Hamburg with flashes of the Elbe River. He was tremendously proud of his aeroplane. He wanted to make flying history. Young officers from the local casern began to come to the parade grounds to watch Houdini fly. He got to know some of them by name. And then the Commandant, whose permission had been required for the use of the parade grounds, asked Houdini if he would be interested in giving a few lectures to these young officers on the art of flying. The magician readily agreed. He arranged his schedule accordingly and began a series of informal sessions. He liked the young officers. They were highly intelligent and very respectful. They laughed at his jokes. His German was faulty and Yiddish-inflected but they seemed not to notice.

One morning after a flight Houdini taxied his plane to the shed and noticed waiting there a Mercedes staff car carrying general officers of the Imperial German Army. Before he could disembark his friend the Commandant stood up from the jump seat of the car, saluted him and asked him in a most formal manner if he would mind taking the Voisin up again for a demonstration flight. Houdini looked at the two elderly men, heavily medaled, sitting in the rear of the car. They nodded at him. Sitting at attention in the front seat next to the driver was an enlisted man who wore the spiked helmet and held a carbine across his lap. At this moment a white Daimler landau with an enclosed carriage for the passengers slowly pulled up behind the staff car. Its brass fittings were polished to a brilliance and even its white wooden wheel spokes were clean. A gold-fringed flag of rank flew from the right front fender. Houdini could not see into the passenger cab. Of course, he said. He ordered his mechanic to refuel and in a few minutes was aloft once more, making wide stately banks around the field. He tried to imagine how he must look from the ground. He felt the thrill of performance. He whirred over the cars at a height of a hundred feet and came around again at fifty feet waggling his wings and waving. He flew for who-ever it was in that white car.

When he landed he was escorted to the big Daimler. The chauffeur opened the door and stood at attention. Sitting in the car was the Archduke Franz Ferdinand, heir to the Austro-Hungarian throne. The Archduke was dressed in the uniform of a field marshal of the Austrian Army. He held in the crook of his arm a plumed helmet. His hair was cut very short and flat on top, like a brush. He had large waxed moustaches that curled upward and he gazed at Houdini with stupid heavy-lidded eyes. Sitting next to him was his wife, the Countess Sophie, a stately matron yawning delicately behind a gloved hand. The Archduke Franz Ferdinand didn't seem to know who Houdini was. He congratulated him on the invention of the aeroplane.

14

When Father returned to New Rochelle he walked up the front steps of his home, passed under the giant Norwegian maples and found his wife holding a brown baby in her arms. Upstairs the colored girl was withdrawn. Melancholy had taken the will out of her muscles. She did not have the strength to hold her baby. She sat all day in her attic room and watched the diamond windowpanes as they gathered the light, glowed with it and then gave it up. Father looked at her through the open door. She ignored him. He wandered through the house finding everywhere signs of his own exclusion. His son now had a desk, as befitted all young students. He thought he heard an Arctic wind but it was the housemaid Brigit pushing an electric suction cleaner across the rug in the parlor. What was strangest of all was the mirror in his bath: it gave back the gaunt, bearded face of a derelict, a man who lacked a home. His shaving mirror on the *Roosevelt* had not revealed this. He removed his clothes. He was shocked by the outlines of his body, the ribs and clavicle, white-skinned and vulnerable, the bony pelvis, the organ hanging there redder than anything else. At night in bed Mother held him and tried to warm the small of his back, curled him into her as she lay against his back cradling his strange coldness. It was apparent to them both that this time he'd stayed away too long. Downstairs Brigit put a record on the Victrola, wound the crank and sat in the parlor smoking a cigarette and listening to John McCormack sing "I Hear You Calling Me." She was doing what she could to lose her place. She was no longer efficient or respectful. Mother marked this change from the arrival of the colored girl. Father related it to the degrees of turn in the moral planet. He saw it everywhere, this new season, and it bewildered him. At his office he was told that the seamstresses in the flag department had joined a New York union. He put on clothes from his closet that ballooned from him as shapeless as the furs he had worn for a year. He had brought home gifts. He gave his son a pair of walrus tusks and a whale's tooth with Esquimo carvings. He gave his wife the fur of a white polar bear. He pulled Arctic treasures from his trunk—notebooks of his journals, their covers curling at the corners, their pages stiff as pages that have been wet; a signed photograph of Commander Peary; a bone harpoon tip; three or four tins of unused tea—incredible treasures in the North, but here in the parlor the embarrassing possessions of a savage. The family stood around and watched him on his knees. There was nothing he had to tell them. On the Northern arc of the world was a darkness and a coldness that had crept upon him and rounded his shoulders. Waiting for Peary to return to the *Roosevelt* he had heard the wind howl at night and had clasped with love and gratitude the foul body, like a stinking fish, of an Esquimo woman. He had put his body into the stinking fish. The old Anglo-Saxon word he had hardly dared think of. That is what he had done. Now in New Rochelle he smelled on himself the oil of fish liver, fish on his breath, fish in his nostrils. He scrubbed himself red. He looked in Mother's eyes to detect there his justice. He found instead a woman curious and alerted to his new being. He realized that every night since he'd returned they had slept in the same bed. She was in some way not as vigorously modest as she'd been. She took his gaze. She came to bed with her hair unbraided. Her hand one night brushed down his chest and came to rest below his nightshirt. He decided God had punishments in store so devious there was no sense trying to anticipate what they were. With a groan he turned to her and found her ready. Her hands pulling his face to hers did not feel the tears.

But the house with its bay windows and beveled corners and three dormers loomed out of the yard like a ship. The rolled awnings were lashed to the windows. He stood on the sidewalk in the morning of a brilliant November day. The fallen leaves were covered with frost and lay like lapping waves about the house. The wind blew. He had come back with a slight limp. He thought about preparing his homecoming lecture for the New York Explorers Club. He found he preferred to sit in the parlor, his feet near a small electric heater. Everyone in the family treated him like a convalescent. His son brought him beef tea. The boy had grown taller. He had lost some of his fat. He was becoming competent and useful. He intelligently discussed Halley's Comet. Father felt childlike beside him.

In the paper was the news of Teddy Roosevelt's African safari. The great conservationist had bagged seventeen lions, eleven elephants, twenty-one rhinos, eight hippos, nine giraffes, forty-seven gazelles, twenty-nine zebras, and kudu, wildebeest, impala, eland, waterbuck, wart hog and bushbuck, beyond number.

As for the business during Father's absence, it seemed to have got on well. Mother could now speak crisply of such matters as unit cost, inventory and advertising. She had assumed executive responsibilities. She had made changes in certain billing procedures and contracted with four new sales agents in California and Oregon. Everything she had done stood up under his examination. He was astounded. On Moth-

er's bedside table was a volume entitled *The Ladies' Battle* by
Molly Elliot Seawell. He found also a pamphlet on the subject
of family limitation and the author was Emma Goldman, the
anarchist revolutionary. Down in the shop, under a translucent
window, he discovered his brother-in-law hunched over a drawing table. Mother's Younger Brother was losing his blond hair.
He was pale, and thin, and more uncommunicative than ever.
Most remarkable was the time he now spent at work, twelve
and fifteen hours a day. He had taken for his province the
fireworks division of the business and had designed dozens of
new rockets, firewheels, and an unusual firecracker packed not
cylindrically but in a spherical container. With its fuse looking
like a stem it was named a Cherry Bomb. The two men went
one morning to Younger Brother's testing ground at the end
of the trolley line, in the salt marshes. They wore heavy black
coats and bowlers. Father stood on a slight rise at the edge of
the tall grass. On a dried mud flat fifty yards away Younger
Brother bent down and prepared his demonstration. He had
arranged with Father that the first combustion would be that
of the standard firecracker and the second of the cherry bomb
design. He suddenly stood up, held one arm aloft and backed
away a few paces. Father heard the faint pop of the firecracker
after he saw a wisp of smoke erased by the wind. Younger
Brother now moved forward again, bent down and backed
away, this time more quickly. He held up two arms. An explosion then occurred like a bomb. Sea gulls were suddenly wheel-
ing through the air and Father felt the after-concussion as a
ringing in his ears. He was quite alarmed. When Younger
Brother rejoined him, his face was flushed and his eyes glis-
tened. Father suggested that perhaps the charge was too powerful and might do injury. I don't want to produce something
that would put a child's eye out, Father said. Younger Brother
said nothing but walked back to his proving ground and lit
another cherry bomb, this time standing up a bare pace or two

from the fuse. He stood as if in a shower bath, his face upturned to the water. He held out his arms. The bomb exploded.
Again he bent down and again held out his arms. The bomb
exploded. The birds turned in widening circles, soaring out
over the Sound, swooping over whitecaps and hovering on the
wind.

The young man was in mourning. Gradually Evelyn Nesbit
had become indifferent to him and when he persisted in his
love she had become hostile. Finally one day she had gone off
with a professional ragtime dancer. She left a note. They were
going to put together an act. Brother brought home to his
room in New Rochelle a wooden crate filled with silhouette
portraits and a pair of small beige satin shoes that Evelyn had
discarded. Once, standing in nothing but these shoes and
white embroidered stockings, she had placed her hands on her
thighs and stared at him over her shoulder. He lay on his bed
for days after his return. At times he would grab himself as if
to pull his sex out by the roots. He would pace his room and
hold his hands over his ears and hum loudly when he heard her
voice. He could not look at the silhouettes. He wanted to pack
his heart with gunpowder and blow it up. Without warning
one dawn he awoke with her scent in his nostrils. This of all
his memories was the most vicious. He ran downstairs and
threw the stack of silhouettes and the satin shoes in the trash
can. Then he shaved and went off to the flag and fireworks
factory.

The silhouette portraits were recovered by his nephew.

15

The boy treasured anything discarded. He took his education peculiarly and lived an entirely secret intellectual life. He had his eye on his father's Arctic journals but would not attempt to read them unless Father no longer cared about them. In his mind the meaning of something was perceived through its neglect. He looked over the silhouettes, examining them carefully, and chose one of them to hang on the inside of his wardrobe door. It was a study of the artist's most frequent model, a girl with hair like a helmet and the posture of someone who might run at any moment. She wore the battered high-lace shoes and sagging socks of poor children. He hid the rest of the silhouette collection in the attic. He was alert not only to discarded materials but to unexpected events and coincidences. He learned nothing at school but he did well because nothing was demanded of him. His teacher was an iron-haired woman who trained her students in declamation and clapped her hands as they practiced in their notebooks the curved lines that were thought to encourage good penmanship. At home he showed a fondness for the Motor Boys books and rarely missed an issue of *Wild West Weekly*, and for some reason these tastes, which the family found unexceptional, were a comfort to them. Mother suspected he was a strange child, although she shared this sense of him with no one, not even Father. Any indication that her son was ordinary heartened her. She wished he had friends. Father was still not himself and Younger Brother was too tormented by his own concerns to be of use, so it was left to Grandfather to cultivate what might be the boy's oddity or merely his independence of spirit.

The old man was very thin and stooped, and he emitted a mildewed smell, possibly because he had few clothes and refused to buy or accept anything new. Also his eyes were constantly watering. But he would sit in the parlor and tell the boy stories from Ovid. They were stories of people who became animals or trees or statues. They were stories of transformation. Women turned into sunflowers, spiders, bats, birds; men turned into snakes, pigs, stones and even thin air. The boy did not know he was hearing Ovid, and it would not have mattered if he had known. Grandfather's stories proposed to him that the forms of life were volatile and that everything in the world could as easily be something else. The old man's narrative would often drift from English to Latin without his being aware of it, as if he were reading to one of his classes of forty years before, so that it appeared nothing was immune to the principle of volatility, not even language.

The boy thought of his grandfather as a discarded treasure. He accepted the stories as images of truth, and therefore as propositions that could be tested. He found proof in his own experience of the instability of both things and people. He could look at the hairbrush on the bureau and it would some- times slide off the edge and fall to the floor. If he raised the window in his room it might shut itself at the moment he thought the room was getting cold. He liked to go to the moving picture shows downtown at the New Rochelle Theatre on Main Street. He knew the principles of photography but saw also that moving pictures depended on the capacity of humans, animals or objects to forfeit portions of themselves, residues of shadow and light which they left behind. He listened with fascination to the Victrola and played the same record over and over, whatever it happened to be, as if to test the endurance of a duplicated event.

And then he took to studying himself in the mirror, perhaps expecting some change to take place before his eyes. He could not see that he was taller than he had been even a few months before, or that his hair was darkening. Mother noticed his new attention to himself and understood it as the vanity of a boy beginning to think of himself as a man. Certainly he had passed the age of sailor suits. Always discreet, she said nothing. But she was very pleased. In fact he continued the practice not from vanity but because he discovered the mirror as a means of self-duplication. He would gaze at himself until there were two selves facing one another, neither of which could claim to be the real one. The sensation was of being disembodied. He was no longer anything exact as a person. He had the dizzying feeling of separating from himself endlessly. He would entrance himself so deeply in this process that he would be unable to come out of it even though his mind was lucid. He would have to rely on some outside stimulus, a loud noise or a change in the light coming through the window, to capture his attention and make him whole again.

And what of his own father, the burly self-confident man who had gone away, and came back gaunt and hunched and bearded? Or of his uncle shedding his hair and his lassitude? Down at the bottom of the Broadview Avenue hill one day the city fathers unveiled a bronze statue of some old Dutch governor, a fierce-looking man with a square-topped hat, a cape, pantaloons and buckled shoes. The family was on hand for that. There were other statues in the city parks and the boy knew them all. He believed that statues were one way of transforming humans and in some cases horses. Yet even statues did not remain the same but turned different colors or lost bits and pieces of themselves.

It was evident to him that the world composed and recomposed itself constantly in an endless process of dissatisfaction.

The winter turned extremely cold and dry and the ponds of New Rochelle became ideal for skating. On Saturdays and Sundays, Mother and Younger Brother and the boy would skate on the pond in the woods at the bottom of Paine Avenue, the street adjoining Broadview. Younger Brother would skate off by himself, taking long solemn and graceful strides across the ice, his hands behind his back, his head bowed. Mother wore a fur hat and a long black coat and held her hands in a muff and skated with her son holding her arm. She hoped to divert him from his lonely indoor pursuits. It was a merry scene with children and adults from all over the neighborhood skating over the white ice, long colorful scarves streaming from their necks, cheeks and noses red. People fell and laughed and were picked up. Dogs struggled to keep their balance as they followed the children about. There was the constant cut-cut of the skate blades on the ice. Some families had wicker chairs on runners for the elderly or less daring, and these were pushed about with solicitude. But the boy's eyes saw only the tracks made by the skaters, traces quickly erased of moments past, journeys taken.

16

This same winter found Tateh and his daughter in the mill town of Lawrence, Massachusetts. They had come there the previous autumn, having heard there were jobs. Tateh stood in front of a loom for fifty-six hours a week. His pay was just under six dollars. The family lived in a wooden tenement on a hill. They had no heat. They occupied one room overlooking an alley in which residents customarily dumped their garbage. He feared she would fall victim to the low-class elements of the neighborhood. He refused to enroll her in school—it was easier here than in New York to avoid the authorities—and made her stay home when he was not there to go out with her. After work he'd walk with her for an hour through the dark streets. She became thoughtful. She held her shoulders straight and walked like a woman. He was torturing himself anticipating her maturity. At such time when the girl becomes a woman she needs a mother to instruct her. Would she have to go through this difficult change alone? Alternatively, if he found someone to marry, how would she take to the new person? It might be the worst thing in the world for her.

The dismal wooden tenements lay in endless rows. Everyone from Europe was there—the Italians, the Poles, the Belgians, the Russian Jews. The feeling was not good between the different groups. One day the biggest of the mills, American Woolen Company, gave out envelopes with short pay, and a tremor went through the workers in the plant. Several Italian workers left their machines. They ran through the mill calling for a strike. They pulled out wires and threw lumps of coal through the windows. Others followed them. The anger spread. Throughout the city people left their machines. Those who couldn't make up their minds were carried along in the momentum. In three days every textile mill in Lawrence was virtually shut down.

Tateh was overjoyed. We were going to starve to death or freeze to death, he told his daughter. Now we'll be shot to death. But people from the I.W.W. who knew how to run a strike quickly came up from New York and organized things. A strike committee was formed with every one of the races represented and the message went out to the workers: no violence. Taking the girl with him Tateh joined the thousands of pickets encircling the mill, a massive brick building that went on for blocks. They trudged under the cold gray sky. Trolley cars came down the street, the drivers peering at the sight of thousands of marchers moving silently through the snow. Overhead the telephone and telegraph wires drooped with ice. Militia with rifles nervously guarded the mill gates. The militia all had overcoats.

There were many incidents. A woman worker was shot in the street. The only ones with guns were the police and the militia, but the two strike leaders, Ettor and Giovanetti, were arrested for complicity in the shooting. They were put in jail pending their trial. Something of the sort had been expected. Tateh went down to the train station to be on hand for the arrival in Lawrence of replacements for Ettor and Giovanetti. There was an immense crowd. Out of the train stepped Big Bill Haywood, the most famous Wobbly of them all. He was a

Westerner and wore a stetson which he now removed and waved. A cheer went up. Haywood raised his hands for quiet. He spoke. His voice was magnificent. There is no foreigner here except the capitalists, he said. The place went wild. Afterward everyone marched through the streets and sang the *Internationale*. The girl had never seen her Tateh so inflamed. She liked the strike because it got her out of the room. She held his hand.

But the battle went on week after week. Relief committees had set up kitchens in every neighborhood. It's not charity, a woman told Tateh when, after the child received her portion, he refused his. The bosses want you weak, therefore you have to be strong. The people who help us today will need our help tomorrow. On the picket line each cold day they wrapped their scarves around their necks and stamped their feet in the cold snow. The girl's little cloak was threadbare. Tateh volunteered for service on the strike display committee and got them off the cold streets by designing posters. The posters were very beautiful. But the man in charge told him they were not right. We don't want art, the man said. We want something to stir the anger. We want to keep the fires stoked. Tateh had drawn pickets, stark figures with their feet in snow. He had drawn families huddled in their tenements. He switched to lettering. All for one and one for all. He felt better. At night he took home scraps of paper, oak tag, pens and India ink, and to take the child's mind off their troubles he began to entertain her with silhouette drawings. He created a streetcar scene, the people getting on and off. She loved it. She leaned it against her bed pillow and looked at it from different angles. This gave him an inspiration. He did several studies of the streetcar and when he held them together and flipped the pages it appeared as if the streetcar came down the tracks from a distance and stopped so that the people could get on and off. His own delight matched the girl's. She gazed at him with such serene approval that he had a fever to create for her. He brought home more scrap paper. He imagined her on ice skates. In two nights he made a hundred and twenty silhouettes on pages not bigger than his hand. He bound them with string. She held the little book and governed the pages with her thumb and watched herself skating away and skating back, gliding into a figure eight, returning, pirouetting and making a lovely bow to her audience. Tateh held her and wept to feel her frail body, her soft lips on his face. What if the truth was that he could do nothing more for her than make pictures? What if they just went on this way in varying degrees of unrealized hope? She would grow up and curse his name.

Meanwhile the strike had become famous. Reporters arrived daily from all over the country. Support was coming in from other cities. But there was a growing weakness in the unity of the strike front. A man with children found it difficult to keep his courage and resolve. A plan was put into effect whereby children of strikers were to be sent to other cities to board with families in sympathy with the strike. Hundreds of families in Boston and New York and Philadelphia offered to take them in. Others sent money. Every family was carefully checked by the strike committee. The parents of the children had to sign permission forms. The experiment began. Wealthy women came up from New York to escort the first hundred on the train. Each child had had a medical examination and wore a new outfit of clothes. They arrived at Grand Central Station in New York like a religious army. A crowd met them and for a moment everyone held the picture of the children hand in hand staring resolutely ahead as if toward the awful fate industrial America had prepared for them. The press coverage was enormous. The mill owners in Lawrence realized that of all the stratagems devised by the workers this one, the children's crusade, was the most damaging. If it was allowed to go on, national sentiment would swing to the workingmen and the owners would have to give in. This would mean an increase in wages that would bring some workers up to eight dollars a week. They would get extra pay for overtime and for machine speed-ups. They would get off without any punishment for their strike. It was unthinkable. The mill owners knew who were the stewards of civilization and the source of progress and prosperity in the city of Lawrence. For the good of the country and the American democratic system they resolved there would be no more children's crusades.

In the meantime Tateh debated with himself: Clearly the best thing for his girl would be to have a place for a few weeks with a settled family. She would be properly fed, she would be warm, and she would get a taste of a normal home life. But he couldn't bear to part from her. The thought gave him forebodings. He went down to the relief committee, a storefront not far from the mill, and talked to one of the women there. She assured him they had more good working-class families who had volunteered to board a child than they knew what to do with. Jewish? Tateh said. You name it we got it, the woman said. But he couldn't bring himself to sign the papers. Every family is investigated, the woman told him. Could we be careless about such things? I've been a socialist all my life, Tateh assured her. Of course, the woman said. A doctor will listen to her chest. For that alone it's worthwhile. She'll eat hot meals and know her father has friends in the world. But no one's pushing you. Look, look at the line behind you, plenty of customers.

Tateh thought Here I am in the middle of brotherhood in action and I'm thinking like some bourgeois from the *shtetl*. He signed the permission papers.

One week later he took the girl down to the railroad station. She was in a contingent of two hundred going to Philadelphia. She was wearing a new cloak and a hat that kept her ears warm. He kept stealing glances at her. She was beautiful. She had a naturally regal posture. She was enjoying her new clothes. He was casual with her and tried not to be hurt. She had accepted the idea of leaving him without one word of protest. Of course, this was good for all concerned. But if she found it so easy, what would the future bring? She had reserves of character he did not elicit from her. She attracted people. Many of the mothers stared. Tateh was proud, but frightened too. They stood in the waiting room, a pandemonium of mothers and children. Someone called Here it comes! and the crowd surged to the doors as the train slid in chuffing and hissing great clouds of steam.

A car reserved for the children was attached to the end of the train. This was the Boston and Maine line. The engine was a Baldwin 4–6–0. Everyone moved down the platform, the registered nurses from the Philadelphia Women's Committee at the head of the procession. Don't forget your manners, Tateh said as they followed along. When people ask you a question answer them. Speak up so they can hear you. Once past the corner of the station he noticed out on the street a line of militia with their blocked hats. They held their rifles across their chests. They were facing away from the platform. The procession stopped and backed up on itself. There was some sort of commotion at the front of the line. Then he heard a scream, police appeared everywhere, and suddenly the crowd was in a terrible turmoil. While amazed passengers looked out from the windows of the train the police started to separate the mothers from their children. They were dragging the mothers kicking and screaming to trucks at the end of the platform. The trucks were army Reo's with pagoda hoods and chain wheel drive. Children were being stepped on. They scattered in all directions. A woman ran by with blood coming from her mouth. Steam drifted back from the engine like patches of fog. The bell quietly rang. A woman appeared in front of Tateh. She tried to say something. She was holding her stomach. She fell. Tateh lifted his daughter bodily and swung her up on the platform of the nearest car, out of harm's way. Then he turned his attention to the fallen woman. He picked her up under the shoulders and dragged her through the crowd to a bench. As he was sitting her down he came to the attention of one of the policemen. The policeman cracked him on the shoulders and the head with his stick. What are you doing, Tateh cried. He didn't know what the maniac wanted of him. He moved back into the crowd. He was followed and beaten. He stumbled away from the crowd and was still beaten. Finally he fell.

The authority for this police action was an order issued by the city marshal prohibiting all children from leaving Lawrence, Massachusetts. It was for their own good. They were on their knees, holding the prostrate forms of their bloodied parents. Some were in hysterics. In a few minutes the police had swept the platform clean, the trucks were driven off, the militia were marched away, and only a few sobbing battered adults and weeping children remained. One was Tateh. He leaned against a pillar to regain his strength. His mind was not clear. He began to hear sounds that had been made minutes before. He heard the little girl's voice: Tateh, Tateh! At that moment it occurred to him that the station platform was unnaturally bright. The train was gone. The realization struck his heart like a chord. He was now completely alert. Still he heard the voice. Tateh, Tateh! He looked down the tracks and saw the last car of the train to Philadelphia some yards beyond the end of the station. It was not moving. He started to run. Tateh, Tateh! As he ran the train slowly began to move. He ran onto the tracks. He ran, stumbling, with his arm out. His hands caught the guardrail of the observation platform. The train was picking up speed. His feet were coming off the ground. The ties began to blur under him. He clung to the railing, finally hoisting his knees to the platform overhang and clinging there with his head pressed against the bars like a man in prison begging to be set free.

17

Tateh was rescued by two conductors who lifted him by the arms and the seat of his pants onto the observation platform. First they had to pry his fingers from the railings. He found his daughter on the train and ignoring everyone around her, conductors, passengers, he gathered her in his arms and wept. Then he noticed that her new cloak was bloody. He looked at her hands. They were smeared with blood. Where are you hurt! he shouted. Where are you hurt! She shook her head and pointed at him and he realized that the blood all over her was his own. It came from his scalp, blackening his white hair.

A doctor who happened to be on board tended Tateh's injuries and gave him an injection. After that he wasn't too clear about what happened. He slept lying on his side across two seats with his arm for a pillow. He was aware of the motion of the train and his daughter sitting in the seat facing him. She looked out the window. They were the only passengers in the special car for Philadelphia. Sometimes he heard voices but he could not bestir himself to understand what they said. At the same time he clearly saw her eyes with hills of snow proceeding slowly, in a curve, over her pupils. In this way he made the trip south to Boston, then to New Haven, through the Westchester towns of Rye and New Rochelle, through the train yards of New York, across the river to Newark, New Jersey, and then to Philadelphia.

When the train arrived the two refugees found a bench in the station and spent the night there. Tateh was not entirely himself. He had in his pockets, fortunately, that part of his week's wages he had set aside for the rent: two dollars and fifty cents. The girl sat beside him on the shiny bench and watched the patterns made by the people moving through the station. By the early morning hours there was only one porter pushing a big broom across the marble floor. As always she seemed to accept totally the situation in which she found herself. Tateh's head ached. His hands were swollen and scraped. He sat with his palms cupping his ears. He didn't know what to do. He couldn't think. Somehow they were in Philadelphia.

In the morning he picked up a discarded newspaper. On the front page was an account of the police terror in Lawrence, Massachusetts. He found his cigarettes in their box in his pocket and smoked and read the paper. An editorial called for an investigation of the outrage by the Federal Government. So that was it, the strike would be won. But then what? He heard the clacking of the looms. A salary of six dollars and change. Would that transform their lives? They would still live in that wretched room, in that terrible dark street. Tateh shook his head. This country will not let me breathe. In this mood he slowly came to the decision not to go back to Lawrence, Massachusetts. His belongings, his rags, he would leave to the landlord. What do you have with you, he said to his daughter. She showed him the contents of her small satchel—things she had taken for her trip away from home. Her underthings, her comb and brush, a hair clasp, garters, stockings, and the books he had made for her of the trolley car and the skater. From this moment, perhaps, Tateh began to conceive of his life as separate from the fate of the working class. I hate machines, he said to his daughter. He stood and she stood and took his hand and together they looked for the exit. The I.W.W. has won, he said. But what has it won? A few more pennies in wages. Will it now own the mills? No.

They cleaned and refreshed themselves in the public lavatories. They went to the station café for a breakfast of rolls and coffee and spent the day walking through the streets of Philadelphia. It was cold and the sun was shining. They looked in the windows of the stores and when their feet began to ache from the cold they walked into a department store to warm up. It was a vast emporium, every aisle crowded with shoppers. The girl noticed with interest that wire baskets swung from moving cables over the counters. They carried the money and receipts back and forth from the counters to the cashier. The sales clerks yanked on wooden-handled rope pulls to bring the baskets down and pulled on other ropes to get them back up. Mannequins, like grown-up dolls, sported satin toques and broad-brimmed hats plumed with egret feathers. One of these hats is more than a week's wages, Tateh said.

Later, on the streets again, they walked past iron-front buildings where trucks were pulled up to warehouse platforms. The windows of supply companies and wholesalers offered little of interest. But then her eye was attracted to the dirty window in which were displayed all the gimcracks of a mail-order novelty company. At this time businessmen were discovering the profit in practical jokes and parlor magic tricks. There were exploding cigars, rubber roses for the lapel that squirted water, boxes of sneezing powder, telescopes that left black eyes, exploding card decks, sound bladders for placing under chair cushions, glass paperweights with winter scenes on which snow fell when you shook them, exploding matches, punchboards, little lead liberty bells and statues of liberty, magic rings, exploding fountain pens, books that told you the meaning of dreams, rubber Egyptian belly dancers, exploding watches, exploding eggs.

Tateh stared at the window long after the girl's interest had waned. He led her into the store. Tateh removed his hat and spoke to a man in a striped shirt with sleeve garters who came forward to meet them. The man was amiable. Sure, he said, let's see it. Tateh took the girl's satchel, put it on the counter and, opening it, withdrew the book of the skater. Standing next to the proprietor he held the book at arm's length and expertly flipped the pages. The little girl skated forward and skated away, did a figure eight, came back, went into a pirouette and made a graceful bow. The man's eyebrows went up. He stuck out his lower lip. Let me try that, he said.

An hour later Tateh walked out of there with twenty-five dollars in cash and a letter of agreement which he had signed calling for four more books at twenty-five dollars each. The company—its name was the Franklin Novelty Company—would publish the books and add them to its line. For purposes of the contract they were called movie books. Come, Tateh said to his child, we'll find a boardinghouse in a good neighborhood and then we'll have ourselves a meal and a hot bath.

18

Thus did the artist point his life along the lines of flow of
American energy. Workers would strike and die but in the
streets of cities an entrepreneur could cook sweet potatoes in
a bucket of hot coals and sell them for a penny or two. A
smiling hurdy-gurdy man could fill his cup. Phil the Fiddler,
undaunted by the snow, cut away the fingers of his gloves and
played under the lighted windows of mansions. Frank the Cash
Boy kept his eyes open for a runaway horse carrying the daughter of a Wall Street broker. All across the continent merchants
pressed the large round keys of their registers. The value of the
duplicable event was everywhere perceived. Every town had its
ice-cream soda fountain of Belgian marble. Painless Parker the
Dentist everywhere offered to remove your toothache. At
Highland Park, Michigan, the first Model T automobile built
on a moving assembly line lurched down a ramp and came to
rest in the grass under a clear sky. It was black and ungainly
and stood high off the ground. Its inventor regarded it from
a distance. His derby was tilted back on his head. He chewed
on a piece of straw. In his left hand he held a pocket watch.
The employer of many men, a good number of them foreign-
born, he had long believed that most human beings were too

dumb to make a good living. He'd conceived the idea of breaking down the work operations in the assembly of an automobile to their simplest steps, so that any fool could perform them. Instead of having one man learn the hundreds of tasks in the building of one motorcar, walking him hither and yon to pick out the parts from a general inventory, why not stand him in his place, have him do just one task over and over, and let the parts come past him on moving belts. Thus the worker's mental capacity would not be taxed. The man who puts in a bolt does not put on the nut, the inventor said to his associates. The man who puts on the nut does not tighten it. He had a way with words. He had gotten his inspiration from a visit to a beef-packing concern where the cows were swung through the plant hanging in slings from overhead cables. With his tongue he moved the straw from one corner of his mouth to the other. He looked at his watch again. Part of his genius consisted of seeming to his executives and competitors not as quick-witted as they. He brushed the grass with the tip of his shoe. Exactly six minutes after the car had rolled down the ramp an identical car appeared at the top of the ramp, stood for a moment pointed at the cold early morning sun, then rolled down and crashed into the rear of the first one. Henry Ford had once been an ordinary automobile manufacturer. Now he experienced an ecstasy greater and more intense than that vouchsafed to any American before him, not excepting Thomas Jefferson. He had caused a machine to replicate itself endlessly. His executives and managers and assistants crowded around him to shake his hand. Tears were in their eyes. He allotted sixty seconds on his pocket watch for a display of sentiment. Then he sent everyone back to work. He knew there were refinements to be made and he was right. By controlling the speed of the moving belts he could control the workers' rate of production. He did not want a worker to stoop over or to take more than one step from his work site. The worker must

have every second necessary for his job but not a single un-
necessary second. From these principles Ford established the
final proposition of the theory of industrial manufacture—not
only that the parts of the finished product be interchangeable,
but that the men who build the products be themselves interchangeable parts. Soon he was producing three thousand cars
a month and selling them to the multitudes. He was to live a
long and active life. He loved birds and animals and counted
among his friends John Burroughs, an old naturalist who studied the humble creatures of the woodland—chipmunk and
raccoon, junko, wren and chickadee.

19

But Ford's achievement did not put him at the top of the business pyramid. Only one man occupied that lofty place.

The offices of the J. P. Morgan Company were at 23 Wall Street. The great financier came to work one morning dressed in a dark blue suit, a black overcoat with a collar of lamb's wool and a top hat. He affected fashions slightly out of date. When he stepped out of his limousine the car robe fell around his feet. One of the several bank officers who had rushed out to meet him disentangled the robe and hung it over the robe rail on the inside of the door. The chauffeur thanked him profusely. Somehow the speaking tube had come off its hook and another officer of the bank replaced it. In the meantime Morgan had marched into the building, assistants, aides and even some of the firm's customers circling him like birds. Morgan carried a gold-headed cane. He was at this time in his seventy-fifth year of life—a burly six-footer with a large head of sparse white hair, a white moustache and fierce intolerant eyes set just close enough to suggest the psychopathology of his will. Accepting the obeisances of his employees, he strode to his office, a modest glass-paneled room on the main floor of the bank where he was visible to everyone and everyone to him. He was helped with his hat and coat. He was wearing a wing collar and an ascot. He sat down behind his desk, and ignoring the depositors' accounts which were usually the first thing he looked at, said to his aides I want to meet that tinkering fellow. What's his name. The motorcar mechanic. Ford.

He had sensed in Ford's achievement a lust for order as imperial as his own. This was the first sign given to him in some time that he might not be alone on the planet. Pierpont Morgan was that classic American hero, a man born to extreme wealth who by dint of hard work and ruthlessness multiplies the family fortune till it is out of sight. He controlled 741 directorships in 112 corporations. He had once arranged a loan to the United States Government that had saved it from bankruptcy. He had single-handedly stopped the panic of 1907 by arranging for the importation of one hundred million dollars in gold bullion. Moving about in private railroad cars or yachts he crossed all borders and was at home everywhere in the world. He was a monarch of the invisible, transnational kingdom of capital whose sovereignty was everywhere granted. Commanding resources that beggared royal fortunes, he was a revolutionist who left to presidents and kings their territory while he took control of their railroads and shipping lines, banks and trust companies, industrial plants and public utilities. For years he had surrounded himself with parties of friends and acquaintances, always screening them in his mind for the personal characteristics that might indicate less regard for him than they admitted. He was invariably disappointed. Everywhere men deferred to him and women shamed themselves. He knew as no one else the cold and barren reaches of unlimited success. The ordinary operations of his intelligence and instinct over the past fifty years had made him preeminent in the affairs of nations and he thought this said little for mankind. Only one thing served to remind Pierpont Morgan of his humanity and that was a chronic skin disease that had colonized his nose and made of it a strawberry of the award-winning giant type grown by California's wizard of horticulture Luther Burbank. This affliction had come to Morgan in his young manhood. As he grew older and richer the nose grew larger. He learned to stare down people who looked at it, but every day of his life, when he arose, he examined it in the mirror, finding it indeed loathsome but at the same time exquisitely satisfying. It seemed to him that every time he made an acquisition or manipulated a bond issue or took over an industry, another bright red pericarp burst into bloom. His favorite story in literature was a tale of Nathaniel Hawthorne's entitled "The Birthmark," which told of an extraordinarily lovely woman whose beauty was perfect except for a small birthmark on her cheek. When her husband, a natural scientist, made her drink a potion designed to rid her of this imperfection, the birthmark disappeared; but as its last faintest outline vanished from her skin and she was perfect, she died. To Morgan, the disfigurement of his monstrous nose was the touch of God upon him, the assurance of mortality. It was the steadiest assurance he had.

Once, years before, he had arranged a dinner party at his residence on Madison Avenue in which his guests were the dozen most powerful men in America besides himself. He was hoping the collected energy of their minds might buckle the walls of his home. Rockefeller startled him with the news that he was chronically constipated and did a lot of his thinking on the toilet. Carnegie dozed over his brandy. Harriman uttered inanities. Gathered in this one room the business elite could think of nothing to say. How they appalled him. How his heart quaked. He heard through his brain the electric winds of an empty universe. He ordered the servants to place garlands of laurel on every pate and crown. Without exception the dozen most powerful men in America looked like horse's asses. But the pomposity that had accrued with their wealth persuaded them that perhaps these ridiculous vines held some significance. Not one of the women thought to laugh. They were hags. They sat on their large draped behinds, breasts drooping under their décolletage. Not an ounce of wit among them. Not a light in their eyes. They were the loyal wives of great men and the hard pull of rampant achievement had sucked the life out of their flesh. Revealing nothing of his feelings Morgan hid behind his fierce and doughty expression. A photographer was summoned to make a picture. There was a flash—the solemn moment was recorded.

He fled to Europe, embarking on the White Star liner *Oceanic*. He had combined the White Star Line, the Red Star Line, the American, Dominion, Atlantic Transport and Leyland lines into one company numbering 120 ocean-going ships. He despised competition no less on the seas than on land. He stood at night by the ship's rail, hearing the heavy sea, feeling its swell but not seeing it. The sea and the sky were black and indistinguishable. A bird, some sort of gull, appeared from the blackness and lighted on the rail a few feet from him. Perhaps it had been attracted by his nose. I have no peers, Morgan said to the bird. It seemed an indisputable truth. Somehow he had catapulted himself beyond the world's value system. But this very fact lay upon him an awesome responsibility to maintain the illusions of other men. For his Episcopal brethren he would build a cathedral, St. John the Divine, on West 110th Street in New York. For his wife and grown children he would continue to provide an image of domestic stolidity. And for the sake of the country he would live in as grand a style as he could summon, dining with kings, or buying art in Rome and Paris, or consorting with beautiful companions at Aix-les-Bains.

Morgan had kept his vows. He spent six months of every year in Europe, moving in majesty from one country to another. The holds of his ships were filled with collections of paintings, rare manuscripts, first editions, jades, bronzes, autographs, tapestries, crystal. He looked into the eyes of Rembrandt burghers and Greco prelates as if to find kingdoms of truth that would bring him to his knees. He fingered the illustrated texts of rare Bibles of the Middle Ages as if to pick up dust from the City of God. He felt if there was something more than he knew, it lay in the past rather than in the present, of whose total bankruptcy of existence he was confident. He was the present. He employed curators to find him art and scholars to teach him of ancient civilizations. He beat his way back through the Flemish tapestries. He fondled Roman statuary. He strode through the Acropolis kicking the loose stones. His desperate studies settled, inevitably, on the civilizations of ancient Egypt, wherein it was taught that the universe is changeless and that death is followed by the resumption of life. He was fascinated. His life took a new turn. He funded Egyptian archaeological expeditions of the Metropolitan Museum. He followed the reclamation from the dry sands of every new stele, amulet and canopic jar containing viscera. He went to the valley of the Nile where the sun never fails to rise nor the river to flood its banks. He studied the hieroglyphs. One evening he left his hotel in Cairo and rode seven miles on a special streetcar to the site of the Great Pyramid. In the clear blue light of the moon he heard from a native guide of the wisdom given to the great Osiris that there is a sacred tribe of heroes, a colony from the gods who are regularly born in every age to assist mankind. The idea stunned him. The more he thought about it the more palpably he felt it. It was upon his return to America that he began to think about Henry Ford. He had no illusions that Ford was a gentleman. He recognized him for a shrewd provincial, as uneducated as a piece of wood.

But he thought he saw in Ford's use of men a reincarnation of pharaohism. Not only that: he had studied photographs of the automobile manufacturer and had seen an extraordinary resemblance to Seti I, the father of the great Ramses and the best-preserved mummy to have been unearthed from the necropolis of Thebes in the Valley of the Kings.

20

Morgan's residence in New York City was No. 219 Madison Avenue, in Murray Hill, a stately brownstone on the northeast corner of 36th Street. Adjoining it was the white marble Morgan Library, which he had built to receive the thousands of books and art objects collected on his travels. It had been designed in the Italian Renaissance style by Charles McKim, a partner of Stanford White's. The marble blocks were fitted without mortar. A snowfall darker than the stones of the Library lay on the streets the day Henry Ford arrived for lunch. All the sounds of the city were muffled by the snow. A city policeman was stationed at the door of the residence. Across the street and on every corner of 36th and Madison small groups of men with their coat collars turned up stood staring at the great man's home.

Morgan had ordered a light lunch. They did not say much as they dined without other company on Chincoteagues, bisque of terrapin, a Montrachet, rack of lamb, a Château Latour, fresh tomatoes and endives, rhubarb pie in heavy cream, and coffee. The service was magical, two of Morgan's house staff making dishes appear and disappear with such self-effacement as to suggest no human agency. Ford ate well but he did not touch the wine. He finished before his host. He gazed frankly at the Morgan nose. He found a crumb on the tablecloth and deposited it in the saucer of his coffee cup. His fingers idly rubbed the gold plate.

At the conclusion of lunch Morgan indicated to Ford that he would like him to come to the Library. They walked out of the dining room and through a kind of dark public parlor where sat three or four men hoping to secure a few moments of Pierpont Morgan's time. These were his lawyers. They were there to advise him on his forthcoming appearance before the House Committee on Banking and Finance then sitting in Washington for the purpose of inquiring into the possibility that a money trust existed in the United States. Morgan waved the lawyers away as they rose upon sight of him. There was also in attendance an art dealer in a morning coat who had traveled from Rome expressly to see him. The dealer rose only to bow.

None of this display was lost on Ford. He was a man of homespun tastes but was not at all put off by what he recognized as an empire different only in style from his own. Morgan brought him to the great West Room of the Library. Here they took chairs on opposite sides of a fireplace that was as tall as a man. It was a good day for a fire, Morgan said. Ford agreed. Cigars were offered. Ford refused. He noticed the ceiling was gilded. The walls were covered in red silk damask. There were fancy paintings hanging behind glass in heavy frames—pictures of yellowish soulful-looking people with golden haloes. He guessed nobody had their pictures made in those days who wasn't a saint. There was a madonna and child. He ran his fingers along the arm of his chair of red plush.

Morgan let him take it all in. He puffed on his cigar. Finally he spoke. Ford, he said gruffly, I have no interest in acquiring your business or in sharing its profits. Nor am I associated with any of your competitors. Ford nodded. I have to allow that is good news, he said, giving off a sly glance. Nevertheless, his host continued, I admire what you have done, and while I must have qualms about a motorcar in the hands of every mongoloid who happens to have a few hundred dollars to spend, I recognize that the future is yours. You're still a young man—fifty years or thereabouts?—and perhaps you understand as I cannot the need to separately mobilize the masses of men. I have spent my life in the coordination of capital resources and the harmonic combination of industries, but I have never considered the possibility that the employment of labor is in itself a harmonically unifying process apart from the enterprise in which it is enlisted. Let me ask you a question. Has it occurred to you that your assembly line is not merely a stroke of industrial genius but a projection of organic truth? After all, the interchangeability of parts is a rule of nature. Individuals participate in their species and in their genus. All mammals reproduce in the same way and share the same designs of self-nourishment, with digestive and circulatory systems that are recognizably the same, and they enjoy the same senses. Obviously this is not to say all mammals have interchangeable parts, as your automobiles. But shared design is what allows taxonomists to classify mammals as mammals. And within a species —man, for example—the rules of nature operate so that our individual differences occur on the basis of our similarity. So that individuation may be compared to a pyramid in that it is only achieved by the placement of the top stone.

Ford pondered this. Exceptin the Jews, he muttered. Morgan didn't think he had heard correctly. I beg your pardon, he said. The Jews, Ford said. They ain't like anyone else I know. There goes your theory up shits creek. He smiled.

Morgan was silent for some minutes. He smoked his cigar. The fire crackled. Gusts of snow blown by the wind gently spattered the Library windows. Morgan spoke again. From time to time, he said, I have retained scholars and scientists to assist me in my philosophical investigations in hopes of reaching some conclusions about this life that are not within the reach of the masses of men. I am proposing to share the fruits of my study. I do not think you can be so insolent as to believe your achievements are the result only of your own effort. Did you attribute your success in this manner, I would warn you, sir, of the terrible price to be paid. You would find yourself stranded on the edge of the world and see as no other man the emptiness of the firmament. Do you believe in God? That's my business, Ford said. Well and good, Morgan said, I would not expect any man of your intelligence to embrace such a common idea. You may need me more than you think. Suppose I could prove to you that there are universal patterns of order and repetition that give meaning to the activity of this planet. Suppose I could demonstrate that you yourself are an instrumentation in our modern age of trends in human identity that affirm the oldest wisdom in the world.

Abruptly Morgan stood and left the room. Ford turned in his chair and looked after him. In a moment the old man was in the doorway and beckoning to him with a vehement gesture. Ford followed him through the central hall of the Library to the East Room, whose high walls were covered with bookshelves. There were two upper tiers with promenades of frosted glass and polished brass balustrades so that any book could be easily removed from its place no matter how high. Morgan walked up to the far wall, pressed the spine of a certain book, and part of the shelving swung away to reveal a passageway through which a man could pass. If you please, he said to Ford, and following him into a small chamber he pressed a button that closed the door behind them.

This was an ordinary-sized room modestly appointed with a round polished table, two spindle-back chairs, and a cabinet with a glass top for the display of manuscripts. Morgan turned on a table lamp with a green metal lampshade. Nobody has ever joined me in this room before, he said. He turned on a floor lamp arranged to light the display cabinet. Come over here, sir, he said. Ford looked through the glass and saw an ancient parchment covered with Latin calligraphy. That, Morgan said, is a folio of one of the first Rosicrucian texts, *The Chemical Wedding of Christian Rosencrutz*. Do you know who the original Rosicrucians were, Mr. Ford? They were Christian alchemists of the Rhenish palatinate whose elector was Frederick V. We are talking about the early seventeenth century, sir. These great and good men promulgated the idea of an ongoing, beneficent magic available to certain men of every age for the collective use of mankind. The Latin for this is *prisca theologia*, secret wisdom. The odd thing is that this belief in a secret wisdom is not the Rosicrucians' alone. We know in London in the middle of the same century of the existence of a society called the Invisible College. Its members were reputed to be the very carriers of the beneficent magic I speak of. You of course do not know of the writings of Giordano Bruno, of which here is a specimen page in his own handwriting. My scholars have traced for me, like the best detectives, the existence of this idea and of various mysterious organizations to maintain it, in most of the Renaissance cultures, in medieval societies and in ancient Greece. I hope you are following this closely. The earliest recorded mention of special people born in each age to ease the sufferings of humankind with their *prisca theologia* comes to us through the Greek in the translated writings of the Egyptian priest Hermes Trismegistus. It is Hermes who gives the historical name to this occult knowledge. It is called the Hermetica. With his thick index finger Morgan thumped the glass above the last display piece in the cabinet, a fragment of pink stone upon which geometric scratchings were faintly visible. That, sir, may be a specimen of Hermes in the original cuneiform. And now let me ask you a question. Why do you suppose an idea which had currency in every age and civilization of mankind disappears in modern times? Because only in the age of science have these men and their wisdom dropped from view. I'll tell you why: The rise of mechanistic science, of Newton and Descartes, was a great conspiracy, a great devilish conspiracy to destroy our apprehension of reality and our awareness of the transcendentally gifted among us. But they are with us today nevertheless. They are with us in every age. They come back, you see? They come back!

Morgan was now florid with excitement. He directed Ford's attention to the furthermost corner of the room where in the shadow stood yet another furnishing, something rectangular that was covered with a gold velvet cloth. Morgan gripped the corner of the cloth in his fist, and staring with fierce proprietary triumph at his guest he pulled it away and dropped it to the floor. Ford inspected the item. It was a glass case sealed with lead. Within the case was a sarcophagus. He heard the old man's harsh panting breath. It was the only sound in the room. The sarcophagus was of alabaster. Topping it was a wooden effigy of the fellow who lay within. The effigy was painted in gold leaf, red ochre and blue. This, sir, said Morgan in a hoarse voice, is the coffin of a great Pharaoh. The Egyptian government and the entire archaeological community believe it resides in Cairo. Were my possession of it known, there would be an international uproar. It is literally beyond value. My private staff of Egyptologists has taken every scientific precaution to preserve it from the ravages of the air. Under the mask that you see is the mummy of the great Pharaoh of the Nineteenth Dynasty, Seti the First, recovered from the Temple of Karnak where it lay for over three thousand years. I will show it to you in due course. Let me now say only that I guarantee the visage of the great king will be of considerable interest to you.

Morgan had to recover his composure. He pulled back one of the chairs and sat down at the table. Slowly his breathing returned to normal. Ford had sat down across from him, and understanding the old man's physical difficulties, remained quiet and stared at his own shoes. The shoes, brown lace-ups, he had bought from the catalogue of L. L. Bean. They were good comfortable shoes. Mr. Ford, Pierpont Morgan said, I want you to be my guest on an expedition to Egypt. That is very much the place, sir. That is where it all begins. I have commissioned a steamer designed expressly for sailing the Nile. When she's ready I want you to come with me. Will you do that? It will require no investment on your part. We must go to Luxor and Karnak. We must go to the Great Pyramid at Giza. There are so few of us, sir. My money has brought me to the door of certain crypts, the deciphering of sacred hieroglyphs. Why should we not satisfy ourselves of the truth of who we are and the eternal beneficent force which we incarnate?

Ford sat slightly hunched. His long hands lay over the wooden arms of his chair as if broken at the wrists. He considered everything that had been said. He looked at the sarcophagus. When he had satisfied himself that he understood, he nodded his head solemnly and replied as follows: If I understand you right, Mr. Morgan, you are talking about reincarnation. Well, let me tell you about that. As a youth I was faced with an awful crisis in my mental life when it came over me that I had no call to know what I knew. I had grit, all right, but I was an ordinary country boy who had suffered his McGuffey like the rest of them. Yet I knew how everything worked. I could look at something and tell you how it worked and probably show you how to make it work better. But I was no intellectual, you see, and I had no patience with the two-dollar words.

Morgan listened. He felt that he mustn't move.

Well then, Ford continued, I happened to pick up a little book. It was called *An Eastern Fakir's Eternal Wisdom*, published by the Franklin Novelty Company of Philadelphia,

Pennsylvania. And in this book, which cost me just twenty-five cents, I found everything I needed to set my mind at rest. Reincarnation is the only belief I hold, Mr. Morgan. I explain my genius this way—some of us have just lived more times than others. So you see, what you have spent on scholars and traveled around the world to find, I already knew. And I'll tell you something, in thanks for the eats, I'm going to lend that book to you. Why, you don't have to fuss with all these Latiny things, he said waving his arm, you don't have to pick the garbage pails of Europe and build steamboats to sail the Nile just to find out something that you can get in the mail order for two bits!

The two men stared at each other. Morgan sat back in his chair. The blood drained from his face and his eyes lost their fierce light. When he spoke, it was with the weak voice of an old man. Mr. Ford, he said, if my ideas can survive their attachment to you, they will have met their ultimate test.

Nevertheless the crucial breakthrough had been made. About a year after this extraordinary meeting Morgan made his trip to Egypt. Although Ford did not go with him he had conceded the possibility of an awesome lineage. And together they had managed to found the most secret and exclusive club in America, The Pyramid, of which they were the only members. It endowed certain researches which persist to this day.

21

Of course at this time in our history the images of ancient Egypt were stamped on everyone's mind. This was due to the discoveries being reported out of the desert by British and American archaeologists. After the football players in their padded canvas knee pants and leather helmets, archaeologists were the glamour personages of the universities. Mummification was described in detail in the Sunday supplements and the funerary concerns of the papyri were analyzed by cub reporters. Egyptian art, its look, was chosen for the interior decoration of homes. Out went the Louis Quatorze and in came the throne chairs with the carved serpent arms. In New Rochelle, Mother was not immune to the fashion, and finding the floral print in the dining room oppressively dull she replaced it with an elegant pattern of sloe-eyed Egyptian males and females in headdresses and short skirts. Colored red ochre, blue and tan, they paraded along the walls in that peculiar frontal way of Egyptians, with vultures on their palms, sheaves of wheat, water lilies and lutes. They were accompanied by lion, scarabs, owl, oxen and dismembered feet. Father, sensitive to every change, found his appetite diminished. It seemed to him inappropriate to entomb oneself in order to dine.

The boy, however, loved the design and was inspired to study the hieroglyphic alphabet. He abandoned *Wild West Weekly* for magazines that published tales of violated tombs and the coming to fruition of mummies' curses. He had become intrigued with the black woman in the attic and in his quiet secret games incorporated her as a Nubian princess now captured for a slave. Unaware, she sat in her room by the window, while he passed her door in a beaked papier-mâché mask of an ibis which he had made himself.

One afternoon, a Sunday, a new Model T Ford slowly came up the hill and went past the house. The boy, who happened to see it from the porch, ran down the steps and stood on the sidewalk. The driver was looking right and left as if trying to find a particular address; he turned the car around at the corner and came back. Pulling up before the boy, he idled his throttle and beckoned with a gloved hand. He was a Negro. His car shone. The brightwork gleamed. There was a glass windshield and a custom pantasote top. I'm looking for a young woman of color whose name is Sarah, he said. She is said to reside in one of these houses.

The boy realized he meant the woman in the attic. She's here. The man switched off the motor, set the brake and jumped down. Then he climbed the stone steps under the two Norwegian maples and walked around the side of the house to the back door.

When Mother came to the door the colored man was respectful, but there was something disturbingly resolute and self-important in the way he asked her if he could please speak with Sarah. Mother could not judge his age. He was a stocky man with a red-complected shining brown face, high cheekbones and large dark eyes so intense as to suggest they were about to cross. He had a neat moustache. He was dressed in the affectation of wealth to which colored people lent themselves. He wore a fitted black overcoat, a black and white hound's-tooth suit, gray spats and pointed black shoes. He held in his hand a charcoal-gray cap and driving goggles. She told him to wait and closed the door. She climbed to the third floor. She found the girl Sarah not sitting at the window as she usually did but standing rigidly, hands folded in front of her, and facing the door. Sarah, Mother said, you have a caller. The girl said nothing. Will you come to the kitchen? The girl shook her head. You don't want to see him? No, ma'am, the girl finally said softly while she looked at the floor. Send him away, please. This was the most she had said in all the months she had lived in the house. Mother went back downstairs and found the fellow not at the back door but in the kitchen where, in the warmth of the corner near the cookstove, Sarah's baby lay sleeping in his carriage. It was a wicker carriage on four wooden tapered spoke wheels and it had a faded upholstery of blue satin with a plush roll. Her own son had slept in it and her brother before him. The black man was kneeling beside the carriage and staring at the child. Mother, not thinking clearly, was suddenly outraged that he had presumed to come in the door. Sarah is unable to see you, she said, and she held the door open. The colored man took another glance at the child, rose, thanked her and departed. She slammed the door harder than she should have. The baby woke and began to cry. She picked him up, comforting him, astonished by her extreme reaction to the visitor.

Such was the coming of the colored man in the car to Broadview Avenue. His name was Coalhouse Walker Jr. Beginning with that Sunday he appeared every week, always knocking at the back door, always turning away without complaint upon Sarah's refusal to see him. Father considered the visits a nuisance and wanted to discourage them. I'll call the police, he said. Mother laid her hand on his arm. One Sunday the colored man left a bouquet of yellow chrysanthemums which in this season had to have cost him a pretty penny.

Before she took the flowers up to Sarah, Mother stood at the parlor window. Out on the street the black man dusted his car, cleaned the wheel spokes, the headlamps and the windshield. He glanced up at the third-floor window and drove away. Mother now had cause to remember the expression on the faces of the Ohio seminarians who called on her when she was a girl of seventeen. She said to Father I think what we are witnessing is, in fact, a courtship of the most stubborn Christian kind. Father replied Yes, if you can call a courtship what has already produced a child. I find that an unkind remark, Mother said. There was suffering, and now there is penitence. It's very grand and I'm sorry for you that you don't see it.

The black girl would say nothing about her visitor. They had no idea where she had met him, or how. As far as they knew she had no family nor any friends from the black community in the downtown section of the city. There was a settled society of Negroes there but also, on its margins, a transient element. Apparently she was a transient and had come by herself from New York to work as a servant. Mother was exhilarated by the situation. For the first time since the terrible day she had found the brown baby in the flower bed she saw a reason for hope for the young woman's future. She began to regret Sarah's intransigence. She thought of the drive from Harlem, where Coalhouse Walker Jr. lived, and the drive back, and she decided the next time to give him more of a visit. She would serve tea in the parlor. Father questioned the propriety of this. Mother said He is well-spoken and conducts himself as a gentleman. I see nothing wrong with it. When Mr. Roosevelt was in the White House he gave dinner to Booker T. Washington. Surely we can serve tea to Coalhouse Walker Jr.

And so it happened on the next Sunday that the Negro took tea. Father noted that he suffered no embarrassment by being in the parlor with a cup and saucer in his hand. On the contrary, he acted as if it was the most natural thing in the world. The surroundings did not awe him nor was his manner deferential. He was courteous and correct. He told them about himself. He was a professional pianist and was now more or less permanently located in New York, having secured a job with the Jim Europe Clef Club Orchestra, a well-known ensemble that gave regular concerts at the Manhattan Casino on 155th Street and Eighth Avenue. It was important, he said, for a musician to find a place that was permanent, a job that required no traveling. I am through traveling, he said. I am through going on the road. He spoke so fervently that Father realized the message was intended for the woman upstairs. This irritated him. What can you play? he said abruptly. Why don't you play something for us.

The black man placed his tea on the tray. He rose, patted his lips with the napkin, placed the napkin beside his cup and went to the piano. He sat on the piano stool and immediately rose and twirled it till the height was to his satisfaction. He sat down again, played a chord and turned to them. This piano is badly in need of a tuning, he said. Father's face reddened. Oh yes, Mother said, we are terrible about that. The musician turned again to the keyboard. "Wall Street Rag," he said. Composed by the great Scott Joplin. He began to play. Ill-tuned or not the Aeolian had never made such sounds. Small clear chords hung in the air like flowers. The melodies were like bouquets. There seemed to be no other possibilities for life than those delineated by the music. When the piece was over Coalhouse Walker turned on the stool and found in his audience the entire family, Mother, Father, the boy, Grandfather and Mother's Younger Brother, who had come down from his room in shirt and suspenders to see who was playing. Of all of them he was the only one who knew ragtime. He had heard it in his nightlife period in New York. He had never expected to hear it in his sister's home.

Coalhouse Walker Jr. turned back to the piano and said

[132]

"The Maple Leaf." Composed by the great Scott Joplin. The most famous rag of all rang through the air. The pianist sat stiffly at the keyboard, his long dark hands with their pink nails seemingly with no effort producing the clusters of syncopating chords and the thumping octaves. This was a most robust composition, a vigorous music that roused the senses and never stood still a moment. The boy perceived it as light touching various places in space, accumulating in intricate patterns until the entire room was made to glow with its own being. The music filled the stairwell to the third floor where the mute and unforgiving Sarah sat with her hands folded and listened with the door open.

The piece was brought to a conclusion. Everyone applauded. Mother then introduced Mr. Walker to Grandfather and to Younger Brother, who shook the black man's hand and said I am pleased to meet you. Coalhouse Walker was solemn. Everyone was standing. There was a silence. Father cleared his throat. Father was not knowledgeable in music. His taste ran to Carrie Jacobs Bond. He thought Negro music had to have smiling and cakewalking. Do you know any coon songs? he said. He did not intend to be rude—coon songs was what they were called. But the pianist responded with a tense shake of the head. Coon songs are made for minstrel shows, he said. White men sing them in blackface. There was another silence. The black man looked at the ceiling. Well, he said, it appears as if Miss Sarah will not be able to receive me. He turned abruptly and walked through the hall to the kitchen. The family followed him. He had left his coat on a chair. He put it on and ignoring them all, he knelt and gazed at the baby asleep in its carriage. After several moments he stood up, said good day and walked out the door.

The visit impressed everyone except Sarah, who gave no sign of relenting in her refusal to have anything to do with the man. The next week he returned, and the week after that. He was

now visiting the family and each time brought them up on the
news of his doings of the previous six days, never once assuming anything but their total and consuming interest. Father
was put off by the man's airs. She won't see him, he told
Mother. Am I to go on entertaining Coalhouse Walker every
Sunday for the rest of my life? But Mother saw signs of progress. Sarah had taken on the duties of the departed
housekeeper and now cleaned rooms so energetically and with
such proprietary competence that Mother laughed with the
momentary illusion that it was Sarah's own house she was
cleaning. She also began to claim her child at other than
feeding time, first taking over his daily bath, then carrying him
upstairs to her room at night. Still she would not see her visitor.
Coalhouse Walker appeared faithfully through the winter.
More than once, when the roads were made impassable by
snow, he came on the train and caught the North Avenue
streetcar to the bottom of the hill. He wore with his fitted
black overcoat a lamb's-wool hat in the Russian style. He
brought outfits for the child. He brought a silver-handled hairbrush for Sarah. Father had to admire his perseverance. He
wondered to what extent a musician's wages could sustain such
gifts.

It occurred to Father one day that Coalhouse Walker Jr.
didn't know he was a Negro. The more he thought about this
the more true it seemed. Walker didn't act or talk like a
colored man. He seemed to be able to transform the customary
deferences practiced by his race so that they reflected to his
own dignity rather than the recipient's. When he arrived at
the back door he gave it a stout rap and when admitted would
solemnly greet everyone and somehow convey to them the
feeling that they were Sarah's family, and that his courtesies
to them simply measured the regard and respect he held for
her. Father recognized certain dangers in the man. Perhaps we
shouldn't encourage his suit, he said to Mother. There is some-

thing reckless about him. Even Mathew Henson knew his place.

By this time, however, the course of events could not be changed. In the late winter Sarah said she would see Coalhouse Walker in the parlor. For days there was a flurry of preparation. Mother gave her one of her own dresses and helped her to take it in. She came downstairs, beautiful and shy. Her hair was combed and pomaded and she sat on the sofa with her eyes lowered as Coalhouse Walker Jr. spoke his formal conversation and played the piano for her. It was only when they were seen together that it became apparent he was a good deal older than she was. Mother insisted that the members of the family excuse themselves so that the courtship could go on in privacy. Nothing was speeded by this. After the visit Sarah looked irritated and even angry. She was slow to forgive, and in some peculiar way her stubbornness seemed the only appropriate response to his persistence. Sarah had attempted to kill her newborn child. Life was not something either of these people took carelessly. They lived in brutal subjection to their hopes and feelings. They suffered themselves. Mother's Younger Brother understood this perhaps more clearly than anyone in the family. He had spoken to Coalhouse Walker just once but admired him immensely. He saw in the way the black man acted upon his intentions more manhood than he himself possessed. He brooded over this. Younger Brother understood the love in some hearts as a physical tenderness in that part of the body, a flaw in the physiological being equivalent to rickets of the bones or a disposition of the lungs to congest. He was afflicted with this and so was Sarah, colored though she was. He thought she was some displaced African queen; her very awkwardness as she moved suggested that it would be grace in another country. And the more reluctant she seemed to accept Coalhouse Walker's offer of marriage, the more Younger Brother understood what a terribly afflicted heart she had.

But one Sunday in March, with the wind blowing softer and small brown buds visible on the branches of the maple trees, Coalhouse arrived in his shining Ford and left the motor idling. Neighbors in their yards came out to watch the strange intense black man, burly and correct, with his dark, dark eyes on the verge of crossing, and the beautifully awkward Sarah, wearing a pink shirtwaist and a black skirt and jacket and one of Mother's wide-brimmed hats, as they walked under the Norwegian maples and down the concrete steps to the street. She carried her baby. He helped her into the car and got up behind the wheel. They waved to the family and drove off through the suburban streets to the farmlands at the north end of town. They parked at the side of the road. They watched a cardinal skim the hard brown earth, then beat its way to the highest thinnest branch of a tree. This was the day he asked her to marry and she accepted. The appearance of these magnificent lovers in the family's life had been startling; the conflict of their wills had exercised an almost hypnotic effect.

22

And now Mother's Younger Brother began again his trips to New York. He would work at his drawing table past the dinner hour and then catch an evening train. He had made friends of some ordnance officers on duty at the armory on Lexington Avenue and 34th Street. They complained about the Springfield rifle. They showed him their small arms and their grenade bombs. He knew immediately that he could design better weapons. He drank with the officers. He became known at the stage doors of several Broadway theatres. He stood in the alleys, like others, never so well-groomed as some of the older men, nor so carelessly handsome as the collegians from Princeton or Yale. But there was an intensity of expectation about his eyes that attracted a fair number of women. He was always so serious and unhappy that they were persuaded he loved them. They took him for a poet.

Still, his salary couldn't support these tastes. Broadway was alive with lights and entertainments and everyone connected with the theatre and charged by its excitement lived to the limit. He learned where to find women who would go to bed with him for a modest price. One of these places was the Bethesda Fountain in Central Park. They walked in twos whenever the weather was mild. The days were beginning to lengthen. In cold luxurious sunsets they strolled about the fountain, shadows filling the great steps, the water already black, the paving stones brown and pink. He amused them by taking them seriously. He was gentle with them and they didn't mind his oddity because it was gentle. He would take a woman to his hotel room and then sit in a chair with one shoe in his hand and completely forget about her. Or he would not attempt to make love but only inspect her intimate places. He drank wine until he was insensible. He dined in steakhouses with sawdust on the floor. He went to cellar clubs in Hell's Kitchen where hoodlums bought everyone drinks. He walked Manhattan at night, his eyes devouring passers-by. He stared in the windows of restaurants and sat in hotel lobbies, his restless eyes picking out motion and color before it defined itself.

Eventually he found the offices of the *Mother Earth* magazine published by Emma Goldman. They were on 13th Street in a brownstone that served now as the anarchist's residence when she was in New York. He stood in the street under the lamppost and stared at the windows. He did this for several nights. Finally a man came out of the door, walked down the steps and crossed the street to where he stood. He was a tall cadaverous man, with long hair and a string tie. He said It gets cold in the evenings—come in, we have no secrets. And Younger Brother was led across the street and up the steps.

It turned out that in his vigil he had been mistaken for a police spy. He was treated with elaborate irony. He was offered tea. Numbers of people were standing about in the apartment in their hats and coats. Then Goldman appeared in a doorway and her attention was directed to him. Good God, she said. That's no policeman. She began to laugh. She was putting on a hat and setting it in place with hatpins. He was thrilled that she remembered him. Come with us, she called.

A while later Younger Brother found himself in the Cooper Union down near the Bowery. The hall was hot, crowded to overflowing. There were lots of foreigners. Men wore their derbies though indoors. It was a great stinking congress garlicked and perfumed in its own perspiration. It had met in support of the Mexican Revolution. He hadn't known there was a Mexican Revolution. Men waved their fists. They stood on benches. Speaker after speaker arose. Some spoke in languages other than English. They were not translated. He had trouble hearing. What seemed to have happened was that the Mexican peons had spontaneously revolted against Díaz the President of Mexico for the past thirty-five years. They needed guns. They needed ammunition. They were striking from the hills, attacking the Federals and the supply trains with wooden staves and muzzle-loading muskets. He thought about this. Finally Emma Goldman got up to speak. Of all the orators she was the best. The hall went quiet as she described the complicity of the wealthy landowners and the despised tyrant Díaz, the subjugation of the peons, the poverty and starvation and, most shameful of all, the presence of representatives of American business firms in the national counsels of the Mexican government. Her voice was strong. As she moved her head and gesticulated the light flashed from her glasses. He pushed his way forward to be closer to her. She described one Emiliano Zapata, a simple farmer of the Morelos district who had turned revolutionary because he had no choice. He wore the share farmer's bleached pajama coat and trousers, bound over the chest with bandoleers and belted with a cartridge belt. My comrades, she cried, that is not a foreign costume. There are no foreign lands. There is no Mexican peasant, there is no dictator Díaz. There is only one struggle throughout the world, there is only the flame of freedom trying to light the hideous darkness of life on earth. The applause was deafening. Younger Brother had no money. He turned out his pockets, mortified to see all around him people who reeked of their poverty coming up with handfuls of change. He found himself standing at the foot of the speaker's platform. The speeches were done, she stood surrounded by colleagues and admirers. He saw her hug a swarthy man who wore a dark suit and tie but also an enormous sombrero. She turned and her glance fell on the balding blondish young man whose head came just above the platform stage, as if severed like a French republican's, the eyes turned upward in a kind of ecstasy. She laughed.

He thought at the end of the rally that she would speak to him but there was a reception for the Mexican back at the offices of *Mother Earth*. He was the *zapatista* representative. He wore boots under his cuffless trousers. He did not smile but drank tea and then wiped his long moustaches with the back of his hand. The rooms were crowded with journalists, bohemians, artists, poets and society women. Younger Brother was not aware that he was following Goldman about. He was desperate for her attention. But she was enormously busy with everyone else. Each new person who came in the door had to be seen. She had lots on her mind. She introduced people to each other. To different persons she proposed different things they must do, others they should speak with, places they ought to go, situations they ought to look into or write about. He felt incredibly ignorant. She went into the kitchen and whipped up the batter for a cake. Here, she said to Younger Brother, take these cups and put them on the table in the big room. He was grateful to be taken into her network of useful people. There were posters of *Mother Earth* magazine covers on every wall. A tall long-haired man was dispensing the punch. He was the one who had come out to the street to invite Younger Brother upstairs. He looked like a Shakespearean actor down on his luck. His fingernails were outlined in black. He was drinking as much as he dispensed. He greeted people by singing a line or two from a song. Everyone laughed who spoke to him. His name was Ben Reitman, he was the man Goldman lived with. There was something the matter with the top of his head, there was a shaven patch. Noticing Younger Brother's glance he explained that he had been in San Diego and had been tarred and feathered. Emma had gone there to speak. He acted as her manager, renting the halls, making the arrangements. They had not wanted Emma to speak. They had kidnapped him, driven him somewhere, stripped him and tarred him. They had burned him with their cigars, and worse. As he gave this account his face darkened, his smile disappeared. An audience had gathered. He was holding the punch ladle and it began to click against the side of the bowl. He couldn't seem to let go of it. He gazed at his hand with a peculiar smile on his face. They did not want my momma to speak in Kansas City or Los Angeles or Spokane, he said. But she spoke. We know every jail. We win every case. My momma will speak in San Diego. He laughed as if he couldn't believe his own hand shook as it did. The ladle clicked against the bowl.

At this point a man pushed his way to the table and said You think, Reitman, the world is well-served by your being tarred and feathered? He was a short, totally baldheaded man with thick eyeglasses, a large full mouth and a very sallow complexion with skin like wax. The issue has become Emma's right to speak rather than what she has to say. All our energies go into defending ourselves. That is their strategy, not our own. I'm afraid you don't understand that. What is so glorious, poor Reitman, about being bailed out of the tank by some guilty liberal. So that then he can congratulate himself. How is the world advanced? The two men stared at each other. Goldman's voice called cheerfully from the back of the gathering: Sacha! She came around the table wiping her hands on her apron. She stood next to Reitman. She gently removed the ladle from his hand. Sacha, my dear, she said to the sallow man, if first we have to teach them their own ideals, perhaps then we may teach them ours.

The party went on into the early hours. Younger Brother despaired of getting her attention. He sat, Indian style, on an old couch with sagging springs. After some time he realized the room was quiet. He looked up. Goldman was sitting on a kitchen chair directly in front of him. The room was otherwise empty, he was the last guest. Unaccountably, tears came to his eyes. You actually asked if I remembered you, Emma Goldman said. But how could I forget. Could anyone forget a sight such as that, my pagan. She touched his cheek with her thumb and mashed away a tear. So tragic, so tragic. She sighed. Is that all you want from your life? Her large magnified eyes peered at him through the lenses of her eyeglasses. She sat with her legs apart, her hands on her knees. I don't know where she is. But if I could tell you, what good would that do? Suppose you got her to come back to you? She would only stay awhile. She would run away from you again, don't you know that? He nodded. You look terrible, Goldman said. What have you been doing to yourself? Don't you eat? Don't you get any fresh air? He shook his head. You have aged ten years. I cannot sympathize. You think you are special, losing your lover. It happens every day. Suppose she consented to live with you after all. You're a bourgeois, you would want to marry her. You would destroy each other inside of a year. You would see her begin to turn old and bored under your very eyes. You would sit across the dinner table from each other in bondage, in terrible bondage to what you thought was love. The both of you. Believe me you are better off this way. Younger Brother was crying. You're right, he said, of course you're right. He kissed her hand. She had a small hand but the fingers were swollen

and the skin was red and the knuckles were enlarged. I have
no memories of her, he sobbed. It was something I dreamed.
Goldman was unappeased. This way you can feel sorry for
yourself, she said. And what a delicious emotion that is. I'll tell
you something. In this room tonight you saw my present lover
but also two of my former lovers. We are all good friends.
Friendship is what endures. Shared ideals, respect for the
whole character of a human being. Why can't you accept your
own freedom? Why do you have to cling to someone in order
to live?

He bowed his head as she talked. He stared at the floor.
He felt her fingers under his chin. His head was lifted,
tilted up. He found himself staring into the faces of Goldman and Reitman. From Reitman's scatterbrained smile a
gold tooth gleamed. They peered at him, curious and interested. Goldman said He reminds me of Czolgosz. Reitman
said He is educated, a bourgeois. But the same poor boy in
the eyes, Goldman said. The same poor dangerous boy.
Younger Brother saw himself standing in line to shake the
hand of William McKinley. A handkerchief was wrapped
around his hand. In the handkerchief was a gun. McKinley
fell back. Blood dyed his vest. There were screams.

When he left she hugged him at the door. Her lips, surprisingly soft, pressed his cheek. He was overcome. He stepped
back. The literature under his arm fell to the floor. There was
laughter between them as they crouched in the doorway and
gathered it up.

But an hour later he stood between the cars on the milk train
going up to New Rochelle. He considered throwing himself
under the wheels. He listened to their rhythm, their steady
clacking, like the left hand of a rag. The screeching and pound-
ing of metal on metal where the two cars joined was the

syncopating right hand. It was a suicide rag. He held the door handles on either side of him listening to the music. The cars jumped under his feet. The moon raced with the train. He held his face up to the sky between the cars, as if even moonlight could warm him.

23

One Sunday afternoon the colored man Coalhouse Walker said goodbye to his fiancée and drove off to New York in his Ford. It was about five o'clock in the evening and shadows of the trees darkened the road. His route took him along Firehouse Lane, past the station house of the Emerald Isle Engine, a company of volunteer firemen known for the dash of their parade uniforms and the liveliness of their outings. In the many times he had gone this way the Emerald Isle volunteers would be standing and talking outside the firehouse, a two-story clapboard building, and as he drove past they would fall silent and stare at him. He was not unaware that in his dress and as the owner of a car he was a provocation to many white people. He had created himself in the teeth of such feelings.

At this time private volunteer companies were maintained as auxiliaries to the municipal fire department; and these companies, which relied upon private subscription, had yet to motorize their equipment. As the Negro came along a team of three matching gray engine horses cantered out of the firehouse into the road pulling behind them the big steam pumper for which the Emerald Isle was locally renowned. They were immediately reined, causing Coalhouse Walker to brake his car abruptly.

Two of the volunteers came out of the building to join the driver of the pumper who sat up on his box looking at the Negro and yawning ostentatiously. They all wore blue work shirts with green handkerchief ties, dark blue trousers and boots. Coalhouse Walker released the clutch pedal and climbed down to crank his car. The volunteers waited until this was done and then advised him that he was traveling on a private toll road and that he could not drive on without payment of twenty-five dollars or by presenting a pass indicating that he was a resident of the city. This is a public thoroughfare, Walker said, I've traveled it dozens of times and no one has ever said anything about a toll. He got up behind the wheel. Tell the Chief, one of the men said to another. Walker decided to put the Ford into reverse gear, back up to the corner and go another way. He turned in his seat. At this moment two of the firemen carrying a twenty-foot ladder between them came into the street behind the car. Two others followed with another ladder and others came out with carts of coiled hose, buckets, axes, hooks and other fire-fighting equipment, all of which was deposited in the street, the company having chosen this particular moment to sweep out its quarters.

The Chief of the company was distinguished by a white military cap he wore at a cocky angle. He was also somewhat older than the rest. He was courteous to Coalhouse and explained that while the toll had never before been collected from him it was nevertheless in force, and that if Coalhouse did not pay up he would not pass. With his two hands he lifted his hat from his head and reset it so that the visor covered his eyes. This caused him to tilt his chin upwards in order to see, giving him a pugnacious look. He was a heavyset man with thick arms. Many of the volunteers were grinning. We need the money for a firetruck, the Chief explained. So we can drive to fires just like you drive to whorehouses.

The Negro calmly considered the courses of action available to him. The Emerald Isle firehouse looked across the street to an open field that sloped down to a pond. Conceivably he might drive off the road, turn in the field and circumnavigate the ladders and hose cart. But he was wedged in tightly, and even if he could pull the wheel hard enough to clear the horses the severe angle of the turn might tilt the car over on the downhill slope. Apparently it did not occur to him to ingratiate himself in the fashion of his race.

Playing down at the edge of the pond were a couple of Negro boys, ten or twelve years old. Hey, Coalhouse Walker called to them. Come on up here! The boys came running. They stared at Coalhouse as he switched off the engine, set the brake and stepped down to the road. I want you to watch this car, he told them. When I come back you tell me if anyone touched it.

The musician quickly strode back to the corner and headed toward the business district. After ten minutes he found a policeman operating a stop-and-go traffic signal. The policeman listened to his complaint and shook his head and spent some time removing his handkerchief from under his frock coat and blowing his nose. Those boys don't mean no harm, he finally said. I know them all. Go on back now, they're probably tired of the sport. Walker may have realized this was probably the maximum support he could expect from a policeman. At the same time he may have wondered if he'd been oversensitive to what was intended as no more than a prank. So he went back to Firehouse Lane.

The fire engine and horses were withdrawn. The road was empty of volunteers and his car stood off the road in the field. He made his way to the car. It was spattered with mud. There was a six-inch tear in the custom pantasote top. And deposited in the back seat was a mound of fresh human excrement.

He went across the street to the firehouse door. Standing there with his arms folded was the Chief in his white military cap and green bohemian tie. The Police Department advises me there is no toll road anywhere in this city, Coalhouse Walker said. That's right, said the Chief. Anyone is free to come and go on this road anytime he thinks he has to. The sun having set, the electric lights were on inside the firehouse. Through the glass panels in the door the Negro could see the three matching grays in their stalls, the great nickel-plated pumper with its brass fittings backed up to the rear wall. I want my car cleaned and the damage paid for, he said. The Chief began to laugh and a couple of his men came out to join the fun.

At this moment a police van drove up. It carried two officers, one of them the traffic policeman to whom Coalhouse Walker had appealed. He went into the field, looked at the car and came back to the firehouse. Willie, the policeman said to the Fire Chief, did you or your boys do any desecratin? I'll tell you exactly what happened, the Chief said. The nigger here parked his damn car in the middle of the road right in front of the firehouse. We had to move it. It's a serious business blocking a fire station, ain't that so, boys? The volunteers nodded righteously. The big policeman came to a decision. He took Coalhouse aside. Listen, he said, we'll push your tin lizzie back on the road and you be on your way. There's no real damage. Scrape off the shit and forget the whole thing. I was on my way when they stopped me, Coalhouse said. They put filth in my car and tore a hole in the top. I want the car cleaned and the damage paid for. The officer had now begun to appreciate Coalhouse's style of speech, his dress, and the phenomenon of his owning a car in the first place. He grew angry. If you don't take your automobile and get along out of here, he said loudly,

I'm going to charge you with driving off the road, drunkenness, and making an unsightly nuisance. I do not drink, Coalhouse said. I did not drive my car off the road nor slash the roof nor defecate in it. I want the damage paid for and I want an apology. The policeman looked at the Chief, who was grinning at his discomfiture, so that the issue for him was now his own authority. He said to Coalhouse I'm placing you under arrest. You'll come with me in the wagon.

Early that evening the telephone rang at Broadview Avenue. The caller was Coalhouse and after quickly explaining that he was at Police Headquarters and why, he asked Father if he would consider putting up bail so that he could get to the city and not miss work that evening. It is to Father's credit that he responded at once, holding back his questions until there was the leisure to have them answered. He called for a cab and went down to the station house and there wrote a cheque for the amount, which was fifty dollars. But as he reported the incident to Mother he was put off because Coalhouse Walker was barely civil in his gratitude and rushed off to the train station saying only he'd make good the sum.

The next evening the household experienced the oddness of a visit by Coalhouse Walker that was not on a Sunday. He sat in the parlor with his arms folded and told the story in detail. There was no aggrieved tone in his voice, he recited calmly and objectively, as if he were describing something that had happened to someone else. Mother said Mr. Walker, I am ashamed that this community is represented in your mind by that bunch of toughs. Father said The company has a bad reputation. They are an exception, the other volunteer engines being in all ways upright and responsible. Younger Brother sat on the piano stool with his legs crossed. He leaned forward, totally engaged by the problem. Where is the car now? he said. And what about those two boys? They are witnesses for you. But the pianist had spent the afternoon tracking down the boys only to find their parents refusing to have them involved in the matter. I'm a stranger to the Negroes here, he said matter-of-factly. They have to live here and they want no trouble. As for the car I have not looked at it again. And I won't until it is returned to me as it was when I drove away from this house yesterday evening.

Standing in the hallway just out of sight during this interview was Sarah. She held her baby on her hip and she listened. She perceived as no one in the family could the enormity of the misfortune. She heard Father say to Coalhouse that if he intended to pursue his claim he should engage a lawyer. There was such a thing as the power of subpoena for witnesses. Are there any colored lawyers here? Coalhouse asked. I don't know of one, Father said. But any lawyer who loves justice will do, I should think. He paused. I will underwrite the expense, he said in a gruff voice. Coalhouse stood. I thank you but that won't be necessary. He put an envelope on the side table. In it was fifty dollars in cash. This, Mother learned afterward, had come out of the money he was saving toward the wedding.

The next day Mother's Younger Brother took it upon himself to go to the site of the incident and see the car. After work he rode his bicycle to Firehouse Lane. The Model T had been thoroughly vandalized, whether by the volunteers or others it was impossible to determine. It sat with its front end in the tall weeds at the edge of the pond. The wheels were sunk in the mud. The headlamps and the windshield were shattered. The rear tires were flattened, the tufted upholstery had been gutted and the custom pantasote top was slashed to ribbons.

24

Younger Brother stood at the pond. Since his evening with Emma Goldman he had been in considerable difficulty. People at work were surprised by his animation. He fixed his attention on anything that could sustain it. He produced small talk that verged on hysteria. He sat at his drawing table and turned out designs in endless modifications for rifles and grenades. He measured the small squares and made his computations and watched the point of his pencil as it impressed the paper. When there was no other recourse he would begin to sing, just to hear the sound. Thus with continuous concentration and the expenditure of enormous amounts of energy he tried to keep himself from slipping into the vast distances of his unhappiness. It was all around him. It was a darkness as impudently close as his brow. It choked him by its closeness. And what was most terrifying was its treachery. He would wake up in the morning and see the sun coming in the window, and sit up in his bed and think it was gone, and then find it there after all, behind his ears or in his heart.

He decided he was on the verge of a nervous collapse. He prescribed for himself a regimen of cold baths and physical exertion. He bought a Columbia bicycle and rode it to work.

At night, before bed, he would do calisthenics until he was exhausted.

On the floor below, Mother and Father felt the house shake. They realized he was jumping up and down. They were used to his eccentricities. He had never confided in them or shared his hopes or feelings and so they saw no marked change in his behavior. Mother did ask him to join them in the parlor after dinner when he had no plans for the evening. He tried this. He heard them address him, heard himself answer. He saw them in their suffocating parlor with its chaise and its mounted heads and fringed lampshades and he felt he couldn't breathe. He despised them. He thought they were complacent, ordinary and inconsiderate. One evening Father read to everyone the editorial in the local newspaper. Father liked to read aloud when he found something particularly instructive or well-written. The title of the editorial was THE SPRING PEEPER. So that diminutive visitor to our ponds and fields has come to call once again, Father read. In truth he is no less ugly than his older brothers Frog and Toad. But we welcome the gallant little fellow and laud his beauty. For is he not in advance of Robin and even hardy Crocus in his proclamation of the Spring? The young man rushed from the room convinced he was strangling to death.

There is no question then that Younger Brother was fortunate to conceive a loyalty to the colored man. Standing at the pond he heard the lapping of the water against the front fenders of the Model T. He noted that the hood was unlatched, and lifting and folding it back, saw that the wires had been torn from the engine. The sun was now setting and it threw a reflection of blue sky on the dark water of the pond. There ran through him a small current of rage, perhaps one one-hundredth, he knew, of what Coalhouse Walker must have felt, and it was salutary.

Here, given subsequent events, it is important to mention

what little is known about Coalhouse Walker Jr. Apparently he was a native of St. Louis, Missouri. As a young man he had known and admired Scott Joplin and other St. Louis musicians and had paid for his piano studies with money he earned as a stevedore. There is no information about his parentage. At one point a woman in St. Louis claimed to be his divorced wife but that was never proved. There were never located any of his school records in St. Louis and it still is not known how he acquired his vocabulary and his manner of speaking. Perhaps by an act of will.

It was widely reported when he was achieving his notoriety that Coalhouse Walker had never exhausted the peaceful and legal means of redress before taking the law into his own hands. This is not entirely true. He went to see three different attorneys recommended by Father. In all cases they refused to represent him. He was advised to recover his automobile before it was totally wrecked and to forget the matter. To all three he insisted that he didn't want to forget the matter but to bring suit against the Fire Chief and men of the Emerald Isle Engine.

Father himself telephoned one of these attorneys, a man who had represented his firm in several business matters. Is there not a case there, he asked. When he goes for his hearing, the lawyer said to Father, you can go with him. You don't need me for this. When a property owner in this city walks into court with a Negro, a charge like this is usually dismissed. But he is not interested in the charge, Father said. He wants to sue. At that point Father realized the attorney was involved in a conversation with someone in his office. Glad to be of help, the attorney said, and rang off.

It is known also that Coalhouse Walker consulted a black attorney in Harlem. He had learned that the Emerald Isle Chief, whose name was Will Conklin, was a stepbrother of the Judge of the City Court and a nephew of a County Alderman in White Plains. The Harlem attorney advised him there were ways to divert the case to other jurisdictions but these were expensive and time-consuming. And the outcome was not at all predictable. You have the money for that? the lawyer said. I am soon to be married, Coalhouse Walker said. That is an expensive proposition, the lawyer said. Surely your responsibilities to your intended are more important than the need to redress a slight on the part of white folks. Then Walker apparently made a remark not entirely courteous to the black lawyer. The counselor stood up behind his desk and told him to leave. I have charity cases you know nothing of, he shouted. I want justice for our people so bad I can taste it. But if you think I would go to Westchester County to plead on a colored man's behalf that someone deposited a bucket of slops in his car, you are very much mistaken.

It is known too that Coalhouse made a preliminary attempt to see the matter through as his own counsel. He had filed a complaint but did not know how to go about getting a place on the court calendar or what steps had to be taken to assure that it was correct in form in order to be heard. He appeared at City Hall for an interview with the Office of the County Clerk. It was suggested that he return another day when there was less pressing business in the office. But he persisted and was then told that his complaint was not on file and that several weeks would be required to trace it. Come back then, the clerk told him. Instead he went to the police station where he had originally filed and wrote out a second complaint. The policemen on duty regarded him with amazement. An older officer took him aside and confided to him that he was probably filing in vain since the volunteer fire companies were not municipal employees and therefore did not come under the jurisdiction of the city. The contemptuousness of this logic did not escape Coalhouse but he chose not to argue with it. He signed his complaint and left and heard laughter behind him as he walked out the door.

All of this happened over a period of two to three weeks. Later, when the name Coalhouse Walker came to symbolize murder and arson, these earlier attempts to find redress no longer mattered. Even at this date we can't condone the mayhem done in his cause but it is important to know the truth insofar as that is possible. Conversation at the family's dinner table was now obsessive on the subject of this strange proud black man's attempts to have his property restored. It seemed like such a foolish thing to have happened. It seemed to be his fault, somehow, because he was Negro and it was the kind of problem that would only adhere to a Negro. His monumental negritude sat in front of them like a centerpiece on the table. While Sarah served, Father told her that her fiancé would have done better after all to drive away his car when he could and forget the matter. Younger Brother bristled. You speak like a man who has never been tested in his principles, he said. Father was so outraged by this remark that he could find no words. Mother said, gently, that no one would be helped by the voicing of intemperate feelings. A peculiar kind of unseasonably warm breeze blew the window curtain in the Egyptian dining room. It had that breath of menace which makes the beginning of the spring so unsettling. Sarah dropped a serving tray of filet of sole. She retreated to the kitchen and held her baby. Sobbing she told Younger Brother, who followed her there, that the preceding Sunday Coalhouse had said he could not marry until he had been satisfied by the return of the Model T in exactly the same condition as when the firehorses had been driven across his path.

25

Nobody knew Sarah's last name or thought to ask. Where had she been born, and where had she lived, this impoverished uneducated black girl with such absolute conviction of the way human beings ought to conduct their lives? In the few weeks of her happiness, between that time she accepted Coalhouse's proposal and the first fears that her marriage would never happen, she had been transformed to the point of having a new, a different face. Grief and anger had been a kind of physical pathology masking her true looks. Mother was awed by her beauty. She laughed and spoke in a mellifluous voice. They worked together on her wedding dress and her movements were altogether graceful and lithe. She had an excellent figure and she gazed at herself in the mirror with pride. She laughed in joy of her own being. Her happiness flowed in the milk of her breasts and her baby grew quickly. He was pulling himself to his feet and the carriage was no longer safe for him. He stayed with her in her room. She picked him up and danced with him. She was a girl of perhaps eighteen or nineteen years, now satisfied that the circumstances of life gave reason to live. She was, Mother realized, the kind of moral being who understood nothing but goodness. She had no guile and could act only in total and helpless response to what she felt. If she loved she acted in love, if she was betrayed she was destroyed. These were the shining and dangerous facts of the life of an innocent. The boy was attracted to her more and more, and to her baby. He played gently with the child and there was solemn recognition between them. The mother sang. She sewed her wedding costume and tried it on and removed it. Underneath she wore a shift which rose to her hips as she pulled the white dress over her head. She saw the boy's honest and attentive regard of her limbs and she smiled. To Younger Brother she offered the unspoken complicity of two members of the same generation. Her husband to be was an older man and Younger Brother was set apart by age from the others in his family. And that was why he followed her into the kitchen and she confided to him the news of Coalhouse's vow not to marry until he had his car back.

What will he do? Younger Brother said. I don't know, Sarah said. But she had perhaps detected the violence underlying all principle.

The following Sunday, Coalhouse Walker did not appear for his visit. Sarah returned to her room. It was now clear to Father that the situation was deteriorating. He said it was ridiculous to allow a motorcar to take over everyone's life as it now had. He decided to go the next day and talk to the Emerald Isle contingent, especially to Chief Conklin. What will you do, Mother said. I will make them see they are dealing with a property owner of this city, Father said. If that doesn't work I will quite simply bribe them to repair the car and return it to my door. I will pay them money. I will buy them off. Mr. Walker would not like that, Mother said. Nevertheless, said Father, that's what I'm going to do. We will worry about explanations later. They are the town dregs and will respect money.

But before the plan could be undertaken Sarah decided on

a course of action of her own. As it happened, this particular season was the spring of an election year: a candidate on the national Republican ticket, Mr. Taft's Vice-President, James Sherman, was to be in New Rochelle that evening to speak at a Republican party dinner to be held at the Tidewaters Hotel. She had remembered overhearing Father discuss his reasons for not attending the event. Knowing little of government, nor appreciating the degree of national unimportance of her Coal-house's trials, Sarah conceived the idea of petitioning the United States on his behalf. It was the second of the frightened and desperate acts provoked from her innocence. She waited in the evening until her child was safely asleep, and wrapping a shawl about her head, left the house without telling any member of the family and ran down the hill to North Avenue. She was shoeless. She ran swiftly as a child. She was prepared to run all the way to the hotel but instead found a streetcar coming along, its interior lights flickering, the driver tolling its bell angrily as she dashed across the tracks just in front of it. She paid the fare and rode downtown.

An evening wind came up and in the dark sky great heavy clouds massed for a rainstorm. She stood in front of the hotel among a small crowd of people awaiting the arrival of the great man. Car after car drove up and gave forth this dignitary or that. A few windswept drops of rain spattered the sidewalk. A carpet had been laid from the curb to the hotel doors. Not only the local police in their white evening gloves but a platoon of militia were on hand, keeping the entrance cleared and pushing the crowd back from the street in anticipation of the arrival of the Vice-President's car. The militia were in constant attendance, as well as plainclothesmen of the Secret Service which had been commissioned to protect presidents and vice-presidents by Theodore Roosevelt after the assassination of President McKinley. As a matter of fact Roosevelt had come out of retirement this season to run against his old friend Taft.

Wilson was the Democratic candidate, Debs the Socialist, and the four campaigns whipped back and forth across the country, blowing up hopes on the land like the winds that ruffled the great plains. In Milwaukee, Wisconsin, just a week or so before, Roosevelt had arrived to make a speech. Leaving the railroad station and walking to a car he had been kept separate from a welcoming crowd. One man stepped out of the crowd and aimed a pistol at point-blank range. Shots rang out. A bullet tore through the spectacle case in Roosevelt's breast pocket, ripped a hole in the fifty folded pages of his speech and lodged in his rib. He was stunned. The assassin was wrestled to the ground. There were shouts. Roosevelt examined his wound and was satisfied it was not serious. He went on to make his speech before he allowed doctors to treat him. But the acrid smoke of the act still lingered in the public mind. Anyone commissioned to guard a personage could not help thinking of the shooting of Teddy Roosevelt. New York City's mayor, William J. Gaynor, had been bloodied by an assassin's bullets not too long before. Guns were going off everywhere.

When the Vice-President's car, a Panhard, rolled up to the curb and the man himself stepped out, a cheer went up. Sunny Jim Sherman was a New York State politician with many friends in Westchester. He was a round balding man and in such ill health that he would not survive the campaign. Sarah broke through the line and ran toward him calling, in her confusion, President! President! Her arm was extended and her black hand reached toward him. He shrank from the contact. Perhaps in the dark windy evening of impending storm it seemed to Sherman's guards that Sarah's black hand was a weapon. A militiaman stepped forward and, with the deadly officiousness of armed men who protect the famous, brought the butt of his Springfield against Sarah's chest as hard as he could. She fell. A Secret Service man jumped on top of her. The Vice-President disappeared into the hotel. In the confusion and shouting that followed, Sarah was put in a police wagon and driven away.

Sarah was held at the police station overnight. She was coughing blood and in the early-morning hours it occurred to the sergeant in charge that perhaps she ought to be looked at by a doctor. She had puzzled them all, answering no questions, looking at them with eyes of fear and pain, and had one of them not recalled hearing her cry President! President! they were prepared to regard her as a deaf-mute. What were you doing, they asked her. What did you think you were doing? She was transferred to the hospital in the morning. It was a gray overcast day, the Vice-President was gone, the festivities were over, the street sweepers pushed their brooms in front of the hotel, and the charge against Sarah was reduced from attempted assassination to disturbing the peace. She lay in the hospital. Her sternum and several ribs were fractured. At home, on Broadview Avenue, Mother heard the baby cry and cry, and finally she went upstairs to see what was the matter. Some hours passed before the family's alarms were connected by a police officer to the colored girl who had been put in the hospital. Father coming from his business and Mother from the house, they found Sarah in a bed on the public ward. She was sleeping, her forehead was dry and hot and a bubble of blood on the corner of her mouth inflated and deflated with each breath. By the next day Sarah had developed a pneumonia. They pieced together the story from the few things she said. She paid little attention to them and kept asking for Coalhouse. They arranged to have her placed in a private room. Not knowing where Coalhouse lived they put in a call to the Manhattan Casino and reached the manager of the Clef Club Orchestra. In this way Coalhouse was located and a few hours later he was sitting by Sarah's bedside.

Mother and Father waited outside the room. When they looked in again Coalhouse was on his knees beside the bed. His head was bowed and with his two hands he held the hand of Sarah. They retreated. Afterward they heard the sepulchral sounds of a grown man's grief. Mother went home. She held the baby constantly. The family was devastated. They could not seem to keep warm. Everyone wore sweaters. Younger Brother fired the furnace. Toward the end of the week Sarah died.

26

The funeral was made in Harlem. It was lavish. Sarah's coffin
was bronze. The hearse was a custom Pierce Arrow Opera
Coach with an elongated passenger compartment and a driver's cab open to the weather. The top was railed with brass and
banked with masses of flowers. Black ribbon flew from the four
corners of the roof. The car was so highly polished the boy
could see in its rear doors a reflection of the entire street.
Everything was black including the sky. The street curved to
a precipitous horizon. There were several town cars for carrying the mourners to the cemetery. The mourners were mostly
musicians, associates of Coalhouse in the Clef Club Orchestra.
They were Negro men with closely cropped hair, tightly buttoned dark suits, rounded collars and black ties. The women
with them wore dresses that brushed the tops of their shoes,
wide-brimmed hats, and small furs around their shoulders.
When the mourners were in the cars and the doors were shut
and the chauffeurs had got in behind their wheels, everyone
heard a fanfare and there came up the street to take its place
in the procession an open omnibus with a five-piece brass band
in tuxedos. Coalhouse Walker paid for the funeral with the
money he had saved for his wedding. He had secured a plot

for Sarah through his membership in the Negro Musicians'
Benevolent Association. The cemetery was in Brooklyn. The
band played dirges through the quiet streets of Harlem and all
the way downtown. The cortege moved slowly. Children ran
behind it and people on the sidewalks stopped to stare. The
band played as the cars slowly crossed the Brooklyn Bridge
high over the East River. Passengers on the trolley cars along
the outer lanes of the bridge stood up in their seats to see the
grand parade. The sun shone. Gulls rose from the water. They
flew between the suspension cables and settled along the railing as the last of the cars went by.

27

Spring, spring! Like a mad magician flinging silks and colored rags from his trunk the earth produced the yellow and white crocus, then the fox grape, the forsythia flowering on its stalks, the blades of iris, the apple tree blossoms of pink and white and green, the heavy lilac and the daffodil. Grandfather stood in the yard and gave a standing ovation. A breeze came up and blew from the maples a shower of spermatozoic soft-headed green buds. They caught in his sparse gray hair. He shook his head with delight, feeling a wreath had been bestowed. A joyful spasm took hold of him and he stuck his leg out in an old man's jig, lost his balance, and slid on the heel of his shoe into a sitting position. In this manner he cracked his pelvis and entered a period of declining health from which he would not recover. But the spring was joyful and even in pain he wore a smile. Everywhere the sap rose and the birds sang. Upstate, at Matteawan State Prison Farm, Harry K. Thaw nimbly jumped over a ditch in a road and stepped on the running board of a waiting Locomobile. He hooked his elbow about the roof post, gave an exultant cry, and the car drove off. Thaw escaped to Canada, leaving a trail of outraged waitresses and stunned *hôteliers*. He abducted and whipped a teenage boy—he was beginning to work out his problems. Eventually he came back across the border. He was discovered on a train near Buffalo and ran through the cars giggling and panting as police detectives set up pursuit. In the dining car he turned and threw heavy silvered individual coffeepots he plucked from the tables of astonished diners. He climbed up between the cars and ran along the top of the train in a kind of simian lope, leaping down upon the observation platform and standing with his arms outstretched to the sun as the police burst through the door and grabbed him.

Thaw would not divulge the name of the person who helped him escape. Just call me Houdini, he said. An enterprising reporter decided to find the great magician and solicit a comment. He was that kind of reporter expert in the stupid and inconsequential news story so loved by the papers of the time. Houdini was found in a cemetery in Queens where he was observing the spring on his knees beside his mother's grave. He looked up with the swollen and laughable face of grief. The reporter stole away. All around the graveyard the dogwood was in flower and the fallen magnolia petals lay in circles under the trees.

Houdini wore a black wool suit and the sleeve of the jacket was torn near the shoulder. His mother had been dead for some months but every morning he awoke with his wound as fresh and painful as if she had died the night before. He had canceled several bookings. He shaved only when he remembered to, which was not often, and with his reddened eyes and stubble and baggy suit he looked like anything but the snappy magician of international fame.

It is a Jewish custom to leave small stones at the gravesite to show that a visit has been made. Mrs. Cecelia Weiss's burial mound was covered with pebbles and small stones, one upon another, so that a kind of pyramid was forming. He thought of her at rest in the coffin under the earth. He wept bitterly.

He wanted to be next to her. He remembered his attempt to escape from a coffin, the terror when he realized he could not. The coffin had a trick lid but he had not anticipated the weight of the earth. He had clawed at the earth, feeling its monumental weight. He had screamed into its impenetrable silence. He knew what it was to be sealed in the earth but he felt now it was the only place for him. What good was life without his beloved little mother?

He hated the spring. The air filled his nose and mouth like clotted soil.

In his brownstone on 113th Street near Riverside Drive, Houdini arranged framed photographs of his mother to suggest her continuing presence. One close-up he laid on the pillow of her bed. He placed an enlarged photo of her seated in a chair and smiling in the very chair in which she had posed. There was a picture of her in a hat and coat walking up the stairs from the street to the front door. He hung this on the inside of the door. One of her prized possessions had been an oak music box with a glass window in its lid so that one could see the large tined disc in rotation. There were several discs to choose from, but her favorite had been the one that played "Gaudeamus Igitur" on one side and "Columbia the Gem of the Ocean" on the other. Houdini cranked up the music box and played these tunes every evening. He dreamed they were her voice. He had saved the letters she had written to him over the years and now had them translated into English and typed so that he could read them easily and relive them without fear of their turning to dust from overuse. He stood in the door of her closet and breathed the redolence of her wardrobe.

The old woman had taken ill while Houdini was in Europe. He had looked forward to describing to her his meeting with the Archduke Franz Ferdinand, heir to the Austro-Hungarian Empire, but before he could write her she had died. He secured a release from his performing contracts and sailed home as quickly as he could. He remembered nothing of the voyage. He was out of his mind with grief. The burial had been delayed until his return. He learned that she had called for him moments before her death. She had suffered a paralytic stroke. Erich, she had moaned. Erich, Erich. He was tormented with guilt. He was obsessed with the idea that she had wanted to tell him something, that she had something to tell him that she could reveal only then, at the moment of her death.

He had always been skeptical of occultists and the spiritual claims of clairvoyants and mediums. In his early days with the Welsh Brothers Circus in Pennsylvania he had himself exploited the gullibility of rubes by claiming transcendental powers for his tricks. Blindfolded he would tell a confederate what item had been held for identification by someone in the audience. What is this, Mr. Houdini, the confederate would say, and he'd know. It was all done by code. Sometimes he would claim to speak with the dead and give some poor sucker whose name and circumstances they had managed to figure out a message from a loved one who had passed on. So he knew what spiritual fraud was. He could recognize it. Spiritual fraud had been rampant in the United States since 1848 when two sisters, Margaretta and Kate Fox, invited neighbors to hear the mysterious rappings in their house in Hydesville, New York. But it was the very fact of his expertise that persuaded him now to consider the possibility of finding someone who had genuine gifts as a medium. If it was possible to communicate with the dead he would find out. He could recognize and unmask any fake act in the world. Therefore if he found the real thing he would know it. He wanted to see his mother Cecelia's tiny figure and feel her hands touch his face. But since that could not be, he decided to see if it was really possible to speak with her.

And at this time in our history communication with the dead was not as far-fetched an idea as it had once been. America was in the dawn of the Twentieth Century, a nation of steam shovels, locomotives, airships, combustion engines, telephones and twenty-five-story buildings. But there was an interesting susceptibility to occult ideas of the most famous pragmatists in the land. Of course it was all very hush-hush. A rumor in certain circles had it that Pierpont Morgan and Henry Ford had formed a secret society. And he knew that the horticultural wizard Luther Burbank, who crossbred and developed hybrids with increased crop yields, talked secretly to plants and believed they could understand him. The great Edison himself, the man who invented the Twentieth Century, had theorized that irreducible particles of life-charged matter, which he called *swarms*, subsisted after death and could never be destroyed. Houdini tried to get in touch with Edison. He asked for an interview. But the great man was too busy. He was working on an invention so secret that there was frequent speculation in the press as to what it might be. One news story came out claiming the new invention was something called a vacuum tube by which Edison hoped to receive messages from dead people. Houdini desperately sent off telegrams begging and pleading for an interview. He was rebuffed. He offered money to help fund the work. He was rebuffed. He swore to himself that he would invent his own instrument, just as he had learned to fly his own aeroplane. Whatever Edison began with came from the storehouse of technology available to everyone. Houdini bought books and began a study of mechanical physics and the principles of the storage battery. He vowed that by whatever medium, mechanical or human, if there was life after death he would discover it.

His passion in no time at all came to the attention of various people who kept abreast of such things. He met a man from Buffalo, New York, who claimed to have worked at one time with Steinmetz, the dwarf immigrant genius of the General Electric Company. Physicists all over the world were discovering waves, the man told him. There was a tremendously important theory from abroad in which it was supposed matter and energy were but two aspects of the same primal force. That is my idea too, the man told Houdini. He was a physicist with a university degree from Transylvania. All he needed was to devise the properly sensitive instrument, and primal waves could be detected and decoded that nobody as yet knew anything about. Houdini signed an agreement with him giving him two thousand dollars for the exclusive rights to his research. Another man, a chemist, he established in the basement of his own home. Letters came to him from people claiming to have mediumistic gifts and asking for any item of his mother's—a brooch or a lock of hair—to work with. He employed a detective agency to look into the most reasonable-sounding of these. He told the agents how to recognize spirit fraud. He told them about trumpets, and trick photography, hidden recording megaphones, levitation of tables by means of pulleys. Why should a medium need the room dark, he told them. When he turns out the lights it's to hide something.

Soon Houdini had generated enough activity of this kind to make him think about working again. I'm feeling stronger, he told his manager. I'm beginning to feel like my old self. The bookings were soon arranged. Those who saw Houdini's performances in this period of his career say they surpassed anything he had ever done. He brought masons onstage who built a brick wall ten feet high which he then walked through. He made a full-sized elephant disappear with a clap of his hands. Coins poured from his fingers. Doves flew from his ears. He stepped into a packing case previously examined by the audience. It was nailed shut and tied with a stout rope. No drape was set up in front of the packing case. It was pried open. It was empty. A collective gasp went up from the audience as Houdini was seen running into the theatre from the lobby. He leaped onstage. His eyes seemed to gleam the color of blue diamonds. Slowly he lifted his arms. His feet rose from the floor. He stood six inches above the floor. Women panted. Suddenly he collapsed in a heap. There were exclamations of disbelief followed by prolonged applause. His assistants helped him to a chair. Houdini asked for a glass of wine to restore his strength. He held the wine up in the spotlight. It turned colorless. He drank it. The wineglass disappeared from his hand.

In fact his performances were now of such intensity and had so strange and disquieting an effect on his audiences, that in some cases children were hurried out before the end of the show. Houdini never noticed. He drove himself beyond his own physical capacity and would do eight or a dozen of his major tricks in a show that was supposed to have three. He had always billed his tricks as death-defying and now reporters from the New York dailies, fully expecting him to overextend himself, followed him on his one-night stands from the Brooklyn Pantages, to Fox's Union City, to the Main Street Theatre in New Rochelle. He did his famous milk-can escape in which he was padlocked in one of the ordinary forty-quart cans used to deliver milk to grocery stores. The can was filled with water. He had to escape or he would die. He lay in a glass tank shaped like a coffin, shown to be airtight, and in which a candle's flame could not be sustained. He lay in there sometimes for as much as six minutes after the candle went out. People shouted from the audience. Women closed their eyes and put their hands over their ears. They begged his assistants to stop him. When the pleas were finally heeded the fitted top of the glass coffin made a popping sound as it came off. He was helped out shaking and covered with sweat. Every feat enacted Houdini's desire for his dead mother. He was buried and reborn, buried and reborn. One night, at a single performance only in New Rochelle, his wish for his own death was so apparent that people began to scream and a local clergyman stood up and shouted Houdini, you are experimenting with damnation! Perhaps it is true that he could no longer distinguish his life from his tricks. He stood in his long belted robe, and glistening with sweat, his wet hair in spirals, he looked like a creature from another universe. Ladies and gentlemen, he said in an exhausted voice, please forgive me. He wanted to explain his mastery of an ancient Eastern breathing regimen that allowed him to suspend his animation. He wanted to explain that his feats looked far more dangerous than they really were. He raised his hands in appeal. But at that moment there was an explosion of such force that the theatre shook on its foundations and chunks of plaster fell from the proscenium arch; and the distracted and nerve-shattered audience, thinking it was another of his satanic tricks, retreated up the aisles in terror of him.

28

Actually the blast occurred two miles away at the borders of the city in its west end. The station house of the Emerald Isle Engine had exploded, firing the field across the street with burning timbers and lighting the sky over Westchester. Companies from every section of the city responded and from the adjoining communities of Pelham and Mount Vernon. Little could be done. Fortunately the clapboard structure on Firehouse Lane was no closer than a quarter-mile to the nearest residence. But two of the volunteers were in the hospital, one with burns so severe that he was not expected to live through the day. And at least five men were known to have been on duty at the time. It was the night of the week, Thursday, when the company gathered for its regular game of poker.

By the following dawn the field was scorched and the building was a pile of charred ruins. The entire area had been roped off and police detectives now began to go through the debris recovering bodies and deducing from the evidence what it was that had caused the disaster. It soon became apparent that homicide had been committed. Of the four bodies recovered two showed that not the fire or the explosion but buckshot had been the cause of death. The matching horses were in harness and attached to the pumper and they lay where they had fallen halfway into the street. The alarm signal machine was recovered from the ruins showing that an alarm had been given from a box at the north end of town, yet there had been no other fire anywhere in the city that night. From this and several other bits of evidence, some secured with the help of a doctor of forensic medicine from the New York City Police Department, the following reconstruction was made: At approximately 10:30 P.M. six members of the engine company had been gathered in their quarters playing cards when the alarm rang. The cardplayers scrambled into their boots and helmets. The horses were trotted out of their stalls and hitched to the steam engine. The harness was a special snap-on variety developed for firehorses by the P. A. Setzer Company of Hickory, North Carolina. Like all firemen the Emerald Isle were proud of the speed with which they answered alarms. There was always a small fire going under the boiler so that the steam could be raised to full pressure by the time the apparatus arrived at the site. If the company were normally efficient on this evening not one minute would have elapsed before the doors were swung open and the driver, hollahing his horses, would have whipped them into the road. Someone was standing in the street directly in the engine's path. He or they were armed with shotguns which were fired directly in the faces of the oncoming horses. Two of the horses went down immediately, the third reared, wounded in the neck so that its blood sprayed over the street like a fine rain. The driver of the rig was fatally shot, and fell forward to the ground. Of the three firemen aboard, two incurred fatal wounds and a third was crushed to death as the engine, pulled awry by the panicked horses, toppled over on its side. When the steam boiler went over, it made a terrible clang that was heard by residents in the neighborhood already startled by the boom of guns. The firebox was scattered and flaming coals ignited the clapboard

E. L. Doctorow

firehouse. The blaze quickly grew and the heat of the burning
building exploded the boiler and sent burning timbers flying
across the road into the field. That was the moment Houdini
lost the affection of his audience.

As it happened the family had retired early that night. They
had been sleeping poorly. The brown baby cried for his mother
and did not take to the milk of a wet nurse. Father heard the
distant explosion and looking out of his bedroom window saw
the lighted sky. His first thought was that his plant with its
store of fireworks had blown. But the glow was brightest in a
different direction. It wasn't until the next morning that he
learned what it was that had burned. The fire seemed to be the
only topic of conversation throughout the city. At the lunch
hour Father went to the site. Crowds were standing at the
police barriers. He circled the ropes and came to the pond at
the bottom of the field across the road from the demolished
firehouse: in the pond, the sunken structure of the Model T
appeared and disappeared as the water, raised to a small chop
by the prevailing breeze, erased and then re-formed its waver-
ing outlines. Father went home for the day although the
twelve-noon whistle had only just blown. Mother could not
look at him. She was seated with the baby on her lap. Her head
was bent in a meditative attitude unconsciously suggestive of
the dead Sarah. Father wondered at this moment if their lives
might no longer be under their control.

At four in the afternoon the newsboy ran by and tossed the
folded evening paper to the porch. The killer arsonist was
believed to be an unidentified Negro male. From his hospital
bed, the sole survivor of the attack had been able to describe
him to the police. Apparently the Negro put out the fire
burning the clothes of the injured man. And then, lest that be
interpreted as an act of mercy, he had held his head by the hair
and demanded to know where the Fire Chief was hiding. But
it was Fire Chief Conklin's good fortune not to be at the

station house that evening. It was not known how the Negro knew Conklin or what he had against him.

The professional consensus was that there had to have been accomplices—this from the fact that a false alarm had been set to bring the volunteers out of the station. Nevertheless an editorial described the disaster as the work of a lone crazed killer. Citizens were called upon to lock their doors and maintain their vigilance, but to remain calm.

The family sat at the dinner table. Mother held the baby in her arms. Without realizing it she did not now expect ever to put the child down. She felt the touch of his tiny fingertips on her cheek. Upstairs in his room Grandfather groaned in pain. There was no dinner this evening, nobody wanted to eat. A cut-glass carafe of brandy was set in front of Father. He was drinking his third glass. He felt that something, some sort of small bone or piece of dust, was lodged in his throat and he had conceived of the brandy as the only thing that would fix it. He had taken from his bureau drawer his old army pistol from the Philippine campaign. It lay on the table. We are suffering a tragedy that should not have been ours, he said to his wife. What in God's name possessed you on that day? The county has facilities for indigents. You took her in without sufficient thought. You victimized us all with your foolish female sentimentality. Mother regarded him. She could not remember any time in their long acquaintance when he had reproached her. She knew he would apologize; nevertheless tears filled her eyes and eventually ran down her face. Wisps of her hair had come undone and lay on her neck and over her ears. Father looked at her and she was beautiful in the way she had been as a girl. He did not realize the pleasure he felt in having made her cry.

Younger Brother was sitting with his elbow on the arm of his chair and his head propped in his hand. His index finger was extended and pointed at his temple. He watched his brother-in-law. Are you going out to find him and shoot him? he said. I'm going to protect my home, Father said. This is his child here. If he makes the mistake of coming to my door I will deal with him. But why should he come here, Brother said in a goading tone of voice. We did not desecrate his car. Father looked at Mother. In the morning I will go to the police and have to tell them this murdering madman was a guest in my home. I will have to tell them we are keeping his bastard child. Younger Brother said I think Coalhouse Walker Jr. would want you to tell the police everything you know. You can tell them he's the same Negro maniac whose car is lying at the bottom of Firehouse Pond. You can tell them he's the fellow who visited their own headquarters to make a complaint against Will Conklin and his thugs. You can tell them he's the same crazed black killer who sat by the bedside of someone who died in the hospital of her injuries. Father said I hope I misunderstand you. Would you defend this savage? Does he have anyone but himself to blame for Sarah's death? Anything but his damnable nigger pride? Nothing under heaven can excuse the killing of men and the destruction of property in this manner! Brother stood so abruptly that his chair fell over. The baby started and began to cry. Brother was pale and trembling. I did not hear such a eulogy at Sarah's funeral, he said. I did not hear you say then that death and the destruction of property was inexcusable.

But the fact was that Coalhouse Walker had already taken several steps to identify himself with the crime. It turned out that within an hour of the explosion he, or some other black man, left identical letters at the offices of the two local newspapers. The editors after conferring with the police chose not to print them. The letters were written in a clear firm hand and told of the events leading up to the attack on the firehouse. I want the infamous Fire Chief of the Volunteers turned over to my justice, the letter said. I want my automobile returned to me in its original condition. If these conditions are not met I will continue to kill firemen and burn firehouses until they are. I will destroy the entire city if need be. The newspaper editors and police officials believed it was in the interest of the public welfare not to print the letter. An isolated crazed killer was one problem. An insurrection was another. Squads of police quietly went through the Negro neighborhoods and asked questions about Coalhouse Walker Jr. At the same time police of neighboring towns with Negro populations did the same. To headquarters the word filtered back: Not one of our Negroes. Not one of ours.

In the morning Father took the North Avenue streetcar downtown. He strode to City Hall. He went in the door a widely respected businessman in the community. His career as an explorer had been well reported in the newspapers. The flag that flew from the cupola on top of the building had been his gift to the city.

29

Father had been born and raised in White Plains, New York. He was an only child. He remembered moments of light and warmth in the days of summer at Saratoga Springs. There were gardens there with paths of washed gravel. He would stroll with his mama down the large painted porches of the great hotels. On the same day every year they went home. She was a frail woman who died when he was fourteen. Father attended Groton and then Harvard. He read German Philosophy. In the winter of his sophomore year his studies ended. His father had made a fortune in the Civil War and had since used his time losing it in unwise speculations. It was now entirely gone. The old man was the sort who thrived on adversity. His confidence rose with every loss. In bankruptcy he was beaming and triumphant. He died suddenly, all his expectations intact. His flamboyance had produced in his lonely son a personality that was cautious, sober, industrious and chronically unhappy. Coming into his majority, the orphan took the few dollars left to him and invested it in a small fireworks business owned by an Italian. Eventually he took it over, expanded its sales, bought out a flag manufacturing firm and became quite comfortable. He had also found the time to secure an army commission in the Philippine campaigns. He was proud of his life but never forgot that before going into business he had been to Harvard. He had heard William James lecture on the principles of Modern Psychology. Exploration became his passion: he wanted to avoid what the great Dr. James had called the habit of inferiority to the full self.

Now every morning Father rose and tasted his mortal being. He wondered if his dislike for Coalhouse Walker, which had been instantaneous, was based not on the man's color but on his being engaged in an act of courtship, a suspenseful enterprise that suggested the best of life was yet to come. Father noted the skin mottling on the back of his hand. He found himself occasionally asking people to repeat to him what they'd said. His bladder seemed always to demand emptying. Mother's body did not arouse his lust, only his quiet appreciation. He admired her shape and softness but was no longer inflamed. He noted that she had grown heavier in the upper arms. Once accustomed to life together after his return from the Arctic, they had slipped into an undemanding companionship in which he felt by-passed by life, like a spectator at an event. He found distasteful her promotion of the black girl's marriage. And now that Sarah was dead he felt altogether invisible, Mother's grief having directed her attention solely on Sarah's boy.

He recognized that he took satisfaction in going to the police. It was not an entirely righteous feeling. Perhaps in compensation, he represented Coalhouse as a peaceful man driven mad by circumstances not of his own doing. This was exactly the argument Younger Brother made at home. Father confirmed the account of events in Coalhouse's letter. He was a pianist, Father said, using the historical tense. He was always courteous and correct in his dealings. The police nodded gravely. They wanted to know if the Negro was likely to strike

[182]

again. That is what the Police Chief said, strike again. Father said that once Coalhouse had set a course for himself he was nothing if not persevering. Largely upon this advice a defense was organized. Police guards were assigned to all the firehouses in the city. The main roads were placed under watch. In the headquarters a wall map was installed showing the deployment of forces. On the basis of Father's information the New York City Police Department was persuaded to assign detectives to look for Coalhouse in Harlem.

Father had expected criticism from the police. This was not forthcoming. They regarded him as an expert on the character of the criminal. They encouraged him to spend as much time at headquarters as he could. They wanted him to be on hand for their deliberations. The walls of the rooms were painted light green to a line at waist level, dark green below. There were cuspidors in every corner. Father agreed to make himself as available as he could. This was his busiest time of year. All the orders for rockets, sparklers, Roman candles, crackers, flares and bombs had to be shipped in time for the Fourth of July celebrations. He went back and forth between his office and the police. To his disgust he found himself at the station in the company of the Emerald Isle Chief, Will Conklin. Conklin smelled of whiskey and the experience of being a hunted man had turned his florid face the color of veal. He was by turn bombastic and craven. He offered counsel of the same level of wisdom that had triggered the crisis in the first place. He wanted to go to the black neighborhood and clean all the niggers out once and for all. The officers heard this with disinterest. They teased him about his fate. We may have to give you to the boogie man, Willie, they said. Just to get some peace around here. Conklin could take little of this. Are we not in this together? he said. God love you, you were cruel lads at St. Catherine's and yer cruel now. Willie, the Police Chief said, we had to wait to hear from the black man himself that one of your shenanigans is what started this, you dumb Mick, telling us now we're in this together.

But the Fire Chief's character and mentality seemed appropriate to the place. There was a constant traffic through the glass doors of felons, lawyers, bondsmen, policemen and hapless relatives. Drunks were brought in by the collar and thieves with their hands cuffed. Voices were loud and language was vile. Conklin owned a coal and ice business and lived with a wife and several children in an apartment over his yard office. It dawned on Father that the man was spending so much time at the police station because he felt safe there. Of course he would not admit it. He boasted of the precautions he had taken at his yard. Not relying on the two posted policemen, he had enlisted all the survivors of the Emerald Isle to billet themselves at his place. They were armed. The nigger might as well attack West Point, he said.

Father felt demeaned by the man. Conklin spoke to him differently from the way he addressed the policemen. His diction improved. His assumption of social equality was galling. It's a tragic thing, Captain, he would say. A tragic thing indeed. Once he actually put his hand on Father's shoulder, a gesture of such alarming brotherhood that it felt like an electric shock.

Nevertheless Father found himself spending more and more time here. He found it difficult to go home. On the day of the mass funeral for the victims of the Emerald Isle fire, he went to hear the eulogies. Half the city turned out. A large brass cross swayed over the heads of the crowd. Will Conklin did not leave the police station. I'd be a perfect target for the rifle shot, he said. Questions about his behavior began to circulate through the city. Then the news that the killings of the Night of the Emerald Isle stemmed from a grievance was published in the New York City dailies, where reporters were not constrained by the interests of the local chamber of commerce. The *World* and the *Sun* printed the text of Coalhouse's letter. Will Conklin became a despised person everywhere. He was hated as the stupid perpetrator of events leading to the death of men whom he ostensibly commanded. On the other hand, among certain elements he was scorned as someone who knew how to bait a Negro but not to put the fear of God into him.

A man wearing a derby now sat in a car every day up the street from the house on Broadview Avenue. Father had not been officially told of this but he advised Mother that he had asked for a police guard, feeling it would be less wise to share with her his speculation that for all their gratitude at his coming forward the police weren't entirely above keeping an eye on him. He wondered what suspicion they might be entertaining.

Exactly one week after Coalhouse's attack on the Emerald Isle, at six in the morning, a White town car drove slowly up Railroad Place, a narrow cobblestone street in the West End. In the middle of the block was Municipal Fire Station No. 2. As the car drew abreast of the building it stopped and the two policemen standing sleepily before the doors were astounded to see several black men disembark holding shotguns and rifles. One of the policemen had the presence of mind to drop to the ground. The other just stood open-mouthed as the raiders efficiently formed a line, like a firing squad, and upon signal fired their weapons in unison. The blast killed the standing policeman and shattered the windowpanes of the firehouse doors. One of the Negroes then ran up and tossed several small packages through the broken windows.

The man who had given the command to fire came up to the terrified survivor lying on the sidewalk. He placed a letter in his hand and said calmly This must be published in the newspaper. Then he joined the other Negroes, who had returned to the car. As it drove off two or perhaps three explosions, coming one on top of another, blew out the doors of the firehouse and instantly turned it into an inferno. The flames quickly engulfed an adjoining saloon and the establishment of a coffee distributor who also roasted his blends for customers off the street. The sacks of beans produced a yellow pall and left a fragrance of roasted coffee over the neighborhood for several weeks. Eventually four bodies were recovered, all of city firemen. An elderly woman, presumably dead of fright, was found in her rooms across the way. A Reo fire engine and an ambulance were destroyed.

And now the city was truly in panic. Children did not appear for school. Cries of outrage were directed against the city administration and against Willie Conklin. A delegation of firemen marched to City Hall and demanded to be sworn in as police deputies and given arms to defend themselves. The flustered Mayor sent a telegram to the Governor of New York appealing for help. The story of Coalhouse's second attack made the front pages of every newspaper in the country. Reporters in droves came up from New York. The Chief of Police was condemned for allowing the black killer to do his murderous work again. The Chief made a statement to reporters gathered in his office. The man uses automobiles to get around, he said. He strikes and disappears, God knows where. For several years the Association of Police Chiefs of the State of New York has passed a resolution calling for the licensing of automobiles and automobilists. If that were the law today we could track the brute down. The Chief as he spoke emptied the drawers of his desk. He puffed a cigar. He walked out with the reporters. The next day a bill to license automobiles was introduced in the State Legislature.

Father employed two Negroes at his manufactory, one as a janitor, the other as an assembler of rocket tubes. Neither reported to work the day of the second disaster. In fact Negroes were to be seen nowhere in the city. They stayed home behind locked doors. That night police arrested on the street several white citizens carrying pistols and rifles. The Governor responded to the Mayor's appeal by sending in two companies of militia from New York City. They arrived the next morning and immediately set up their tents on the baseball field behind the high school. Children gathered to watch. Special editions of the local papers were published and each carried prominently the text of Coalhouse's second letter. This is what it said: One, that the white excrescence known as Willie Conklin be turned over to my justice. Two, that the Model T Ford with its custom pantasote top be returned in its original condition. Until these demands are satisfied, let the rules of war prevail. Coalhouse Walker Jr., President, Provisional American Government.

At this point everyone's most urgent need was to know what Coalhouse Walker looked like. The newspapers competed fiercely. Newsmen stormed the offices of the Clef Club Orchestra in Harlem. There were no pictures to be had that included the face of the infamous pianist. Hearst's *American* triumphantly went to press with a portrait of the composer Scott Joplin. Friends of Joplin threatened to sue, the composer being in the last stages of a terminal illness and unable to see to his own interests. Apologies were tendered. Finally a newspaper in St. Louis came up with a picture that was reprinted widely. Father recognized it to be accurate. It showed a somewhat younger Coalhouse sitting at an upright piano in white tie and tails. His hands were on the keyboard and he was smiling for the camera. Grouped around the piano were a banjo player, a cornetist, a trombonist, a violinist and a drummer bent over a snare drum. They were all in white tie. They were posed as if playing but were clearly not. A circle was drawn around Coalhouse's head. This became the standard photo. The ironies of a smiling black man with a neat moustache, an altogether cheerful and forthright physiognomy, were too delicious for the caption writers to resist. Smile of a killer, they said. Or the President of the Provisional American Government in happier days.

Under the intense and widespread investigation by the press the family's role in the entire affair could not be kept hidden. Reporters, first in ones and twos, later in larger groups, began to knock on the door, and then, being refused admittance, to camp outside under the Norwegian maples. They wanted to see the brown child, they wanted statements of any kind about Coalhouse and his visits to Sarah. They peeked through the windows of the parlor and came around to the kitchen door to try the lock. They wore straw boaters and carried pads in their pockets. They chewed tobacco and spit it on the ground and crushed cigarettes under their heels in the grass. Pictures of the house appeared in the New York papers. There were inaccurate accounts of Father's explorations. The blinds were drawn and the boy was not allowed to go out. The house was stifling and in the night Grandfather moaned in his sleep.

Mother might have withstood all of this if a debate did not rise concerning the family's sheltering of Coalhouse Walker's son. A steady parade of cars came up the hill in the long evenings as sightseers craned their necks for a glimpse of a face in the window. An official of the Child Welfare Board in New York gave the opinion that the still-unchristened illegitimate child should be given over to one of the excellent asylums that existed for the care of orphans, waifs and children born out of wedlock. Mother kept the baby in her room. She would no longer take him downstairs. She enlisted her son to watch over him when she had to see to something. She did not take the time to put her hair up but let it hang to her shoulders all day. She was uncharacteristic in her bitterness toward Father. Why don't you unlock your treasure chest, she said, and get me some proper help. This was a reference to his financial conservatism which she had never before questioned. Always they had lived less well than he could afford. Father was stung by the remark but he went out and found a woman to do the cooking and another woman to be laundress and housemaid, both to live in. He hired the man who had been the part-time gardener and installed him in the rooms above the garage stable. Grandfather already had a registered nurse to tend him in the day. The house, under siege, now bustled like a wartime camp. The boy was constantly admonished to get out from under people's feet. He watched his mother pace her room, her hands clasped in front of her, her unbound hair hanging down the sides of her face. She looked gaunt, and her chin, which had always inclined to roundness, seemed ungenerous, even pointed.

It was clear the crisis was driving the spirit from their lives. Father had always felt secretly that as a family they were touched by an extra light. He felt it going now. He felt stupid and plodding, available simply to have done to him what circumstances would do. Coalhouse ruled. Yet he had been to the Arctic, to Africa, to the Philippines. He had traveled out west. Did that mean only that more and more of the world resisted his intelligence? He sat in his study. Everyone he thought about, even Grandfather, he saw in terms of his own failed concern. He had treated Grandfather with the arrogant courtesy one gives to the senile even before the condition had set in. From Younger Brother he was completely estranged. Toward his wife he felt drastically slipped in her estimation, an explorer in body only, the spirit trapped in his own father's prejudices. He was beginning to look like him, too, going dry and juiceless in everything, with a mad glint showing in the corner of his eye. Why did that have to be?

He condemned himself most for the neglect of his son. He never talked to the boy or offered his companionship. He had always relied on his presence in the child's life as a model for emulation. How smug that was, how stupid, as the tactic of a man who had acted in his life to distinguish himself from his own father. He looked for the boy and found him on the floor of his room reading in the evening paper an account of the successful play of the New York baseball nine under the masterful coaching of John J. McGraw. Would you like to see that team? he said. The boy looked up, startled. I was just thinking of it, he said. Father went to Mother's room. Tomorrow, he announced, I am taking the boy to see a game of baseball. He said this with such resolve in its rightness that she was checked in her response, which was to condemn him for an idiot, and when he left the room she could only wonder that she had had that thought in the first place, so separated from any feeling of love.

30

The next afternoon, when father and son left the house, two reporters followed them part of the way on their brisk walk to the railroad station on Quaker Ridge Road. We're going to the Giants baseball game, Father advised them. That's all I will say. Who's pitching? one of the reporters asked. Rube Marquard, the boy said. He's won his last three chances.

Just as they reached Quaker Ridge a train pulled in. This was the New York Westchester and Boston railway. It did not go anywhere near Boston, nor did it provide service all the way to New York. But it gave a smooth ride to the Bronx and left them with a trolley connection, the 155th Street crosstown, which went over the Harlem River to the Polo Grounds at Coogan's Bluff.

It was a fine afternoon. Large white clouds moved briskly under a clear blue sky. As the trolley came across the bridge they could see on the bluff overlooking the wooden stands several huge trees which, lacking leaves even in this season, supported derbied figures of men who preferred not to pay to enter the park but to watch the game festooned in the branches like black flowers swaying in the wind. Father caught some of the boy's excitement. He was immensely pleased to be out of New Rochelle. When they reached the park crowds were streaming down the stairs from the El, cabs were pulling up and discharging their passengers, newsboys were hawking programs of the game, and there was a raucous energy everywhere in the street. Horns blew. The overhead tracks of the El left the street mottled with sun. Father bought the expensive fifty-cent admission, then paid extra for a box, and they entered the park and took their seats behind first base in the lower of the two decks where the sun would for an inning or two cause them to shade their eyes.

The Giants were dressed in their baggy white uniforms with black pin stripes. The manager, McGraw, wore a heavy black cardigan over his barreled trunk with the letters NY emblazoned on the left sleeve. He was short and pugnacious. Like his team he wore socks with thick horizontal stripes and the small flat cap with a peak and a button on the crown. The opponents of the afternoon were the Boston Braves, whose dark blue flannels were buttoned to the neck with the collar turned up. A brisk wind blew the dirt of the field. The game began and almost immediately Father regretted the seats he had chosen. The players' every ragging curse could be heard clearly by his son. The team at bat shouted obscene taunts at the opposing pitcher. McGraw himself, the paternal figure and commander of his team, stood at third base unleashing the most constant and creative string of vile epithets of anyone. His strident caw could be heard throughout the park. The crowd seemed to match him in its passions. The game was close, with first one team then the other assuming the lead. A runner sliding into second base upended the Giant second baseman, who rose howling, limping in circles and bleeding profusely through his stocking. Both teams came running from their dugouts and the game was stopped for some minutes while everyone fought and rolled in the dirt and the crowd yelled its encouragement. An inning or two after the fight the

Giant pitcher Marquard seemed to lose his control and threw the ball so that it hit the Boston batsman. This fellow rose from the ground and ran out toward Marquard waving his bat. Again the dugouts emptied and players wrestled with each other and threw their roundhouse punches and beat clouds of dust into the air. The audience this time participated by throwing soda pop bottles onto the field. Father consulted his program. On the Giant side were Merkle, Doyle, Meyers, Snodgrass and Herzog, among others. The Boston team boasted a player named Rabbit Maranville, a shortstop who he noted roamed his position bent over with his hands at the end of his long arms grazing the grass in a manner that would more properly be called simian. There was a first baseman named Butch Schmidt, and others with the names Cocrehan, Moran, Hess, Rudolph, which led inevitably to the conclusion that professional baseball was played by immigrants. When play was resumed he studied each batsman: indeed, they seemed to be clearly from the mills and farms, rude-featured, jug-eared men, sunburned and ham-handed, cheeks bulging with tobacco chew, their intelligence completely absorbed in the effort of the game. The players in the field wore outsized flapping leather gloves which made them look like half-dressed clowns. The dry dust of the diamond was blotched with expectorant. Woe to the campaigns of the Anti-Spitting League in the example of these men. On the Boston side the boy who picked up the bats and replaced them in the dugout was, upon second look, a midget, in a team uniform like the rest but proportionately minute. His shouts and taunts were piped in soprano. Most of the players who came to bat first touched him on the head, a gesture he seemed to invite, so that Father realized it was a kind of good luck ritual. On the Giant side was no midget but a strange skinny man whose uniform was ill-fitting, who had weak eyes that did not align properly and who seemed to shadow the game in a lethargic pantomime of

[193]

his own solitude, pitching imaginary balls more or less in time to the real pitches. He looked like a dirt eater. He waved his arm in complete circles, like a windmill turns. Father began to watch the game less than he did this unfortunate creature, obviously a team pet, like the Boston midget. During dull moments of the game the crowd yelled to him and applauded his antics. Sure enough, he was listed in the program as mascot. His name was Charles Victor Faust. He was clearly a fool who, for imagining himself one of the players, was kept on the team roster for their amusement.

Father remembered the baseball at Harvard twenty years before, when the players addressed each other as Mister and played their game avidly, but as sportsmen, in sensible uniforms before audiences of collegians who rarely numbered more than a hundred. He was disturbed by his nostalgia. He'd always thought of himself as progressive. He believed in the perfectability of the republic. He thought, for instance, there was no reason the Negro could not with proper guidance carry every burden of human achievement. He did not believe in artistocracy except of the individual effort and vision. He felt his father's loss of fortune had the advantage of saving him from the uncritical adoption of the prejudices of his class. But the air in this ball park open under the sky smelled like the back room of a saloon. Cigar smoke filled the stadium and, lit by the oblique rays of the afternoon sun, indicated the voluminous cavern of air in which he sat pressed upon as if by a foul universe, with the breathless wind of a ten-thousand-throated chorus in his ears shouting its praise and abuse.

Out in center field, behind the unroofed or bleacher seats, a great display board indicated the number of outs and the inning and the hits and runs made. A man went along a scaffold and hung the appropriate marked shingles that summarized the action. Father sank into his chair. As the afternoon wore on he entertained the illusion that what he saw was not baseball but an elaborate representation of his own problems accounted, for his secret understanding, in the coded clarity of numbers that could be seen from a distance.

He turned to his son. What is it you like about this game, he said. The boy did not remove his gaze from the diamond. The same thing happens over and over, he said. The pitcher throws the ball so as to fool the batter into thinking he can hit it. But sometimes the batter does hit it, the father said. Then the pitcher is the one who is fooled, the boy said. At this moment the Boston hurler, Hub Perdue, threw a pitch which the New York batter, Red Jack Murray, swung at. The ball soared into the air in a high narrow arc and seemed then to stop in its trajectory. With a start Father realized it was coming directly at them. The boy jumped up and held out his hands and there was a cheer behind them as he stood with the leather-covered spheroid resting in his palms. For one instant everyone in the park looked in their direction. Then the fool with the weak eyes who imagined he was a player on the team came up to the fence in front of them and stared at the boy, his arms and hands twitching in his baggy flannel shirt. His hat was absurdly small for his abnormally large head. The boy held out the ball to him and gently, with a smile almost sane, he accepted it.

An interesting note is that this poor fellow, Charles Victor Faust, was actually called upon to pitch one inning in a game toward the end of this same season when the Giants had already won the pennant and were in a carefree mood. For a moment his delusion that he was a big-leaguer fused with reality. Soon thereafter the players became bored with him and he was no longer regarded as a good luck charm by Manager McGraw. His uniform was confiscated and he was unceremoniously sent on his way. He was remanded to an insane asylum and some months later died there.

31

At the end of the ball game a great anxiety came over Father.
He felt it had been stupid to leave his wife alone. But as they
left the park borne by the streaming crowd he realized his son
had taken his hand. He felt an uplift of his spirit. On the open
trolley he put his arm around the boy's shoulders. Arriving in
New Rochelle they walked briskly from the train station and
when they came in the door they gave a loud hello! and for the
first time in days Father felt like himself. Mother appeared
from the back of the house. Her hair was bound, she was
groomed and smiling and neat. She embraced him and said
Look, I have something to show you. Her face was radiant. She
stepped aside and walking down the hall, holding the hand of
the housemaid, was Sarah's child in his nightshirt. He tottered
and swung against her skirt, righted himself and looked at
Father in triumph. Everyone laughed. We can't hold him,
Mother said. He wants to walk everywhere.

The boy knelt and held out his arms and the child shook his
hand free of the housemaid and lurched toward him, picking
up speed as he went, outracing his instability and falling hap-
pily against the boy's chest.

A kind of resolute serenity carried them through the evening. In the quiet of Mother's room toward midnight she and Father discussed everything on their minds. The chances were that Coalhouse would continue for some time to elude capture. In that case they foresaw a community from which they would be increasingly alienated. Already a few of Mother's acquaintances from her service league had reacted to the publicity given the family. She dreaded actions of spite and bitterness in which Sarah's baby would be taken away under protection of a vengeful authority. Father could not deny that might happen. But they were in this moment so calmly in possession of themselves that there was no need for false assurances or for either of them to dissemble an optimism not truly felt. Father said he would not put it past the authorities to decide to use the child in some way to persuade Coalhouse to surrender. What we have to do, Father said, is get away. But how can we, Mother said. My father is invalided, school is not yet out, we have just taken on the responsibilities of a household staff. Each of these problems she enumerated with her right index finger tolling the fingers of her left hand. So she had been thinking the same thing and Father now perceived that she awaited his solutions in good faith. He told her to leave everything to him. His assumption of responsibility produced in her warm feelings of gratitude. Their conversation reminding them that they were after all friends of long standing, they went to bed and spent the night together. She let him make love to her, responding with such cooperative huggings and movements of her hips, and with so many caresses of encouragement to represent her best wishes to have him succeed in his efforts, that he felt for the first time in many months she appreciated she had a good man in her arms.

The answer to everything seemed to be Atlantic City. Father located a fine hotel there, the Breakers, which had available a suite of rooms facing the ocean for something less than would be expected, the season having barely begun. The South

Jersey shore was easy to reach, a few hours by rail, not too near, but not too far to keep him from going back Sunday evening as his business dictated. The change of air would do everyone good. Grandfather's doctor, who had submitted him to the latest orthopedic procedure for broken hips, a metallic pin implanted like an internal splint, advised them that he should be on his crutches or in his chair as much as possible, bed rest comprising the greatest danger for one his age. The boy would have to leave school a few weeks early but was so adept at his studies that this was not considered a serious disadvantage. The house would not be closed with the covering up of furniture and shutting off of rooms this required, but maintained with the staff for those periods in which Father would have to be in New Rochelle. The housekeeper would stay with Mother at the shore. She was a stolid, conscientious Negro woman who would provide, in addition, the obvious and erroneous explanation for the presence of a brown child in their party.

Thus armed with a plan of action the family prepared for their departure. They maintained a good cheer that became almost hysterical as the situation grew in its ugliness. The new Police Chief, a retired inspector from the New York City Department of Homicide, proposed lines of investigation that were ominous. His first day on the job he told reporters that the explosive used on Municipal Station No. 2 was very sophisticated, a combination of gun cotton and fulminate of mercury that could only have been concocted by someone who knew his stuff, which Coalhouse Walker, a piano player, did not. He asked where the Negro got the money for the car he used or for the assistance of a gang of colored men all armed and all presumably motivated by hard cash. He has to pay his cohorts. He has expenses. Where does he get his money? Where does he stay between his mad raids on this gentle city? I know a half-dozen Reds I would love to have in detention here. I bet I would get some of my answers.

[198]

These remarks, which were widely disseminated, had in their suggestion of a conspiracy of radicals the worst possible effect on an already agitated townspeople. Militia patrolled the streets. There were several instances of abuse of Negroes who were seen out of their neighborhoods. There was a rash of false alarms from fireboxes all over the city, each bringing out engines with police guards and a convoy of reporters in cars. Reporters were everywhere, and along with the troopers and the highly visible police in their wagons, produced in the community a painfully swollen sense of itself. The churches on Sunday mornings had never known such crowds. The hospital emergency room reported a higher than usual number of household accident victims. People were burning themselves, cutting themselves, tripping on rugs and falling down flights of stairs. Several men were brought in with gun wounds inflicted in the cleaning and handling of old weapons.

Meanwhile the press seemed to be ahead of the authorities in dealing with the specifics of Coalhouse's letters. Probably for the pictures it would make they agitated for several editions to raise the Model T from Firehouse Pond. This was finally done. A crane was moved to the site and the automobile was brought up like a monstrous artifact, mud dripping from its tires, water and slime pouring out of its hood. It was swung over to the bank and deposited on the ground for everyone to see.

But now the authorities were embarrassed. The Ford stood as tangible proof of the black man's grievance. Waterlogged and wrecked, it offended the sensibilities of anyone who respected machines and valued what they could do. After its picture was published people began to come to see it in such numbers that the police had to cordon off the area. Feeling that they had compromised themselves the Mayor and the Board of Aldermen issued a new series of condemnations of the colored madman and said that to negotiate with him in any way at all, to face him with less than an implacable demand that he surrender himself, would be to invite every renegade and radical and black man in the country to flout the law and spit upon the American flag.

Even if there was at this point a public demand for a strategy of negotiation, which there was not—not even the press suggested it—no one could have had any idea of how to get in touch with the killer. Coalhouse had not announced how much time he granted them till the next attack. Indeed, there was an opinion delivered by an alienist hired by the New York *World* that the second of the letters, signed *Coalhouse Walker, President, Provisional American Government,* was much advanced beyond the first in its signals of mental deterioration, and that to deal with someone in the throes of a progressive delusionary madness as if he were open to reason would be a tragic mistake.

However, it was left to the plain citizenry of New Rochelle to come up with the most practical idea for dealing with the problem. From every neighborhood and every class the cry arose for Willie Conklin to leave town. Some irate citizens even communicated with Conklin himself. He brought into police headquarters several unsigned letters delivered to his mailbox, all suggesting that if he did not pack up and leave New Rochelle they, the writers, would do Coalhouse Walker's job for him. Like all of Conklin's moves, sharing his correspondence with the authorities was a mistake. It did not generate their sympathy, as he had hoped, but simply made up their minds to sponsor the idea. From the beginning Conklin had been unable to understand how anyone who was white could feel for him less than the most profound admiration. The more unpopular he became the more piteous his bewilderment. The miserable fellow understood nothing and saw the public outcry for his exile not in its larger strategy, as a means of defusing the situation, nor even in the small, as a means perhaps of saving his own life. He felt martyred by what he called the nigger lovers, even though these now seemed to constitute virtually the entire population of the city. He drank himself into a state of torpor and became dumbly complaisant as his wife and associates made arrangements for their departure.

Thus, with no one completely in command of the situation, with municipal authorities, police, state militia and citizenry all nervous and unsure in their continuing vulnerability to the black guerrilla, two things were caused to happen more or less by public consensus that were roughly analogous to a recognition of his demands: the Model T Ford had been raised, possibly foretelling some kind of negotiation, and he could read, if he was in range of the New Rochelle papers, both of which gave the largest headlines in their history to the intelligence, that the Conklin family had gone into hiding in New York City. No concessions had been made and the streets bristled with military and paramilitary deployments. But the situation was altered. Let him now burn down the entire metropolis of New York, one editorial said. Or accept the principle that any man who takes the law into his own hands places himself against a civilized and resolute people and defames the very justice he seeks to enforce.

In contrast to all of this the family's departure was private and unreported. Father contracted with the Railway Express to transport their baggage—a matching pair of wicker trunks he had bought for the occasion, each with several drawers and compartments and a commodious closet for hanging clothes, a brass-studded footlocker and several suitcases and hatboxes —and they rode out of New Rochelle on a train that came through at the crack of dawn. Later that morning in New York they made connections with an Atlantic City train in Pennsylvania Station. This was the station designed by the firm of Stanford White and Charles McKim. Its stone colonnade façades, modeled on the Roman baths at Caracalla, spanned

31st to 33rd Street, and 7th to 8th Avenue. Porters helped with Grandfather's wheelchair. Mother was wearing a white ensemble. The laundress held Sarah's child. The station on the inside was so vast that although it was filled with people their voices were no more than a murmur. The boy gazed at the roof, an exposition of corrugated green glass vaults and arches supported by steel ribs and needlelike steel columns. The light fell through this roof like a soft crystal dust. Descending to the concourse of trains he looked right and left and saw as far as he could see in either direction the encouched locomotives waiting in an impatience of steam and shouts and tolling bells to be released on their journeys.

32

And what of Younger Brother? His absence from home since his passionate defense of Coalhouse had caused no undue concern. They were used to his sullen temper. He appeared intermittently at the flag and fireworks plant. He drew his salary. He was not on hand for their departure and so Mother sealed a note and left in on the table in the front hall. The note was never claimed.

Some days after the attack on the firehouse Younger Brother had gone back to the Harlem funeral parlor from which Sarah had been buried. He was met at the door by the proprietor. I should very much like to speak with Mr. Coalhouse Walker, Younger Brother said. I shall wait every evening under the arcade of the Manhattan Casino until he is satisfied that it is safe to receive me. The mortician listened impassively and gave no sign that he knew what Younger Brother was talking about. Nevertheless, every evening thereafter the young man stood at the Casino enduring the stares of the black patrons and timing the intervals between trains of the Eighth Avenue El that periodically rumbled past the building. The weather was warm and through the ornate glass doors of the theatre, which were opened sometime after the evening concert began, he could hear strains of the syncopated music of Jim Europe and the applause of the audience. Of course Coalhouse had quit his orchestra job and moved out of his rooms weeks before his attack on the firehouse. To the police who tried to trace him it was as if he had never existed.

On the fourth night of Younger Brother's vigil a well-dressed colored youth approached him and asked him for a dime. Hiding his astonishment that someone so well turned out should beg for a coin, he dug in his pocket and produced it. The fellow smiled and said he seemed to have more change than that, could he manage another quarter? Younger Brother looked in his eyes and saw there the intelligent appraisal of someone empowered to make a decision.

The next night he looked for the colored fellow but did not see him. Instead he became aware of someone else standing under the arcade after the audience had gone inside. He too was a young man in a suit and tie with a derby upon his head. He suddenly began to walk away and Younger Brother impulsively followed him. He followed him along streets of shabby row houses, across intersections paved in brick, down alleys and around corners. He was aware of going down several streets more than once. Finally on a quiet side street he followed him down under the front steps of a brownstone to a basement door. The door was open. He stepped inside, and went through a short hall to another door and found himself facing Coalhouse, who was seated at a table with his arms crossed. The room was otherwise bare of furniture. Standing about Coalhouse, like a guard, were several Negro youths, all dressed as he was in his characteristically neat and well-groomed manner, with well-pressed suit, clean collar, tie and stickpin. Younger Brother recognized both the one he had followed and the one who had asked for a dime the night before. The door was closed behind him. What is it you want? Coalhouse said. Younger Brother had prepared himself for this question. He had composed an impassioned statement about justice, civilization and the right of every human being to a dignified life. He remembered none of it. I can make bombs, he said. I know how to blow things up.

Thus did Younger Brother commence his career as an outlaw and revolutionary. The family was for a while spared knowledge of this. Only one thing was to link him circumstantially to the black man and that was the disappearance from Father's factory storeroom of several kegs of gunpowder and packages of dry chemicals of various kinds. The pilferage was duly reported to the police and duly forgotten by them. They were busy working on the Coalhouse case. Over a period of several days Younger Brother transported the materials to the basement apartment in Harlem. He then went to work and concocted three powerful package bombs. He shaved his blond moustache and he shaved his head. He blackened his face and hands with burnt cork, outlined exaggerated lips, put on a derby and rolled his eyes. Having in this way suggested his good faith to Coalhouse's other young followers by appealing to their sense of irony, he went out with them and threw the bombs into Municipal Firehouse No. 2, thereby proving himself to everyone including himself.

Our knowledge of this clandestine history comes to us by Younger Brother's own hand. He kept a diary from the day of his arrival in Harlem to the day of his death in Mexico a little more than a year later. Coalhouse Walker had militarized his mourning. His grief for Sarah and the life they might have had was hardened into a ceremony of vengeance in the manner of the ancient warrior. It was Younger Brother's impression that Coalhouse's eyes with their peculiar gaze of unswervable intention appeared now to be looking beyond what they saw to the grave. His command of the young men's loyalty was absolute, probably because he had not asked for it. None of them was a mercenary. There were five besides Younger Brother, the oldest in his twenties, the youngest not yet eighteen. Their respect for Coalhouse bordered on reverence. They lived together there in the basement of the brownstone pooling their wages as stock clerks and delivery boys. Younger Brother added several comparatively munificent pay envelopes from the flag and fireworks plant before he abandoned New Rochelle altogether. The bookkeeping of the communal treasury was scrupulous. Every penny was accounted for. They mimicked Coalhouse's dress and so the suit and carefully brushed black derby was a kind of uniform. They came and went from their rooms like soldiers on patrol.

At night they sat for hours and discussed their situation and what it could lead to. They studied the reactions of the press to what they had done.

Coalhouse Walker was never harsh or autocratic. He treated his followers with courtesy and only asked if they thought something ought to be done. He dealt with them out of his constant sorrow. His controlled rage affected them like the force of a magnet. He wanted no music in the basement quarters. No instrument of any kind. They embraced every discipline. They had brought in several cots and laid out a barracks. They shared kitchen chores and housecleaning chores. They believed they were going to die in a spectacular manner. This belief produced in them a dramatic, exalted self-awareness. Younger Brother was totally integrated in their community. He was one of them. He awoke every day into a state of solemn joy.

On both of Coalhouse's attacks he used automobiles the young men stole for him in Manhattan. The autos were returned without damage to their garages and if the phenomenon of their disappearance and return was reported to the New York Police it was never connected by them to the events in Westchester. After the bombing of the Municipal Fire Station, when Coalhouse's picture was published on every front page in the country, he sat down with a sheet over his shoulder and permitted one of the young men to shave his head and his neat moustache. The change in him was striking. His shaven head seemed massive. Younger Brother understood that whatever its practical justification this was no less than a ritualistic grooming for the final battle. A day or two later one of the band brought in the daily papers with photographs of the Model T raised from the pond. This tangible proof of the force of Coalhouse's will made them all feel holy. By the time they received news of Willie Conklin's flight and sat down to discuss the proper response, they were so transformed as to speak of themselves collectively as Coalhouse. Coalhouse gone to that coal and ice yard, one of them said, Willie be a dead man now. We missed our chance. Naw, Brother, another said, he better to us alive. He keeping Coalhouse in the folks' minds. He a plague. Now we going do something so terrible bad in this town, no one ever mess with a colored man for fear he belong to Coalhouse.

33

Ah, what a summer it was! Each morning Mother opened the white-curtained glass doors of her room and stood looking at the sun as it rose above the sea. Gulls skimmed the breakers and strutted on the beach. The rising sun erased the shadows from the sand as if the particled earth itself shifted and flattened, and by the time she heard Father astir in the adjoining room the sky was beneficently blue and the beach was white and the first sea bathers had appeared down at the surf to test the water with their toes.

They breakfasted in the hotel at tables covered with starched white cloths. The service was heavy hotel silver. They dined on half grapefruit and shirred eggs and hot breads, broiled fish, ham slices, sausage, a variety of preserves dispensed to oneself from tiny spoons, coffee and tea. And all the while the breezes from the ocean lifted the bottoms of the window curtains and shivered their salt thrill along the high fluted ceiling. The boy was always eager to be up and out. After the first few days they allowed him to excuse himself and watched from their table as he appeared moments later running down the wide steps of the porch with his shoes held in his hand. They were on nodding acquaintance with several of the guests. This would yield to speech eventually and then the mild curiosity aroused by this one's looks or that one's dress would be satisfied. They were in no rush. They felt they looked grand and prosperous. Mother bought beautiful summer ensembles from the boardwalk shops. She wore white and yellow and in the informality of afternoons abandoned herself to no hat and only carried a sun parasol. Her face was bathed in soft golden light.

They would swim in midafternoon, when the air became still and the heat oppressive. Mother's bathing costume was modest but she required several days to feel comfortable in it. It was black, of course, with skirt and pantaloons that came below her knees and low-cut swim shoes. But her calves were exposed and her neck, almost to the bodice. She insisted that they separate themselves by several hundred yards from the nearest bathers. They encamped under a hotel umbrella with its name imprinted in orange upon its escalloped fringe. The Negro woman sat upon a straw chair some yards away. The boy and the brown child studied the tiny crabs that buried themselves with a bubbly trail in the wet sand. Father wore a horizontal striped blue and white sleeveless one-piece bathing suit that made cylinders of his thighs. Mother found it distasteful to see the outlines of his maleness in that costume when he emerged from the water. Father liked to swim out. He lay on his back beyond the breakers spouting water like a whale. He came in staggering through the waves, laughing, his hair flattened on his head, his beard dripping and his costume clinging to him immodestly; and she felt momentary twinges of dislike, so fleeting she didn't even recognize what they were. After sea bathing everyone retired for a rest. She would remove her costume with relief, having wet it only for a few moments in the foamy surf, and sponge the salt from her skin. She was so fair that the shore was dangerous for her. Yet cooled by her ablutions, powdered and loosely gowned, she could feel the sun stored in her, spreading in her blood, lighting it as at noon it did the sea, with millions of diamond flashes of light. After-the-swim was soon established by Father as the time for amour. He would make his lusty heedless love every day if she allowed it. She silently resented the intrusion, not as in the old days but with some awareness of her own, some sort of expectation on the skin that was only pounded from her. She thought about Father a good deal. The events since his return from the Arctic, his response to them, had broken her faith in him. The argument he had had with her brother still resounded in her mind. Yet at moments, for whole days at a time, she loved him as before—with a sense of the appropriateness of their marriage, its fixed and unalterable character, as something heavenly. Always she had intuited a different future for them, as if the life they led was a kind of preparation, when the manufacturer of flags and fireworks and his wife would lift themselves from their respectable existence and discover a life of genius. She didn't know of what it would consist, she never had. But now she no longer waited for it. During his absence when she had made certain decisions regarding the business, all its mysterious potency was dissipated and she saw it for the dreary unimaginative thing it was. No longer expecting to be beautiful and touched with grace till the end of her days, she was coming to the realization that whereas once, in his courtship, Father might have embodied the infinite possibilities of loving, he had aged and gone dull, made stupid, perhaps, by his travels and his work, so that more and more he only demonstrated his limits, that he had reached them, and that he would never move beyond them.

Yet she was happy to be in Atlantic City. Here Sarah's child was protected. For the first time since Sarah's death she could think of her without weeping. She enjoyed being viewed in public, as in the dining room at the hotel or on the veranda in the evening, or strolling on the boardwalk down to the pavilions and piers and shops. Sometimes they hired a chair in which she and Father sat side by side and were slowly pushed along by a porter. They made lazy examination of the occupants of chairs going in the opposite direction, or glanced discreetly at other riders they happened to pass. Father tipped his straw. The chairs were wicker, with fringed canvas tops that reminded her of the surreys of her childhood. The two side wheels were large, as on a safety bicycle; the small wheel in front swiveled and sometimes squeaked. Her son loved these chairs. They could be hired too without a man, and he loved that best of all, for then he pushed the chair with his mother and father seated in it and he could direct it as he would, at whatever speed, without their feeling the need of instructing him. The great hotels stood behind the boardwalk, one next to the other, their awnings flapping in the sea wind, their immaculately painted porches lined with rocking chairs and white wicker settees. Nautical flags flew from the cupolas and at night they were lighted by rows of incandescent bulbs strung along their roof lines.

One night the family stopped at a pavilion where a brass band of Negroes stoutly played a rag, she didn't know which one, that she remembered ringing from her piano at home under the fine hands of Mr. Coalhouse Walker. She had for days lived not in forgetfulness of the tragedy but in relief from it, as if in this resort city by the sea painful thoughts were blown off by the prevailing breezes as soon as they formed. Now she was almost overcome by the music which was associated in her mind also with Younger Brother. And immediately her love for her brother, a wave of passionate admiration, broke over her. She felt she had neglected him. An image of his lean moody impetuous being flashed in her mind, somewhat reproachful, somewhat disgusted. It was the way he had looked at her over the dining table at home as Father cleaned his pistol. She felt a slight vertigo, and looking into the lights

of the pavilion where the indomitable musicians sat in red and
blue uniforms with their shiny trumpets and cornets, tubas and
saxophones, she thought she saw under each trim military cap
the solemn face of Coalhouse.

After that evening Mother's joy in the seashore was more
tenuous. She had to concentrate on each day as it came. She
attempted by sheer resolve to make it serene. She was affectionate to her son, her husband, her invalid father; she was
affectionate to her Negro woman and most of all to the still-
unchristened and beautiful son of Sarah, who was thriving here
and seemed to be growing visibly. She began to consider the
attentions that were being paid her by various of the hotel
guests. They hovered on the edges of her consciousness, waiting for some recognition from her. For simple occupation she
was now prepared to bestow this. There were several impressive Europeans at the hotel. One was a German military at-
taché to his embassy who wore a monocle and always saluted
her with discreet gallantry. He was tall and wore that cropped
hair they affected and came to dinner in his formal uniform
of white, with a black bow tie. He made a great show of
ordering wines and then rejecting them. There were no women
in his party but three or four men, somewhat coarser-looking,
whose rank was apparently inferior to his. Father said he was
a Captain von Papen and that he was an engineer. They saw
him every day walking the beach and unrolling charts and
pointing to sea and speaking to his aides. Usually there was at
the time a small craft slowly traversing the horizon. It is some
kind of engineering survey, Father said lying on the beach sand
with his face to the sun. I can't imagine why the South Jersey
coast should interest Germans. Father was oblivious to the
man's speculative notice of his wife. Mother was amused by
this. She knew from the first careless glance she returned to the
officer that he presented to her only the most lascivious inten-

tions focused, as it were, in the imperiousness of his monocled gaze. She decided to ignore him.

There was an elderly French couple with whom she learned to exchange pleasantries; she laughed to recall her schoolgirl French and they very generously complimented her accent. They never appeared in the sun except cocooned in endless swaths of linen and gauze topped with Panama hats. For good measure they carried parasols. The man, who was shorter than his wife and quite heavy, had liver spots on his face. He wore thick glasses. He had enormous pendent ear lobes. He carried a butterfly net and jar with a cork stopper and she a picnic hamper so heavy that she could not walk upright with it. Each morning she struggled after him over the dunes and they disappeared in the distant haze where there were no hotels, no boardwalk, only the gulls and sandpipers and the dune grasses, where sat the trembling wings for which he lusted. He was a retired history professor from Lyons.

Mother tried to interest Grandfather in the French couple on the basis of their academic background. The old man would have none of it. He was totally engrossed by his condition and too irritable to engage in civilized discourse. He defeated all the diversions she thought up for him—except one, a daily ride in a boardwalk chair in which he could sit and be wheeled without being thought infirm. But he carried a cane across his lap and whenever the pedestrian traffic did not move fast enough for him he lifted the cane and prodded women and men alike, who would turn and stare, outraged, as he sailed past them.

There were other guests, of course, who were not Europeans: a gigantic stockbroker from New York with a huge wife and three immense children, who spoke not a word when they dined; several family groups from Philadelphia, who could be placed quickly by the nasalities of their speech. But Mother found that the persons who interested her were invariably foreigners. They were not a substantial number but seemed to beam more life than her countrymen. The most fascinating of all was a small, limber man who wore jodhpurs and a white silk shirt open at the neck and a flat white linen cap with a button. He was a flamboyant, excited person whose eyes darted here and there, like a child's, afraid of what they might miss. He carried on a chain around his neck a rectangular glass framed in metal which he often held up to his face as if to compose for a mental photograph what it was that had captured his attention. One cloudy morning on the hotel porch it turned out to be Mother. Caught in the act he came over and in a thick foreign accent made profuse apologies. He was, he said, the Baron Ashkenazy. He was in the moving-picture business and the glass rectangle was a tool of the trade which he could not forbear using even when on vacation. He laughed sheepishly and Mother was charmed. He had shining black hair and his hands were delicate and small. She saw him next on the beach leaping about some distance away, entertaining a child at the edge of the sea, picking up things, running this way and that, and holding up his peculiar rectangular glass. With the sun behind him he was no more than a silhouette. But she immediately recognized his energetic figure, even at that distance, and she smiled.

The Baron Ashkenazy was the first guest to join Mother and Father at their table. He arrived with a beautiful little girl whom he introduced as his daughter. She was astonishingly lovely, about the same age as the boy. Mother had immediate hopes that they would become friends. Of course they sat there and said nothing and didn't look at one another. But she was a remarkable creature, with the darkest eyes and thick black hair like her father's and a Mediterranean complexion. She wore a fine white lace dress with a satin bodice shaped by the smallest suggestion of a bosom. Father could not take his eyes off the girl. Through dinner she said nothing, nor did she smile. But the explanation was soon forthcoming, after the appetizer, in fact, when the Baron in a lowered voice, his hand going out to touch his daughter's hand, explained that her mother had died some years before although he did not say of what. He had never remarried. A moment later he was again his ebullient self. He talked incessantly in his European accent, with malapropisms he himself recognized and laughed over. Life excited him. He dwelled on his own sensations and liked to talk about them: the taste of the wine or the way the candle flames multiplied in the crystal chandeliers. His simple delight in everything was infectious and soon Mother and Father wore constant smiles on their faces. They had forgotten themselves. It was enormously pleasurable to see the world as the Baron did, alive to every moment. He held his rectangular glass aloft, framing Mother and Father, the two children, the waiter walking toward the table and, at the far end of the dining room, a pianist and a fiddler who played for the patrons on a small platform decorated with potted palms. In the movie films, he said, we only look at what is there already. Life shines on the shadow screen, as from the darkness of one's mind. It is a big business. People want to know what is happening to them. For a few pennies they sit and see their selves in movement, running, racing in motorcars, fighting and, forgive me, embracing one another. This is most important today, in this country, where everybody is so new. There is such a need to understand. The Baron lifted his wineglass. He looked at the wine and tasted it. You have of course seen *His First Mistake*. No? *A Daughter's Innocence*. No? He laughed. Don't embarrass! They are my first two picture plays. One-reelers. I made them for under five hundred dollars and each has brought ten thousand dollars in receipt. Yes, he said laughing, it is true! Father had coughed and turned red at the mention of specific sums. Misunderstanding, the Baron insisted on explaining to him how this was a good profit but not unusual. The film business was at this time booming and anyone could make money. Now, the Baron said, I have become myself a company in partnership with the Pathé exchange for a story fifteen reels long! And each reel will be shown, one a week for fifteen weeks, and the customer will come back every week to see what next happens. With a mischievous look he took a shiny coin from his pocket and flipped it into the air. It went nearly as high as the ceiling. Everyone watched it. The Baron caught the coin and flattened his hand on the table with a loud smack. The silver jumped. The water shook in the glasses. He lifted his hand, revealing one of the popular new five-cent pieces, a buffalo nickel. Father couldn't understand why he was doing this. How I named myself, the Baron said with delight. I am the Buffalo Nickel Photoplay, Incorporated!

As the Baron went on talking, Mother looked across the table at the two children sitting next to each other. The idea of examining through a frame what was ordinarily seen by the eye intrigued her. She composed them by her attention, just as if she had been holding the preposterous frame. Her son's hair was combed back from his forehead for the occasion and he wore a large white collar with his little-man suit and flowing tie. His blue eyes, flecked with yellow and green, looked up at her. All the beautiful child next to him needed in her white lace and satin dress was a veil. Her eyes were raised now and she returned Mother's gaze with a directness that verged on defiance. Mother saw them as the bride and groom in a characteristic grade-school exercise of the era, the Tom Thumb wedding.

34

And so the two families met. The sun spread over the sea each
morning and the children sought one another down the wide
corridors of the hotel. When they rushed outside the sea air
struck their lungs and their feet were chilled by the beach sand.
Awnings and pennants snapped in the wind.

Every morning Tateh worked on the scenario of his fifteen-
chapter photoplay, dictating his ideas to the hotel stenogra-
pher and reading the typewritten pages of the previous day's
work. When he was alone he reflected on his audacity. Sometimes he suffered periods of trembling in which he sat alone
in his room smoking his cigarettes without a holder, slumped
and bent over in defeat like the old Tateh. But his new existence thrilled him. His whole personality had turned outward
and he had become a voluble and energetic man full of the
future. He felt he deserved his happiness. He'd constructed it
without help. He had produced dozens of movie books for the
Franklin Novelty Company. Then he had designed a magic
lantern apparatus on which paper strips printed with his silhouettes turned on a wheel. A wooden shuttle passed back and
forth in front of an incandescent lamp like a loom. The apparatus was accepted for mail-order distribution by Sears, Roe-

buck and Company, and the owners of Franklin Novelty offered to make Tateh a partner. In the meantime he had discovered that others were doing animated drawings like his except for projection on celluloid film. From this he became interested in film itself. The images did not have to be drawn. He sold his interests and went into the movie business. Anyone with enough self-assurance could get backing. The film exchanges in New York were desperate for footage. Film companies were forming overnight, re-forming, merging, going to court, attempting to monopolize distribution, taking out patents on technical processes and in all ways exemplifying the anarchic flash and fireworks of a new industry.

There were commonly in America at this time titled European immigrants, mostly impoverished, who had come here years before hoping to marry their titles to the daughters of the *nouveaux riches.* So he invented a baronry for himself. It got him around in a Christian world. Instead of having to erase his thick Yiddish accent he need only roll it off his tongue with a flourish. He dyed his hair and beard to their original black. He was a new man. He pointed a camera. His child was dressed as beautifully as a princess. He wanted to drive from her memory every tenement stench and filthy immigrant street. He would buy her light and sun and clean wind of the ocean for the rest of her life. She played on the beach with a well-bred comely boy. She lay between soft white sheets in a room that looked into an endless sky.

The two friends every morning went to the deserted stretches of beach where the dunes and grasses blocked the hotel from their sight. They dug tunnels and channels for the sea water, walls and bastions and stepped dwellings. They made cities and rivers and canals. The sun rose over their bent backs as they scooped the wet sand. At noon they cooled themselves in the surf and raced back to the hotel. In the afternoons they played in sight of the beach umbrellas, collecting sticks of wood and shells, walking slowly with the little brown boy splashing after them in the ebb tide. Later the adults retired to the hotel and left them alone. Slowly, with the first blue shadows reappearing in the sand, they followed the tide line beyond the dunes and lay down for their most serious pleasure, a burial game. First, with his arm, he made a hollow for her body in the damp sand. She lay in this on her back. He positioned himself at her feet and slowly covered her with sand, her feet, her legs, her belly and small breasts and shoulders and arms. He used wet sand and shaped it in exaggerated projections of her form. Her feet were magnified. Her knees grew round, her thighs were dunes and on her chest he constructed large nippled bosoms. As he worked, her dark eyes never left his face. He lifted her head gently and raised a pillow of sand under it. He lowered her head. From her forehead he built lappets of sand that spread out to her shoulders.

No sooner was the elaborate sculpture completed than she began to destroy it, moving her fingers gently, wiggling her toes. The encrustation slowly crumbled. She raised one knee and then the other, then burst forth altogether and ran down to the water to wash off the crust of sand on her back and the back of her legs. He followed. They bathed in the sea. They held hands and squatted and let the surf break over them. They went back to the beach and now it was his turn to be buried. She built the same elaborate casing for his body. She enlarged the feet, the legs. The small prominence in his bathing suit she built up with cuppings of sand. She built out his narrow chest and widened his shoulders and gave him the lappeted headdress he had designed for her. When the work was done he slowly broke it to pieces, cracking it carefully, as a shell, and breaking out then for the run to the water.

In the evenings, sometimes, their parents took them to the amusements on the boardwalk. They would hear the band concert or see the road show. They saw *Around the World in*

80 Days. Clouds floated through the theatre. They saw *Dr. Jekyll and Mr. Hyde*. But the real excitement was in the attractions the adults would not dream of patronizing: the freak shows, the penny arcades, the *tableaux vivants*. They were too shrewd to express their desires. Then after a few visits downtown, when the trip seemed not so formidable, they persuaded the adults they were capable of making it by themselves. And fortified with fifty cents they ran along the boardwalk in the dusk. They stood looking into the lights of the mechanical fortuneteller's glass case. They put in a penny. The turbaned figure, its mouth clacking open on shining teeth, turned its head right and left and raised its hand in a jerking way; a ticket was extruded and the entire apparatus lurched to a halt in mid-smile. I am the great He-She, the ticket said. They put money in the claw machine, directing it by means of wheels to drop the steel claw where it would clutch the treasure they wanted and release it into the chute. In this way they received a necklace of shells, a small mirror of polished metal, a tiny cat of glass. They viewed the freaks. They walked quietly among the exhibition stalls of the Bearded Lady, the Siamese Twins, the Wild Man from Borneo, the Cardiff Giant, the Alligator Man, the Six-Hundred-Pound Woman. It was this behemoth who stirred on her stool and quivered as the children came before her. She was seized with an irrepressible emotion and rose on her tiny feet and came toward them mountainously. The great gardens of her flesh closed and opened, going out and in, out and in, as she spread her arms in oscillations of sentiment. They moved on. Behind each fence the watchful normal eyes of the creatures tracked their odyssey. From the Giant they bought a ring from his finger which went around their wrists; from the Siamese twins, a signed photo. They ran out.

Their desire for each other's company was unflagging. This was noted with amusement by the adults. They were inseparable until bedtime but uncomplaining when it was announced. They ran off to their separate rooms with not a glance backward. Their sleep was absolute. They sought each other in the morning. He did not think of her as beautiful. She did not think of him as comely. They were extremely sensitive to each other, silhouetted in a diffuse excitement, like electricity or a nimbus of light, but their touching was casual and matter-of-fact. What bound them to each other was a fulfilled recognition which they lived and thought within so that their apprehension of each other could not be so distinct and separated as to include admiration for the other's fairness. Yet they were beautiful, he in his stately blond thoughtfulness, she a smaller, darker, more lithe being, with flash in her dark eyes and an almost military bearing. When they ran their hair lay back from their broad foreheads. Her feet were small, her brown hands were small. She left imprints in the sand of a street runner, a climber of dark stairs; her track was a flight from the terrors of alleys and the terrible crash of ashcans. She had relieved herself in wooden outhouses behind the tenements. The tails of rodents had curled about her ankles. She knew how to sew with a machine and had observed dogs mating, whores taking on customers in hallways, drunks peeing through the wooden spokes of pushcart wheels. He had never gone without a meal. He had never been cold at night. He ran with his mind. He ran toward something. He was unencumbered by fear and did not know there were beings in the world less curious about it than he. He saw through things and noted the colors people produced and was never surprised by a coincidence. A blue and green planet rolled through his eyes.

One day, as they played, the sun grew dim and a wind began to blow in from the sea. They felt the coldness on their backs. They stood up and saw flights of heavy black clouds coming over the ocean. They started back to the hotel. The rain began. Raindrops pelted craters in the sand. Rain left streaks on their salted shoulders. It poured into their hair. They took shelter under the boardwalk a half-mile from the hotel. They crouched in the cold sand and listened to the rain spatter the boardwalk and watched it collect in droplets between the planks. Debris was under the boardwalk. Broken glass and staring putrefied fish heads, torn parts of crabs, rusted nails, broken boards, driftwood, starfish as hard as stone, oiled spots of sand, bits of rags with dried blood. They stared out at the sea from their cave. A storm had risen and the sky glowed with a green light. Lightning broke the sky as if it were a cracking shell. The storm punished the ocean, flattened it, cowed it. There were no waves now but aimless swells that did not break or roll into the beach. The weird light increased in intensity; the sky was yellow. The thunder broke as if the surf were in the sky and the wind now blew the rain along the beach, whipped it into the sand, rolled it down the boardwalk. Coming through the wind and water and golden light were two figures walking with their heads down, their arms shielding their eyes. And they would turn and with their backs to the wind look up and down the beach and cup their hands to their mouths. But they could not be heard. The children watched them without moving. They were Mother and Tateh. On they came. They stumbled through the wet sand. They turned and the wind blew their clothes against their backs. They turned and the wind blew their clothes against their chests and legs. They cut away from the water toward the boardwalk. Tateh's black hair, flattened over his forehead, shone in the bright water. Mother's hair had come undone and lay in wet strands about her face and shoulders. They called. They called. They ran and walked and looked for the children. They were distraught. The children ran into the rain. When Mother saw them she dropped to her knees. In a moment the four were together, hugging and admonishing and laughing; Mother laughed and cried at the same time with the rain pouring down her face. Where were you, she said, where were you. Didn't you hear us call? Tateh had lifted his daughter to hold her in his arms. *Gottzudanken,* said the Baron. *Gottzudanken.* They walked back along the beach in this rain and light, happy, huddled all together, soaking wet. Tateh could not help but notice how Mother's white dress and underclothes lay against her so that ellipses of flesh pressed through. She looked so young with her hair down on her shoulders and matted around her head. Her skirts stuck to her limbs and every few moments she would bend to pluck them away from her body and the wind would blow them back against her. When they had discovered that the children were missing they had run down to the beach and she had removed her shoes at the bottom of the boardwalk stairs and held his arm for support. She walked with her arms around the children. He recognized in her wet form the ample woman in the Winslow Homer painting who is being rescued from the sea by towline. Who would not risk his life for such a woman? But she was pointing to the horizon: a lead of blue sky had opened over the ocean. Suddenly Tateh ran ahead of them all and did a somersault. He did a cartwheel. He stood on his hands in the sand and walked upside down. The children laughed.

Father slept through the incident. He was unable to sleep at night lately and had begun to nap in the afternoons. He was restless. He had read in the newspaper of the growing movement in the Congress for a national tax on income. This was his first presentiment of the end of summer. He took to making regular telephone calls to his manager at the plant in New Rochelle. Things were quiet at home. Nothing more had been heard from the black killer. Business was holding up as he would know from the copies of the orders sent out to him every day. None of this put him at ease. He was becoming bored by the beach and no longer cared to bathe in the ocean. In the evenings before bed he went to the game room and practiced billiards. How could they resume their lives if they remained

in Atlantic City? Some mornings he awoke and felt that time
and events had gone on and left him more vulnerable than
ever. He found their new friend, the Baron, a momentary
distraction. Mother thought he was endearing but he felt no
special sympathy from him or for him. He wanted to pack up
and leave but was constrained by Mother's security in the
place. Here she believed it might be possible to wait for the
Coalhouse tragedy to conclude itself and hope it could be
outlasted. He knew this was an illusion. To the consternation
of the *hôtelier* she had taken to having the brown child at her
table in the dining room. Father gazed at the little boy with
grim propriety. At breakfast the morning after the rainstorm
he opened the newspaper and found on the front page a
picture of the father. Coalhouse's gang had broken into one of
the city's most celebrated depositories of art, Pierpont Morgan's library on 36th Street. They had barricaded themselves
inside and commanded the authorities to negotiate with them
or risk having the Morgan treasures destroyed. They had
thrown a grenade into the street to demonstrate the capacity
of their armaments. Father crushed the paper in his hands. An
hour later he was paged to the telephone for a call from the
District Attorney's office in Manhattan. That afternoon, borne
by Mother's anxious good wishes, he climbed aboard the train
for New York.

35

Even to someone who had followed the case from its beginning, Coalhouse's strategy of vengeance must have seemed the final proof of his insanity. By what other standard could the craven and miserable Willie Conklin, a bigot so ordinary as to be like all men, become Pierpont Morgan, the most important individual of his time? With eight people dead by Coalhouse's hand, horses destroyed and buildings demolished, with a suburban town still reverberating in its terror, his arrogance knew no bounds. Or is injustice, once suffered, a mirror universe, with laws of logic and principles of reason the opposite of civilization's?

We know from Brother's journal that the actual plan had been to make Morgan a prisoner in his own home. The band's thinking had been that Conklin hiding in an Irish neighborhood was as undetectable as Coalhouse was in Harlem, and that therefore he had to be flushed out. What was needed was a hostage. Two nights of discussion had turned up the candidacy of Pierpont Morgan. More than any mayor or governor he represented in Coalhouse's mind the power of the white world. For years he had been portrayed in cartoons and caricatures, with his cigar and his top hat, as the incarnation of power. The great fiefdom of New York could be made to pay an army of fire chiefs and a fleet of Model T's for the ransom of its Morgan.

But Coalhouse had entrusted the reconnaissance of the Morgan home to two of the youths who knew little about the city below 100th Street and less about the ways of the wealthy. When they reconnoitered the Morgan establishments, the one a brownstone town house, the other a palace of white marble stone, they chose the white marble for the residence. Younger Brother would have seen the error. But he was the ordnance man; he lay in the back of a covered van loaded with explosives and supplies. He could hear the attack under way. The van was backed up to the Library gates and he was given the signal to unload. When he lifted the canvas flaps and looked out he screamed that it was the wrong building. But at that point there was no turning back. A guard lay dead, police whistles were heard. The sound of gunfire had alerted the entire neighborhood. The conspirators unloaded the van, bolted the great brass doors and took up their assigned positions. Then Coalhouse made a quick inspection of the premises. Nothing is lost, he assured them. We wanted the man and so we have him since we have his property.

As it happened Pierpont Morgan **was not** even in New York. He was two days to sea on the S.S. *Carmania* bound for Rome. He was making a slow pilgrimage to Egypt. Coalhouse had not known this either. So the entire action, misdirected and poorly timed, seemed to enjoy some special grace.

Almost immediately aides of the J. P. Morgan Company were informed of the situation. They cabled the *Carmania* to receive the old man's instructions. For some reason, possibly a breakdown of telegraphy equipment aboard the ship, they could not learn if their message had been received. With Morgan not available to tell them what to do the police did

[226]

nothing but cordon off the block, from 36th to 37th Street, from Madison Avenue to Park Avenue. Traffic was diverted and mounted city policemen galloped back and forth to keep the crowds behind the lines. The sounds of the city, its traffic, its horns, its life, seemed walled out by the silence of the scene. The thousands who gathered were as quiet as people can be who are thoroughly engrossed. When night came, flood lamps run by portable generators were trained on the edifice. The rumbling of the generators was felt under the feet of the onlookers, like the growling of an earthquake. Police were everywhere, in their wagons, on foot, on their mounts, but they seemed to be as much spectators as the crowds they held back.

The grenade that was thrown, after the shouted warning by Younger Brother, had ripped up the sidewalk and left an enormous crater in the street in front of the Library gates. At the bottom of the crater a broken water main bubbled like a spa. Windows had been blown out all up and down the block. There was a brownstone across the street, a private residence, that had been particularly hard-hit by the blast. Its owners had fled and had given the Police Department permission to establish its headquarters on the ground floor. The police discovered that they could run up and down the brownstone steps with impunity and move freely along that side of 36th Street if they did not attempt to step over the curb. The house filled with Police Department officials and other city authorities, and gradually, as the nature of the confrontation became clear, one authority after another ceded his responsibility to one higher. Until finally, with lieutenants and precinct captains and inspectors and the Police Commissioner, Rhinelander Waldo, all present, the control of the operation fell to the District Attorney of New York, Charles S. Whitman. Whitman had gained considerable fame prosecuting a corrupt police lieutenant named Becker and securing for him the death sentence for ordering four thugs—Gyp the Blood, Dago Frank, Whitey Lewis and Lefty Louie—to murder a well-known gambler named Herman Rosenthal. This monumental case had made Whitman a natural candidate for governor of New York. There was even talk of his eventual nomination for the Presidency. He had been about to leave New York with his wife for a vacation in Newport at the forty-room summer cottage of Mrs. Stuyvesant Fish. He had recently been introduced to society by Mrs. O. H. P. Belmont. He valued these connections but could not resist dropping over to 36th Street when the news reached him. He thought it was his duty as President-to-be. He liked to be photographed at the scene of the action. Upon his arrival everyone immediately deferred to his judgment, including an enemy of his, the choleric Mayor William J. Gaynor. He thought this was a significant acknowledgment of political realities. He looked at his watch and decided he had a few minutes to take care of this matter of the mad coon.

Whitman called for the plans of the Library from the architectural firm of Charles McKim and Stanford White. After a study of these he authorized a reconnaissance by a single athletic patrolman who was to gain access to the Library roof and look in the domed skylight over the central hall and the East Room to determine how many niggers were in there. A patrolman was found and dispatched through the garden that separated the Library from the Morgan residence. Whitman and the other officials waited in the improvised headquarters. No sooner had the officer entered the garden than the sky flashed and there was a loud report followed by an agonized scream. Whitman went pale. They've got the goddamn place mined, he said. An officer came in. From what anyone could tell, the patrolman in the garden was dead, which was his only bit of luck because nobody could have gone in to get him out of there. The police officials were grim. They looked at Whitman. He now knew that the numerical strength of Coalhouse's band was not crucial intelligence. But he called the press around and announced that they numbered a dozen and perhaps as many as twenty men.

36

In the hours following, District Attorney Whitman conferred
with several advisers. The colonel in command of the New
York militia in Manhattan urged a full-scale military action.
This so alarmed one of Mr. Morgan's curators, a tall nervous
man with a pince-nez who held his hands clasped at his chest
as if he were a diva at the Metropolitan, that he began to
tremble. Do you know the value of Mr. Morgan's acquisitions!
We have four Shakespeare folios! We have a Gutenberg Bible
on vellum! There are seven hundred incunabula and a five-page
letter of George Washington's! The colonel waved his finger
in the air. If we don't take care of that son of a bitch, if we
don't go in there and cut off his balls, you'll have every nigger
in the country at your throat! Then where will you be with your
Bibles? Whitman paced back and forth. A city engineer told
him that if they could repair the broken main they might be
able to tunnel in through the Library foundations. How long
would that take, Whitman asked. Two days, the engineer said.
Someone else thought of poison gas. That might get him,
Whitman agreed. Of course every one else on the East Side
would die, too. He was beginning to feel fretful. The Library
was built of fitted marble blocks. You couldn't get a knife blade

between the stones. The place was wired for dynamite and a pair of watchful coon eyes looked out of every window.

Whitman now had the good sense to ask for ideas from the police officers in the room. An old sergeant with many years on the street, a veteran of Hell's Kitchen and the Tenderloin, said The crucial thing, sir, is to get this Coalhouse Walker engaged in conversation. With an armed maniac, talking calms him down. You get him talking and keep him talking and then you have a wedge into the situation. Whitman, who was not without courage, took a megaphone and stepped into the street and shouted to Coalhouse that he wanted to speak with him. He waved his straw hat. If there's a problem, he cried, we can solve it together. He repeated such sentiments for several minutes. Then for a moment the small window adjacent to the front entrance opened. A cylindrical object came flying into the street. Whitman flinched and the men in the house behind him dropped to the floor. To everyone's astonishment there was no explosion. Whitman retreated to the brownstone and only after several minutes did someone using binoculars make the object out as a silver tankard with a lid. An officer ran into the street, picked up the tankard and sprinted back up the brownstone stairs. The object, now dented, was a medieval drinking stein of silver with a hunting scene in relief. The curator asked to see it and advised that it was from the seventeenth century and had belonged to Frederick, the Elector of Saxony. I'm really pleased to hear that, Whitman said. The curator then raised the lid and found inside a piece of paper with a telephone number that he recognized as his own.

The District Attorney himself took the telephone. He sat on the edge of a table and held the speaker in his left hand and the receiver attached by a cord in his right. Hello, Mr. Walker, he said heartily, this is District Attorney Whitman. He was stunned by the calm businesslike tone of the black man. My demands are the same, said the voice on the phone. I want my car returned in just the condition it was when my way was blocked. You cannot bring back my Sarah, but I want for her life the life of Fire Chief Conklin. Coalhouse, Whitman said, you know that I as an officer of the court could never give over to you for sentencing outside the law a man who has not had due process. That puts me in an untenable position. What I can promise is to investigate the case and see what statutes apply, if any. But I can't do anything for you until you're out of there. Coalhouse Walker seemed not to have heard. I will give you twenty-four hours, he said, and then I will blow up this place and everything in it. And he rang off. Hello, Whitman said. Hello? He ordered the operator to get the number again. There was no answer.

Whitman next sent off a telegram to Mrs. Stuyvesant Fish in Newport. He hoped she read the newspapers. His eyes, which tended to bulge when he was exercised, were now quite prominent. His face was florid. He removed his jacket and unbuttoned his vest. He asked one of the patrolmen to find him some whiskey. He knew that Red Emma Goldman, the anarchist, was in New York. He ordered her arrested. He stared out the window of the brownstone. The day was overcast and unnaturally dark. The air was close and a fine rain made the streets glisten. The lights of the city were on. The compact white Grecian palace across the street shone in the rain. It looked very peaceful. At this moment Whitman came to the realization that the deference shown by Commissioner Rhinelander Waldo and everyone else in the Police Department had tricked him into identifying himself with a politically dangerous situation. He had on one hand to guard the interests of Morgan, whose various Simon Pure reform committees of wealthy Republican Protestants had funded his investigations of corruption in the Democratic Catholic Police Department. He had on the other hand to preserve his own reputation as a tough D.A. who dealt handily with the criminal classes. For that nothing would do but the speediest unhorsing of the colored man. A glass of whiskey was brought to him. Just this one, to calm my nerves, he said to himself.

In the meantime police knocked at the door of Emma Goldman on West 13th Street. Goldman was not surprised. She always kept packed and ready to go a small bag with a change of clothes and a book to read. Ever since the assassination of President McKinley she had been routinely accused of fomenting by word or deed most of the acts of violence or strikes or riots that occurred in America. There was a national obsession of law enforcement officers to connect her to every case just as a matter of principle whether they believed she was guilty or not. She put on her hat, picked up her bag and strode out the door. She rode in the police wagon with a young patrolman. You won't believe this, she said to him, but I look forward to a spell in jail. It is the one place where I can get some rest.

Goldman did not know of course that one of the Coalhouse band was the young man she had pitied as the bourgeois lover of an infamous whore. In front of the sergeant's desk at police headquarters on Centre Street, she made a statement to reporters as she was booked for conspiracy. I am sorry for the firemen in Westchester. I wish they had not been killed. But the Negro was tormented into action, so I understand, by the cruel death of his fiancée, an innocent young woman. As an anarchist, I applaud his appropriation of the Morgan property. Mr. Morgan has done some appropriating of his own. At this the reporters shouted questions. Is he a follower of yours, Emma? Do you know him? Did you have anything to do with this? Goldman smiled and shook her head. The oppressor is wealth, my friends. Wealth is the oppressor. Coalhouse Walker did not need Red Emma to learn that. He needed only to suffer.

Within an hour extra editions of the newspapers were on the

streets featuring the news of the arrest. Goldman was liberally quoted. Whitman wondered if it had been wise to give her a forum. But he did derive one clear benefit from the move. The president of Tuskegee Normal and Industrial Institute, Booker T. Washington, was in the city to do some fund-raising. He was delivering an address downtown at the great hall of Cooper Union on Astor Place and he departed from his prepared text to deplore Goldman's remarks and condemn the actions of Coalhouse Walker. A reporter called Whitman to tell him of this. Immediately the District Attorney got in touch with the great educator, asking if he would come to the scene and use his moral authority to resolve the crisis. I will, Booker T. Washington replied. A police escort was sent downtown and Washington, apologizing to the hosts of the luncheon in his honor, left to ringing applause.

37

Booker T. Washington was at this time the most famous Negro in the country. Since the founding of Tuskegee Institute in Alabama he had become the leading exponent of vocational training for colored people. He was against all Negro agitation on questions of political and social equality. He had written a best-selling book about his life, a struggle up from slavery to self-realization, and about his ideas, which called for the Negro's advancement with the help of his white neighbor. He counseled friendship between the races and spoke of the promise of the future. His views had been endorsed by four Presidents and most of the governors of Southern states. Andrew Carnegie had given him money for his school and Harvard had awarded him an honorary degree. He wore a black suit and homburg. He stood in the middle of 36th Street, a sturdy handsome man with all the pride of his achievement in the way he held himself, and he called out to Coalhouse to let him in the Library. He disdained the use of the megaphone. He was an orator and his voice was strong. There was nothing in his manner to indicate any other possibility than that the desperadoes would grant him his demand. I am coming in now, he called. And he stepped around the crater in the street and walked through the iron gates. He climbed the steps between the stone lionesses and stood in the shadow of the arched portico between the double Ionic columns and waited for the doors to open. There was now a silence and a stillness in the scene that allowed the horn of a cab many blocks away to be heard clearly. After some moments the doors opened. Booker T. Washington disappeared inside. The doors closed. Across the street District Attorney Whitman wiped his brow and sank into a chair.

What Booker Washington found was the awesome gilded library of paintings and tiers of rare books, statuary and marbled floors, damask silk walls and priceless Florentine furniture, all wired for demolition. Fascia of dynamite were strapped to the marble pilasters of the entrance hall. Wires led from the East and West rooms along the floor to the rear of the entrance hall, where there was a small alcove. Here sat a man straddling a marble bench. On the bench was a box with a T-shaped plunger which he held with both hands. His back was to the brass doors and he was leaning forward so that if a bullet were to kill him instantly the weight of his falling body would depress the plunger. This fellow now turned to look over his shoulder at Washington and the great educator drew in his breath sharply as he saw it was not a Negro but a white in blackface, as if this were some minstrel show. Washington had entered in a stern and admonitory frame of mind but with the intention to be diplomatic. He disdained persuasion now. He looked in on the West Room and then walked across the hall to the doorway of the East Room. He had expected to find dozens of colored men but saw only three or four youths standing each beside a window with a rifle in his hands. Coalhouse stood waiting upon him in a well-pressed hound's-tooth suit and a tie and collar, although he carried a pistol in his belt. Washington looked him over. His handsome brow furrowed and his eyes flashed. Summoning all his declamatory powers he spoke as follows: For my entire life I have worked in patience and hope for a Christian brotherhood. I have had to persuade the white man that he need not fear us or murder us, because we wanted only to improve ourselves and peaceably join him in enjoyment of the fruits of American democracy. Every Negro in prison, every shiftless no-good gambling and fornicating colored man has been my enemy, and every incident of faulted Negro character has cost me a piece of my life. What will your misguided criminal recklessness cost me! What will it cost my students laboring to learn a trade by which they can earn their livelihood and still white criticism! A thousand honest industrious black men cannot undo the harm of one like you. And what is worse you are a trained musician, as I understand it, one who comes to this infamous enterprise from the lyceum of music, where harmony is reverenced and the strains of the harps and the trumpets of heaven are the models for song. Monstrous man! Had you been ignorant of the tragic struggle of our people, I could have pitied you this adventure. But you are a musician! I look about me and smell the sweat of rage, the impecunious rebellion of wild unthinking youth. What have you taught them! What injustice done to you, what loss you've suffered, can justify the doom you have led them into, these reckless youths? And, may you be damned, you add to this unholy company a white who smears himself with color and adds mockery to your arsenal.

Every word of this speech could be heard by every member of the band. They were not so steeped in revolution that the sentiments of Booker T. Washington, of whom they had heard since they were children, could not awe them. It must have been crucial for them to know Coalhouse's reply. Coalhouse spoke softly. It is a great honor for me to meet you, sir, he said. I have always stood in admiration for you. He looked at the marble floor. It is true I am a musician and a man of years. But I would hope this might suggest to you the solemn calculation of my mind. And that therefore, possibly, we might both be servants of our color who insist on the truth of our manhood and the respect it demands. Washington was so stunned by this suggestion that he began to lose consciousness. Coalhouse led him from the hall into the West Room and sat him down in one of the red plush chairs. Regaining his composure Washington mopped his brow with a handkerchief. He gazed at the marble mantel of the fireplace as tall as a man. He glanced upward at the polychrome carved ceiling that had originally come from the palace of Cardinal Gigli in Lucca. On the red silk walls were portraits of Martin Luther by Lucas Cranach the Elder and several adorations of the Magi. The educator closed his eyes and locked his hands in his lap. Oh Lord, he said, lead my people to the Promised Land. Take them from under the Pharaoh's whip. Free the shackles from their minds and loosen the bonds of sin that tie them to Hell. Over the mantel was a contemporary portrait of Pierpont Morgan himself when he was in his prime. Washington appraised the fierce face. In the meantime Coalhouse Walker had sat down in the adjoining chair and together the two well-dressed black men were the picture of probity and serious self-contemplation. Come out with me now, Booker Washington said in a soft voice, and I will intercede for the sake of mercy that your trial shall be swift and your execution painless. Dismantle these engines of the devil, he said waving his hands at the dynamite packs strapped in the corners of the carved ceiling and against every wall. Take my hand and come with me. For the sake of your young son and all those children of our race whose way is hard, and whose journey is long.

Coalhouse sat lost in thought. Mr. Washington, he finally said, there is nothing I would like more than to conclude this business. He raised his eyes and the educator saw there the tears of his emotion. Let the Fire Chief restore my automobile and bring it to the front of this building. You will see me come out with my hands raised and no further harm will come to this place or any man from Coalhouse Walker.

This statement constituted Coalhouse's first modification of his demands since the night of the Emerald Isle, but Washington did not understand this. He heard only the rejection of his plea. Without another word he rose and walked out. He went back across the street believing his intervention had accomplished nothing. Afterwards Coalhouse paced the rooms. His young men stayed at their posts and followed him with their eyes. One lay on the roof atop the domed skylight of the portico. He lay in the rain on guard and felt, though he could not see, the presence of thousands of quietly watchful New Yorkers. During the night he thought they made a sound, some barely detectable mourning sound, not more than an exhalation, not louder than the mist of fine rain.

38

After Booker T. Washington conferred with the District Attorney he spoke with reporters in the parlor of the temporary headquarters. Mr. Morgan's library is a dynamite bomb ready to go off at any moment, he said. We are faced with a desperately brainsick man. I can only pray the Lord in His Wisdom will bring us safely out of this sad affair. Washington then made a number of phone calls to friends and colleagues in Harlem—church pastors and community leaders—and invited them to come downtown and demonstrate the opposition of responsible Negroes to the cause of Coalhouse Walker. This took the form of a vigil in the street. District Attorney Whitman granted his permission even though the report brought back from the Library was grim enough to cause him to order an evacuation of every house and apartment within a two-block radius. Such was the state of things when Father arrived. He was escorted through the police lines and marched past the bareheaded silent black men standing in prayer. He looked for a moment at the Library and then went up the stairs of the brownstone. Inside he was left to himself. Nobody spoke with him or wanted anything from him. He turned around, facing this way and that, waiting for some word or notice from the authorities. None was forthcoming.

The house was filled with police in uniform and men of indeterminate responsibility. Everyone milled about. Father wandered back to the kitchen. Here were the reporters. They had eaten the food in the icebox. They sat with their feet on the table and stood leaning against the cupboards. They wore their hats. They used the sink for a spittoon. Father listened to the conversation and heard the details of Booker T. Washington's interview with Coalhouse. He marveled at the fame of the man who had played piano in his parlor. But it sounded to him as if Coalhouse had modified his demands. Was this so? Nobody seemed to perceive it. Yet if the life of Willie Conklin the Fire Chief was either conceded or at least negotiable, he ought to inform someone. He looked for an official and came upon the District Attorney himself, whom he recognized from his pictures in the paper. Whitman was at the bay window in the parlor, a pair of binoculars in his hands. I beg your pardon, Father said, and introducing himself he told Whitman what he thought. The District Attorney regarded him with startled eyes. Father noted small broken veins in his face. Whitman turned back to the window and raised his binoculars and stared out like a sea admiral. Not knowing what else to do Father remained with him.

Whitman was waiting for the reply from Mr. Morgan. He kept looking at his watch. Then someone ran by in the street. There was a commotion in the hallway. A boy came into the parlor followed by the curators and several policemen. He had a wireless from the *Carmania*. The District Attorney tore at the envelope. He read the wire and shook his head in disbelief. Goddamnit, he muttered. Goddamnit to hell. Suddenly he was shouting at everyone in the room. Out! Get out! He herded everyone through the doors. But he held Father's arm and kept him there. The doors closed. Whitman thrust the cable into Father's hands. GIVE HIM HIS AUTOMOBILE AND HANG HIM, the text read.

Father looked up and found the District Attorney glaring at him. This is the one way I would never consider, Whitman said. I can't give in to the coon. Even to hang him. I can't afford it. It would finish me. Goddamnit, I took care of that son of a bitch Becker. The crime of the century. That's what the papers called it. And now the D.A. giving in to a nigger? No, sir! It can't be done!

Whitman paced the room. Father experienced an infusion of boldness. He was holding in his hands a private message from J. Pierpont Morgan. It enabled him to accept immediately and without question his investiture as confidant of the District Attorney of New York.

Father saw clearly that the situation was ready to be negotiated. Even across the world Morgan had understood this. Coalhouse seemed to have softened on one of his demands, that Conklin be turned over to him. It was Father's opinion, furthermore, that since Sarah's death Coalhouse Walker's most fervent wish was to die. He informed the District Attorney of this. The whole matter might be resolved quickly, he said. The car has no real value. Besides, it's Mr. Morgan's idea. I'll say, said Whitman. Only Pierpont Morgan could think of it. Who else would have the nerve. No, Father said, I mean it's his idea. Of course I don't know anything about politics, but doesn't that absolve you of the responsibility? Whitman stopped in his tracks and gazed at Father. Right this minute, he said, I am supposed to be in Newport with the Stuyvesant Fishes, he said.

And so it happened just after midnight that a team of dray horses was backed up to Coalhouse Walker's ruined Model T sitting by Firehouse Pond in New Rochelle. The rain had gone and the stars were out. The horses were hitched to the bumper and they pulled the car up to the road. Then they began the long journey to the city, clip-clopping along, the driver standing up in the front seat holding the reins in one hand, grasping the steering wheel with the other. The tires were all flat, the car rocked as it went, and every revolution of the wheels grated on the ears.

Even as the Ford was advancing toward Manhattan, Whitman managed to get Coalhouse on the phone. He told him he wanted to talk about his demands. He proposed Father as the intermediary to carry the discussion back and forth. This was more private than the telephone. You can trust him and I can trust him, Whitman said of Father. After all, he's your former employer. No, Father said in Whitman's other ear. I was never his employer. Father now had grave misgivings. In too few minutes he found himself outside in the chill early morning, walking across the floodlit street around the crater and up the steps past the stone lions. He reminded himself that he was a retired officer of the United States Army. He had explored the North Pole. The brass doors opened, not widely, and he stepped in. He heard his own footsteps ring on the polished marble floor. His eyes took a moment to adjust to the dim light. He looked for the black man and saw instead his brother-in-law undressed to the waist but with his face blackened and a holstered pistol under his arm. You! Father cried. Younger Brother pulled out the pistol and tapped the barrel against his temple in a kind of salute. Father's knees buckled. He was helped to a chair. Coalhouse brought him a canteen with water.

The first agreement between the two sides was that the twenty-four-hour deadline be extended. The second agreement was that wooden planks should be laid over the hole in the street. Father went back and forth doing his job capably but in a state of peculiar numbness, like a sleepwalker. He did not look at his relative. He could feel queer pulses of bitter glee breaking over his back.

While these points were being settled Whitman was on the telephone using all the means at his disposal to find Willie Conklin. He had the police looking for him in every borough. Then he thought of calling Big Tim Sullivan, Fourth Ward leader and the grand old man of the Tammany machine. He roused him out of his sleep. Tim, he said, there's a visitor in town, a Willie Conklin from up in Westchester County. I don't know the feller, Big Tim said, but I'll see what I can do. I'm sure you will, Whitman said. In less than an hour Conklin was brought up the stairs of the brownstone by the scruff of the neck. He was wet and disheveled and frightened. He had lost the lower buttons of his work shirt and his belly protruded over his belt. He was shoved in a chair in the hallway and told to shut up. A policeman stood guard over him. His teeth were chattering and his hands shook. He reached in his back pocket where he carried his pint in a paper bag. The cop grabbed his arm before he could withdraw it and swung a pair of handcuffs like a whip against his head.

By dawn the crowds, somewhat diminished during the night, filled up again four and five deep behind the barricades. The rusted-out Model T stood on 36th Street along the curb in front of the Library. At a designated moment, the door of the brownstone opened and out on the stoop came two policemen holding between them the forlorn figure of Willie Conklin. He was held there on exhibit. Then he was taken back in, and Whitman, having in good faith brought forth the two items of debate, the car and the Fire Chief, now gave his terms. He would urge his counterpart in Westchester to bring charges against Willie Conklin for malicious mischief, vandalism and illegal detainment of a citizen. In addition the Fire Chief would right there in the street in full sight of everyone help to restore the Model T. It would be a humiliation that he would live with for the rest of his life. And the car of course would be made over new. Whitman wanted in return the surrender of Coalhouse and his men. And then I guarantee that you will have your full privileges and rights under the law, he said.

When Father brought these terms to the Library the young men laughed and hooted. We got him, they called to each other. He givin in. We gonna get the whole pie. They had been buoyed by the sight of the car and the exhibit of Conklin. But Coalhouse himself was silent. He sat alone in the West Room. Father waited on him. Gradually Coalhouse's somber reflection overcame the spirits of the young men. They became apprehensive. Finally Coalhouse said to Father I will surrender myself but not my boys. For them I want safe passage away from here and full and total amnesty. But stay here, please, until I have a chance to tell them.

Coalhouse rose from his chair and went out to talk to the young men in the hall. They gathered around the detonation box. They were stunned. You don't have to give him nothing, they said. We got Morgan's balls! You don't have to negotiate nothing. Give us Conklin and that car and let us out of here and you get the Library back! That's the negotiation, man, that's the kind of negotiation!

Coalhouse was calm. He spoke softly. None of you is known to the authorities by name, he said. You can disappear into the city and reclaim your life. So can you, came the answer. No, Coalhouse said. They would never let me out of here, you know that. And if they did they would spare no effort to hunt me down. And everyone with me would be hunted down. And you would all die. To what purpose? For what end?

We always talked before, one of them said. Now you doing this. You can't, man! We all Coalhouse! We can't get out we'll blow it up, another said. Younger Brother said What you are doing is betraying us. Either we all ought to go free or we all ought to die. You signed your letter President of the Provisional American Government. Coalhouse nodded. It seemed to be the rhetoric we needed for our morale, he said. But we meant it! Younger Brother cried. We meant it! There are enough people in the streets to found an army!

Certainly no theorist of revolution could have denied the truth that with an enemy as vast as an entire nation of the white race, the restoration of a Model T automobile was as good a place to start as any. Younger Brother was shouting now. You can't change your demands! You can't reduce the meaning of your demands! You can't betray us for a car! I have not changed my demands, Coalhouse said. Is the goddamn Ford your justice? said Younger Brother. Is your execution your justice? Coalhouse looked at him. As for my execution, he said, my death was determined the moment Sarah died. As for my Godforsaken Ford it is to be made over as it was the day I drove past the firehouse. It is not I who reduce my demands but they who magnified them as long as they resisted them. I will trade your precious lives for Willie Conklin's and thank God for him.

A few minutes later Father walked back across the street. To get justice, Coalhouse Walker was ready to have it done to him. But the people following him were not. They were another generation. They were not human. Father shuddered. They were monstrous! Their cause had recomposed their minds. They would kick at the world's supports. Start an army! They were nothing more than filthy revolutionaries.

Coalhouse's famous stubbornness had now become a fortress against the arguments of his men. It was he who stood between Mr. Morgan and disaster. Father confided none of this to the District Attorney. He felt Whitman would have trouble enough with the official terms. This turned out to be the case. Whitman threw back several shots of whiskey. Stubble covered his face. His protuberant eyes were red and his collar was wilted. He paced. He stood at the window. He made a fist of his right hand and several times smacked the palm of his left. He looked again at the wire from Morgan. Father cleared his throat. It does not say you have to hang the confederates, Father said. What? said Whitman. What? All right, all right. He looked for a chair to sit down in. How many of them are there, did you say? Five, Father said, unconsciously excluding Younger Brother. Whitman sighed. Father said I think this is the best you can do. Sure, said the District Attorney. And what do I tell the newspapers. Why, Father said, you can tell them, one, Coalhouse Walker is captured, and two, Mr. Morgan's treasures are saved, and three, the city is safe, and four, the entire facilities of your office and the police will be used to track down the underlings until every last one of them is behind bars where he belongs. Whitman thought about that. We'll tail them, he muttered. Right back to the woodpile. Well, Father said, that may not be possible. They're taking a hostage and they won't let him go until they know they're safe. Who is the hostage, Whitman said. I am, Father said. I see, Whitman said. And what makes the coon think he can hold the building alone? Well, Father said, he will be out of the sightlines of skylight or windows with his hands on the dynamite box. That would do it, I should think.

Perhaps Father at this moment nourished the hope that after his release he could lead the authorities back to the criminals' lair. He thought without Coalhouse they would lack the spirit and intelligence to continue successfully to defy the law. They were anarchist murderers and arsonists but he was not personally afraid. He knew their stamp and was a better man than any of them. From Younger Brother he was so totally alienated that he felt at this moment only joy in the thought of being responsible for his capture.

Whitman was staring into space. All right, he said. All right.

Maybe if we wait till dark nobody will see what we're doing. For Mr. Morgan's sake, and his goddamn Gutenberg Bible and his five-page goddamn letter from George Washington.

And so the negotiations were completed.

39

Several calls to the Ford motorcar people had brought forth by eight in the morning a truck carrying all the interchangeable parts for a Model T. The Pantasote Company delivered a top. Aides of Morgan had agreed that he would be billed for everything. As the crowd watched from the corner, Fire Chief Conklin, under the direction of two mechanics, piece by piece dismantled the Ford and made a new Ford from the chassis up. A block and tackle was used to hoist the engine. Sweating, grunting, complaining and at times crying, Conklin did the work. New tires replaced old, new fenders, new radiator, magneto, new doors, running boards, windshield, headlamps and upholstered seats. By five in the afternoon, with the sun still blazing in the sky over New York, a shining black Model T Ford with a custom pantasote roof stood at the curb.

All day the followers of Coalhouse had come to him with appeals to change his mind. Their arguments became wilder and wilder. They said they were a nation. He was patient with them. It became apparent they wouldn't know what to do without him. They recognized his decision as suicide. They were forlorn at their abandonment. By the late afternoon the Library was in gloom. The young men watched listlessly from the windows as the automobile in which Coalhouse had done his courting reappeared at the curb.

Coalhouse himself never once went to the window to look at it. He sat at Pierpont Morgan's desk in the West Room and composed his will.

Younger Brother had withdrawn in silent bitterness. Father, who was now closeted in the Library as an official hostage, wanted to talk with him. He was thinking what he would have to tell Mother. Only when it grew dark and the hour of the departure was approaching could he bring himself to confront him. It might be the last privacy they would have.

The young man was in the lavatory behind the entrance hall. He was wiping the burnt cork from his face. He glanced at Father in the mirror. Father said I myself require nothing from you. But don't you feel your sister deserves an explanation? If she thinks about me, Younger Brother said, she will have her explanation. I could not transmit it through you. You are a complacent man with no thought of history. You pay your employees poorly and are insensitive to their needs. I see, Father said. The fact that you think of yourself as a gentleman in all your dealings, Younger Brother said, is the simple self-delusion of all those who oppress humanity. You have lived under my roof and worked in my business, Father said. Your generosity, Younger Brother said, was what you felt you could afford. Besides, he added, I have repaid that debt, as you will discover. Younger Brother washed his face with soap and hot water. He used a vigorous motion, his head over the basin. He dried himself with a hand towel embroidered with the initials JPM. He threw the towel on the floor, put on his shirt, dug in his pockets for cuff links, buttons, placed his collar over the shirt, tied his tie, raised his suspenders. You have traveled everywhere and learned nothing, he said. You think it's a crime to come into this building belonging to another man and to threaten his property. In fact this is the nest of a vulture. The den of a jackal. He put on his coat, ran his palms over his shaved head, placed his derby on his head and glanced at himself in the mirror. Goodbye, he said. You won't see me again. You may tell my sister that she will always be in my thoughts. For a moment he gazed at the floor. He had to clear his throat. You may tell her I have always loved her and admired her.

The band met in the entrance hall. They were dressed now in their Coalhouse uniforms of suit and tie and derby. Coalhouse told them they should pull their brims down and turn up the collars of their jackets to avoid identification. Their means of safe conduct was the Model T. He explained how to set the spark and throttle and how to turn the crank. You will ring the telephone when you're free, he said. Father said Am I not to go? Here is the hostage, Coalhouse said, indicating Younger Brother. One white face looks just like another. They all laughed. Coalhouse embraced each of them before the great brass doors. He embraced Younger Brother with the same fervor he accorded the others. He looked at his pocket watch. At this moment the floodlights in the street went out. He took his place in the alcove at the back of the hall, straddling the white marble bench with his hands on the dynamite detonation box. There is slack in the plunger to a point halfway down, Younger Brother called to him. All right, Coalhouse said. Go on now. One of the young men unbolted the doors and with no further ceremony they filed out. Then the doors closed. Bolt them, please, Coalhouse commanded. Father did so. He put his ear to the doors. All he heard was his own heavy and frightened breathing. Then after what seemed a torturously long interval, in which almost all his hope for his own life flowed from him, he heard the sibilant cough and sputter of a Model T engine. A few moments later the gears were engaged and he heard the car drive off. There was a thump thump as it went over the planks laid over the crater. He ran to the back of the hall. They're gone, he said to Coalhouse Walker Jr. The black man was staring at his hands poised on the plunger of the box. Father sat down on the floor with his back to the marble wall. He raised his knees and rested his head. They sat like that, neither of them moving. After a while Coalhouse asked Father to tell him about his son. He wanted to know about his walking, whether his appetite was good, whether he'd said any words yet, and every detail he could think of.

40

About two hours later Coalhouse Walker Jr. came down the stairs of the Library with his arms raised and started to walk across 36th Street to the brownstone. This was according to the negotiated agreement. The street had been cleared of all observers. Facing him on the opposite sidewalk was a squad of New York's Finest armed with carbines. Lined up from one sidewalk to the other were two troops of mounted police facing each other at a distance of thirty yards, the horses shoulder to shoulder, so that a kind of corridor was formed. Coalhouse was therefore not visible to anyone looking on from the intersections at Madison Avenue or, more remotely, Park Avenue. The generators on the corner made a fearsome roar. In the bright floodlit street the black man was said by the police to have made a dash for freedom. More probably he knew that all he must do in order to end his life was to turn his head abruptly or lower his hands or smile. Inside the Library, Father heard the coordinated volley of a firing squad. He screamed. He ran to the window. The body jerked about the street in a sequence of attitudes as if it were trying to mop up its own blood. The policemen were firing at will. The horses snorted and shied.

Up in their Harlem hideout the Coalhouse band could reason what the outcome would be. They were all there but the man they had followed. The rooms seemed empty. Nothing mattered. They could barely bring themselves to talk. All but Younger Brother thought they would remain in New York. The Model T was hidden in an adjoining alley. They assumed it had been marked. Since Younger Brother wanted to leave town he was awarded the car. He drove that night to the waterfront at 125th Street and took the ferry to New Jersey. He drove south. Apparently he had some money although it is not known how or where he got it. He drove to Philadelphia. He drove to Baltimore. He drove deep into the country where Negroes stood up in the fields to watch him pass. His car left a trail of dust in the sky. He drove through small towns in Georgia where in the scant shade of the trees in the squares citizens spoke of hanging the Jew Leo Frank for what he had done to a fourteen-year-old Christian girl, Mary Phagan. They spit in the dirt. Younger Brother raced freight trains and clumped his car through the cool darkness of covered bridges. He used no maps. He slept in the fields. He drove from gasoline pump to gasoline pump. He collected in the back seat an assortment of tools, tire tubes, gascans, oilcans, clamps, wires and engine parts. He kept going. The trees became more scattered. Eventually they disappeared. There was rock and sagebrush. Beautiful sunsets lured him through valleys of hardened sun-cracked clay. When the Ford broke down and he couldn't fix it he was pulled by children sitting up on wagons drawn by mules.

In Taos, New Mexico, he came upon a community of bohemians who painted desert scenes and wore serapes. They were from Greenwich Village in New York. They were attracted by his exhaustion. He was passionately sullen, even when drinking. He replenished himself here for several days. He enjoyed a brief affair with an older woman.

By now Younger Brother's thinning hair was just long

enough to fall flat on his crown. He wore a blond beard. His
fair skin peeled constantly and he squinted from the sun. He
drove on into Texas. His clothes had worn away. He wore bib
overalls and moccasins and an Indian blanket. At the border
town of Presidio he sold the Ford to a storekeeper and, taking
with him only the desert water bag that he had hung from the
radiator cap, he waded across the Rio Grande to Ojinaga,
Mexico. This was a town that had seen successive occupations
of federal troops and insurgents. The adobe houses of Ojinaga
lacked roofs. There were holes in the church walls made by
field guns. The villagers lived behind the walls of their yards.
The streets were white dust. Here were billeted some of the
forces of Francisco Villa's Division of the North. He attached
himself to them and was accepted as a *compañero*.

When Villa did his march south to Torreón, two hundred
miles along the destroyed tracks of the central railroad,
Younger Brother was in the throng. They rode across the great
Mexican desert of barrel cactus and Spanish bayonet. They
encamped at ranchos and in the coolness of the castellated
abbeys smoked *macuche* wrapped in cornhusks. There was
little food. Women with dark shawls carried water jars on their
heads.

After the victory at Torreón, Younger Brother wore the
cartridge belts crisscrossed over his chest. He was a *villista* but
dreamed of going on and finding Zapata. The army rode on
the tops of railroad freight cars. With the troops went their
families. They lived on the tops of the trains with guns and
bedding and baskets with their food. There were camp followers and babies at the breast. They rode through the desert with
the cinders and smoke of the engine coming back to sting their
eyes and burn their throats. They put up umbrellas against the
sun.

There was a meeting in Mexico City of the insurgent chiefs
from the various regions. It was another moment when the

revolution had to be defined. After the despised tyrant Díaz had been overthrown a reformist, Madero, had taken power. Madero had fallen to a General Huerta, an Aztec. Now Huerta was gone and a moderate, Carranza, was trying to assume control. The capital seethed with proliferating factions, thieving bureaucrats and foreign businessmen and spies. Into this chaos rode Zapata's peasant army of the south. The city was hushed by their arrival. Their reputation was so fierce that the urban Mexicans feared them. Younger Brother stood quietly with the *villistas* and watched them ride in. Then the Mexicans began to laugh. The fearsome warriors of the south could not speak properly. Many of them were children. Their eyes went wide when they saw the palace of Chapultepec. They wore rags. They would not step on the sidewalks of the Paseo de la Reforma, a boulevard of mansions and trees and outdoor restaurants, but walked instead in the street, through the horse droppings. The electric streetcars of the city frightened them. They fired their rifles at fire engines. And the great Zapata himself, sitting for photographs in the palace, let Villa take the President's chair.

The *campesinos* of the south did not like either Mexico City or the revolution of the moderates. When they left, Younger Brother went with them. He had never revealed his special knowledge to the officers of Villa. But to Emiliano Zapata he said I can make bombs and repair guns and rifles. I know how to blow things up. In the desert a demonstration was given. Younger Brother filled four dry gourds with the sand at his feet. He added pinches of a black powder. He rolled corn silk into fuses. He lit the fuses and methodically threw a gourd to each of the four points of the compass. The explosions made holes in the desert ten feet wide. Over the next year Younger Brother led guerrilla raids on oil fields, smelters and federal garrisons. He was respected by the *zapatistas* but was thought also to be reckless. On one of his bombing forays his hearing was damaged. Eventually he grew deaf. He watched his explosions but could not hear them. Spindly mountain railroad trestles crumpled silently into deep gorges. Tin-roofed factories collapsed in the white dust. We are not sure of the exact circumstances of his death, but it appears to have come in a skirmish with government troops near the Chinameca plantation in Morelos, the same place where several years later Zapata himself was to be gunned down in ambush.

By this time of course the President in the United States was Woodrow Wilson. He had been elected by the people for his qualities as a warrior. The people's instinct escaped Teddy Roosevelt. Roosevelt accused Wilson of finding war abhorrent. He thought Wilson had the prim renunciatory mouth of someone who had eaten fish with bones in it. But the new President was giving the Marines practice by having them land at Vera Cruz. He was giving the army practice by sending it across the border to chase Pancho Villa. He wore rimless glasses and held moral views. When the Great War came he would wage it with the fury of the affronted. Neither Theodore Roosevelt's son Quentin, who was to die in a dogfight over France, nor the old Bull Moose himself, who was to die in grief not long thereafter, would survive Wilson's abhorrence of war.

The signs of the coming conflagration were everywhere. In Europe the Peace Palace was opened at The Hague and forty-two nations sent representatives to the ceremonies. A conference of socialists in Vienna resolved that the international working class would never again fight the battles of imperialist powers. The painters in Paris were doing portraits with two eyes on one side of the head. A Jewish professor in Zurich had published a paper proving that the universe was curved. None of this escaped Pierpont Morgan. He debarked at Cherbourg, the incident of the mad black man in his Library quite forgotten, and made his customary way across the Continent, going from country to country in his private train and dining with bankers, premiers and kings. Of this latter group he noted a marked deterioration in spirit. If the royal families were not melancholic they were hysterical. They overturned wineglasses or stuttered or screamed at servants. He watched. The conviction came over him that they were obsolete. They were all related, from one country to the next. They had been marrying one another for so many centuries that they had bred into themselves just the qualities, ignorance and idiocy, they could least afford. At the funeral of Edward VII in London they had pushed and shoved and elbowed each other like children for places in the cortege.

Morgan went to Rome and took his usual floor at the Grand Hotel. Very quickly the butler's silver plate filled with cards. For several weeks Morgan received counts and dukes and other aristocrats. They arrived with pieces that had been in their families for generations. Some of them were impoverished, others merely wished to convert their assets. But they all seemed to want to leave Europe as quickly as possible. Morgan sat in a straight chair with his hands folded upon the cane between his knees and viewed canvases, majolica, porcelain, faïence, brasses, bas-reliefs and missals. He nodded or shook his head. Slowly the rooms filled with objects. He was offered a beautiful golden crucifix that pulled apart to become a stiletto. He nodded. Through the lobby of the hotel and out the doors and around the block stretched a line of aristocrats. They wore morning coats, top hats, spats. They held walking sticks. They carried bundles wrapped in brown paper. Some of the more intemperate of them offered their wives or their children. Beautiful young women with pale skin and the most mournful of eyes. Delicate young men. One individual brought in twins, a boy and girl, done up in gray velvet and lace. He undressed them and turned them in every direction.

Morgan remained in Europe until his agents advised him that his Nile steamer was waiting in Alexandria, outfitted and ready to sail. Before departing he attempted for the last time to persuade Henry Ford to come to Egypt. He composed a lengthy cable. The reply came back from Ford that he could not leave Michigan because he had entered into the most sensitive stage of negotiations with an inventor fellow who was able to power a motorcar's engine with a green pill. Morgan ordered his bags packed. After giving instructions in the crating and shipping of his acquisitions, he set off. It was the autumn of the year. When he reached Alexandria he came up to his boat, a paddle steamer built of steel, and without more than a glance from the pier he went aboard and ordered the captain to cast off.

Morgan's intention in Egypt was to journey down the Nile and choose a site for his pyramid. He stowed in the safe in his stateroom the plans for this structure secretly designed for him by the firm of McKim and White. He expected that with modern construction techniques, the use of precut stones, steam shovels, cranes, and so forth, a serviceable pyramid could be put up in less than three years. The prospect thrilled him as nothing ever had. There was to be a False King's Chamber as well as a True King's Chamber, an impregnable Treasure Room, a Grand Gallery, a Descending Corridor, an Ascending Corridor. There was to be a Causeway to the banks of the Nile.

His first stop was at Giza. He wanted to feel in advance the eternal energies he would exemplify when he died and rose on the rays of the sun in order to be born again. When the boat docked it was nighttime, and he could see from the starboard deck the pyramid field silhouetted against a blue night sky of stars. He went down the ramp and was met by several men in the Arab burnoose. He was installed on the back of a camel and taken in this ancient way up to the north face, to the entrance of the Great Pyramid itself. Against all advice he was determined to spend the night inside. He hoped to learn if he could the disposition by Osiris of his ka, or soul, and his ba, or physical vitality. He followed his guides down the entrance corridor. The light of a torch threw great bounding shadows against the stone-block walls and ceiling. After many turns and twists, some difficult climbs up ramped passageways, and several occasions requiring that he crawl on all fours to squeeze through an aperture, he found himself in the heart of the pyramid. He paid his guides half of the agreed-upon price so that they would come back for him for the balance; and receiving their wishes for a good night's rest he was left suddenly alone in the dark chamber, the only light a dim glimmer of a star or two from the top of a narrow air shaft.

Morgan would not sleep that night. This was the King's Chamber, long since emptied of its furnishings. The earth was so damp that its chill permeated the wool blanket he had brought to sit upon. He had his monogramed gold box of safety matches but refused as a matter of principle to light one. Nor did he drink from his brandy flask. He listened to the dark and stared at the dark and waited for whatever signs Osiris would deign to bring him. After some hours he dozed. He dreamed of an ancient life in which he squatted in the bazaars, a peddler exchanging good-natured curses with the dragomans. This dream so disturbed him that he awoke. He became aware of being crawled upon. He stood up. Places all over his body itched. He decided to light one match. In its small light he saw on his blanket the unmistakable pincered bedbug, in community. After the match went out he continued to stand. He then paced the chamber, holding his hand out before him so as not to bump into the stone walls. He paced from the west to the east, from the north to the south, though he didn't know which was which. He decided one must in such circumstances make a distinction between false signs and true signs. The dream of the peddler in the bazaar was a false sign. The bedbugs were a false sign. A true sign would be the glorious sight of small red birds with human heads flying lazily in the chamber, lighting it with their own incandescence. These would be ba birds, which he had seen portrayed in Egyptian wall paintings. But as the night wore on, the ba birds failed to materialize. Eventually he saw up through the long narrow air shaft that the stars had faded and the rhomboid of night sky had grown gray. He permitted himself a drink of brandy. His limbs were stiff, his back ached and he had caught a chill.

Morgan's aides came along with the Arab guides and he was helped back to the outside world. Surprisingly, the morning was well-advanced. He was placed on his camel and slowly led down from the pyramid. The sky was bright blue and the rock of the pyramid field was pink. As he passed the Great Sphinx and looked back he saw men swarming all over her, like vermin. They were festooned in the claws and sat in the holes of the face, they perched on the shoulders and they waved from the heights of the headdress. Morgan started. The desecrators were wearing baseball suits. Photographers on the ground stood by their tripods with their heads poked under black cloth. What in God's name is going on, Morgan said. His guides had stopped and were calling back and forth to other Arabs and camel drivers. There was great excitement. An aide of Morgan's came back with the intelligence that this was the New York Giants baseball team that had won the pennant and was on a world exhibition tour. The pennant? Morgan said. The pennant? Running toward him was a squat ugly man in pin-striped knee pants and a ribbed undershirt. His hand was outstretched. An absurd beanie was on his head. A cigar butt was in his mouth. His cleated shoes rang on the ancient stones. The manager, Mr. McGraw, to pay his respects, Morgan's aide said. Without a word the old man kicked at the sides of his camel and, knocking over his Arab guide, fled to his boat.

Shortly after these adventures Pierpont Morgan suffered a sudden decline in health. He demanded to be taken back to Rome. But he was far from unhappy, having concluded that his physical deterioration was exactly the sign for which he had been waiting. He was so urgently needed again on earth that he was exempt from the usual entombment rituals. Members of his family met him in Rome. Don't be sad, he told them. War speeds things up. They didn't know what he was talking about. They were at his bedside when he died, not without anticipation, at the age of seventy-six.

Now, it was not long after Morgan's death that the Archduke Franz Ferdinand rode into the city of Sarajevo, the capital of Bosnia, to inspect the troops there. With him was his wife the Countess Sophie. The Archduke held his plumed helmet in the crook of his arm. All at once there was a loud noise and a good deal of smoke and shouting. Archduke Franz Ferdinand and Countess Sophie found themselves covered with chalk dust. Dust coated their faces, it was in their mouths and eyes and all over their clothing. Someone had thrown a bomb. The Mayor was aghast. The Archduke was furious. The day is ruined, he said, and terminating the ceremonies he ordered his chauffeur to leave Sarajevo. They were in a Daimler touring car. The chauffeur drove through the streets and made a wrong turn. He stopped, put the gears into reverse and twisted around in his seat preparatory to backing up. As it happened the car had stopped beside a young Serbian patriot who was one of the same group who had tried to kill the Archduke by bomb but who had despaired of another opportunity. The patriot jumped on the running board of the touring car, aimed his pistol at the Duke and pulled the trigger. Shots rang out. The Countess Sophie fell over between the Archduke's knees. Blood spurted from the Archduke's throat. There were shouts. The green feathers of the plumed helmet turned black with blood. Soldiers grabbed the assassin. They wrestled him to the ground. They dragged him off to jail.

In New York the papers carried the news as one of those acts of violence peculiar to the Balkan states. Few Americans could have had any particular feeling of sympathy for the slain heir to the Austro-Hungarian throne. But the magician Harry Houdini, reading his paper at breakfast, felt the shock of the death of an acquaintance. Imagine that, he said to himself. Imagine that. He saw the moody and phlegmatic Duke staring at him from under his coif of flattened brush-cut hair. It seemed to him awesome that someone embodying the power and panoply of an entire empire could be so easily brought down.

It so happened that Houdini, on this very day, was scheduled to perform one of his spectacular outdoor feats. He was therefore unable to reflect on the Archduke's death to the extent he might have otherwise. He left his house, hailed a cab and rode downtown to Times Square. Here, an hour and a half later, with several thousands watching, he was put in a strait jacket and attached by the ankles to a steel cable and hauled feet first halfway up the side of the Times Tower. With each turn of the winch up on the roof he rose a few feet and swayed in the wind. The crowd cheered. It was a warm day and the sky was blue. The higher he rose the more distant the sounds of the street. He could see his own name upside down on the marquee of the Palace Theatre five blocks to the north. Automobiles honked and trolleys ganged together at Times Square as their drivers stopped to see the excitement. Police on horseback blew their whistles. Everything was upside down —the automobiles, the people, the sidewalks, the police on horseback, the buildings. The sky was at his feet. Houdini rose past the baseball scoreboard attached to the side of the building. He breathed deeply and found the calmness in danger that years of physical discipline had made possible. He had directed his assistants to hoist him approximately twelve stories above the street, truly well up in the air but not too high to be seen clearly. His plan was to wrestle himself out of the strait jacket, fling it away, jackknife his body upwards, like an aerialist, and grab the cable hooked to the chain around his ankles. He would then stand right side up, his feet planted in the curve of the great hook, and wave to the cheering crowd as he descended. Houdini had lately been feeling better about himself. His grief for his mother, his fears of losing his audience, his suspicions that his life was unimportant and his achievments laughable— all the weight of daily concern seemed easier to bear. He attributed this to his new pursuit, the unmasking of spirit fraud wherever he found it. Driven by his feeling for his sainted mother, he had broken up séances, revealed the shoddy practices of mediums and held up to public scorn the trappings and devices that charlatans used to gull the innocent. At every performance he offered ten thousand dollars to the medium who would produce a manifestation he, Houdini, could not duplicate using mechanical means. The press and the public loved this new element in his work, but that was incidental. It was as if, now that his mother was dead, heaven had to be defended. Embattled, he felt he would soon begin to distinguish the borders of the region where she dwelled. His private detectives visited occult parlors in every city in which he played. He himself went to séances disguised as a gray-haired widow in a veil. He would shine a portable electric torch on the thin wire that caused the table to levitate. He tore the covering from the hidden Victrola. He plucked trumpets out of the air and grabbed by the scruff of the neck confederates hidden behind drapes. Then he stood up and dramatically cast off his wig of waved gray hair and announced who he was. He accrued lawsuits by the dozens.

Houdini realized he was now raised to his assigned height. The breeze up here was somewhat stronger. He felt himself revolving. He faced the windows of the Times Tower, then the open spaces over Broadway and Seventh Avenue. Hey, Houdini, a voice called. The wind turned Houdini toward the building. A man was grinning at him, upside down, from a twelfth-floor window. Hey, Houdini, the man said, fuck you. Up yours, Jack, the magician replied. He could actually release himself from a strait jacket in less than a minute. But if he did it too quickly people would not believe he was legitimate. So he took longer. He appeared to struggle. He could hear the oohs and aahs rising from the street as he made the cable jerk and spin. Soon his entire upper half, including his head, was entangled in the restraint. Inside the thick duck of the strait jacket there was no light. He rested for a moment. He was upside down over Broadway, the year was 1914, and the Archduke Franz Ferdinand was reported to have been assassinated. It was at this moment that an image composed itself in Houdini's mind. The image was of a small boy looking at himself in the shiny brass headlamp of an automobile.

We have the account of this odd event from the magician's private, unpublished papers. Harry Houdini's career in show business gave him to overstatement, so we must not relinquish our own judgment in considering his claim that it was the one genuine mystical experience of his life. Be that as it may, the family archives show a calling card from Mr. Houdini dated just a week later. Nobody was home to receive him. The family had by this time entered its period of dissolution. Mother, son and the brown child, who had been christened Coalhouse Walker III, were motoring upstate in a Packard touring car, Mother at the wheel. They were seeing the Howe Caverns, and their ultimate destination for the summer was the Maine shore at Prout's Neck, where the painter Winslow Homer had lived his last years. Mother and Father were now on the most correct and abbreviated speaking terms, the death of Younger Brother in Mexico having provided final impetus for their almost continuous separation. Grandfather had not survived the winter and resided now in the cemetery behind the First Congregational Church on North Avenue in New Rochelle. Father was in Washington, D.C. He had found upon his

return to the flag and fireworks plant a drawerful of blueprints
that was the repayment of his debt to which Younger Brother
had referred, cryptically, in their last conversation at the Morgan Library. In the year and a half of his life before his emigra-
tion, Younger Brother invented seventeen ordnance devices,
some of which were so advanced that they were not used by
the United States until World War II. They included a recoil-
less rocket grenade launcher, a low-pressure land mine, sonar-
directed depth charges, infrared illuminated rifle sights, tracer
bullets, a repeater rifle, a lightweight machine gun, a shrapnel
grenade, puttied nitroglycerine and a portable flame thrower.
It was to arrange for adoption of certain of these weapons that
Father had repaired to Washington and become a familiar of
high-ranking officers of the United States Army and Navy.
What with tests of prototype models, sales contract negotiations, conferences in the halls of the Congress and various
expensive lobbying procedures, including lunches and dinners
and weekend entertainments, Father had had to take an apartment at the Hay-Adams Hotel. His response to his personal
unhappiness was to throw himself more avidly into his work
than he had ever done. With the onset of the Great War in
Europe he was one of those who feared Woodrow Wilson's
lack of fighting spirit and was openly for preparedness before
it became the official view of the Administration. There was
great interest expressed by other governments than our own in
the malign works of Younger Brother's genius, and under the
advice of counselors in the State Department Father tended
to recognize some of these at the expense of others. To the
Germans he was quite rude, to the British friendly and con-
ciliatory of terms. He was anticipating just the final alignment
of American sympathies with the Allies that in fact took place
in 1917, but which began to be inevitable as early as 1915
when the British passenger liner *Lusitania* was torpedoed by
a U-boat off the southwest coast of Ireland. The *Lusitania*,

registered as an armed merchant ship, was secretly carrying a manifest of volatile war matériel in her holds. Twelve hundred men, women and children, many of whom were American, lost their lives, among them, Father, who was going to London with the first shipments for the War Office and the Admiralty of the grenades, depth charges and puttied nitro that undoubtedly contributed to the monstrous detonations in the ship that preceded its abrupt sinking.

Poor Father, I see his final exploration. He arrives at the new place, his hair risen in astonishment, his mouth and eyes dumb. His toe scuffs a soft storm of sand, he kneels and his arms spread in pantomimic celebration, the immigrant, as in every moment of his life, arriving eternally on the shore of his Self.

Mother wore black for a year. At the end of this time Tateh, having ascertained that his wife had died, proposed marriage. He said I am not a baron, of course. I am a Jewish socialist from Latvia. Mother accepted him without hesitation. She adored him, she loved to be with him. They each relished the traits of character in the other. They were married in a civil ceremony in a judge's chambers in New York City. They felt blessed. Their union was joyful though without issue. Tateh made a good deal of money producing preparedness serials—*Slade of the Secret Service* and *Shadows of the U-Boat.* But his great success was still to come. The family found tenants for the house in New Rochelle and moved out to California. They lived in a large white stucco house with arched windows and an orange tile roof. There were palm trees along the sidewalk and beds of bright red flowers in the front yard. One morning Tateh looked out the window of his study and saw the three children sitting on the lawn. Behind them on the sidewalk was a tricycle. They were talking and sunning themselves. His daughter, with dark hair, his tow-headed stepson and his legal responsibility, the schwartze child. He suddenly had an idea for a film. A bunch of children who were pals, white black, fat thin, rich poor, all kinds, mischievous little urchins who would have funny adventures in their own neighborhood, a society of ragamuffins, like all of us, a gang, getting into trouble and getting out again. Actually not one movie but several were made of this vision. And by that time the era of Ragtime had run out, with the heavy breath of the machine, as if history were no more than a tune on a player piano. We had fought and won the war. The anarchist Emma Goldman had been deported. The beautiful and passionate Evelyn Nesbit had lost her looks and fallen into obscurity. And Harry K. Thaw, having obtained his release from the insane asylum, marched annually at Newport in the Armistice Day parade.

E. L. DOCTOROW was born in New York and educated at Kenyon College and Columbia University. His novels include Welcome to Hard Times *and* The Book of Daniel, *which was nominated for a National Book Award.*